ONSET
BLOOD OF THE INNOCENT

BOOK THREE
OF THE ONSET SERIES

ONSET
BLOOD OF THE INNOCENT

BOOK THREE
OF THE ONSET SERIES

GLYNN STEWART

FAOLAN'S PEN
PUBLISHING
faolanspen.com

ONSET: Blood of the Innocent © 2017 Glynn Stewart

All rights reserved. For information about permission to reproduce selections from this book, contact the publisher at info@faolanspen.com or Faolan's Pen Publishing Inc., 22 King St. S, Suite 300, Waterloo, Ontario N2J 1N8, Canada.

This is a work of fiction. All the characters and events portrayed in this book are fictional, and any resemblance to any persons living or dead is purely coincidental.

This edition published in 2018 by:

Faolan's Pen Publishing Inc.

22 King St. S, Suite 300

Waterloo, Ontario

N2J 1N8 Canada

ISBN-13: 978-1-988035-43-7 (print)

A record of this book is available from Library and Archives Canada.

Printed in the United States of America

2 3 4 5 6 7 8 9 10

Second edition

First printing: July 2017

Illustration © 2018 Shen Fei

Faolan's Pen Publishing logo is a trademark of Faolan's Pen Publishing Inc.

Read more books from Glynn Stewart at faolanspen.com

[1]

Dawn broke to the sound of sirens, dozens of black-and-white vehicles screaming through the streets of Reno in response to the evacuation order. None of the officers in those trucks and cars knew the truth of what was going on, only that Homeland Security had ordered one of the Nevadan city's suburbs completely evacuated due to a terrorist threat.

If the police beneath his helicopter had any concerns or problems with the "Feds" sweeping in and giving orders, none of it had come across in their communications with Commander David White, Office of the National Supernatural Enforcement Teams.

Now his Pendragon helicopter, a magically stealthed gunship, led a squadron of six of the eerily silent black aircraft across the same suburb, heading towards the glittering casino in the heart of the area.

"What am I looking at, Control?" he asked over the radio.

"The Golden Twilight Casino shut down at two AM," Cynthia Leitz, the former CIA agent who now worked as the dispatcher for David's ONSET Thirteen strike team, responded. "They don't open again for another two hours, so there should be no civilians on site.

"Number of vampires in the building is unknown," Leitz continued. "The back half of the building either has no windows or has them closed off with security shutters. It's officially kitchens and private entertaining spaces but could easily hold as many as a hundred fangs—and that's assuming no underground facilities."

"What about the intel dump from Dresden?" the stocky team lead asked. The facility they were hitting belonged to the Romanov Vampire Familias...and they'd been provided intelligence on it by the *Dresden* Vampire Familias.

There were advantages to your enemies having a civil war.

"His data says there's about two dozen personal suites, and what looks like a frigging dungeon under the building. Any info from that dump is at least six months out of date, though, and it wouldn't be the first time we've run into an underground structure we have no idea how the vampires built!"

"That's fair, if less than useful," David groused.

"I've had worse briefings," Commander Kate Mason, the leader of ONSET Fifteen, the other strike team attached to this operation, interrupted. "Command says you're in charge, David. What's the call?"

"Is Klein on the channel?" he asked.

"Yo."

Jun Klein was a trained battle Mage, seconded to ONSET from the Elfin Warriors, a paramilitary supernatural organization that wasn't supposed to *have* trained battle Mages. He also commanded the three squads of Elfin Warriors deputized and assigned to this operation.

"Klein, I want your people to ground in the parking lot and lock down the exits," David ordered. "You've got the drawings, same as I do. There are multiple entry and exit points and I want them all secured."

"The fangs won't run in daylight."

"They may try and run via vehicle from the parking lot," the team leader pointed out. "Once you've secured the exterior, move in and take control of the public spaces. Secure civilians, try and keep a low profile."

"Can do."

"And us?" Mason asked.

"You're going to hit the roof above the main casino, punch through and sweep," he answered. "Dresden's intel says we've got at least one hidden floor up there, so our undead friends are almost certainly hiding up there."

"And you?"

"ONSET Thirteen is going to hit the main loading dock and move in. That's where we expect the heaviest resistance and the most likely route of egress. We'll all punch inward and meet in the gooey center.

"Remember, people, there are almost certainly prisoners being held as portable blood supply," he said grimly. "We want to keep those poor bastards alive."

"And the fangs?" Klein asked.

"You know the standing orders," David said flatly. "Take them out."

A STEADY STREAM of cars and busses flowed through the streets away from the Golden Twilight, loaded and guided by the uniformed men and women of the Reno police. At the center of the expanding storm was the area they'd already evacuated, an eerie silence seeming to ripple outward from the casino as the ONSET helicopters came overhead.

The four carrying Klein's Warriors landed first, disgorging twenty armed supernaturals who swarmed the exterior of the building, taking cover behind the scattered vehicles as they moved to lock down the entrances.

The vampires wouldn't be able to come out into daylight, but they almost certainly had blood-bound Thralls who would willingly fire on Federal agents for their undead masters. The sirens and evacuation had robbed them of the chance for surprise, but David wasn't willing to risk civilian casualties—or civilian witnesses to his people's supernatural powers.

Powers that were demonstrated as the helicopter carrying Mason's ONSET Fifteen stooped on the roof of the casino. Mason herself was a powerful Mage, and her second-in-command, Bella Samuels, was a weaker but still potent magic-wielder.

A fifty-meter-square chunk of the casino roof simply vanished, disintegrated into dust by the power of the US government's combat-gear-clad wizards, and then the Pendragon's cannons opened up, walking explosive shells through the wreckage, the ONSET team flagging targets for the guns as they dropped into the chaos.

"Our turn," Shevon McCreery, David's new pilot, lilted as the chopper plummeted towards the loading docks. "Door-knocker preference?"

The lanky and shaven-headed McCreery was Empowered, a member, like David himself, of the grab-bag of supernaturals whose gifts didn't line up with any particular myth or legend. In her case, she was slightly faster and stronger than a regular human, with vision she could dial from microscopic to "read the flag on the moon," and perfect kinesthetic sense.

She was the perfect sniper, pilot—or helicopter gunner.

"Take those loading bay doors down," David ordered.

"Coming right up."

The Pendragon charged across the parking lot toward the industrial-scale loading bay, currently empty, and the cannons spat fire. A different pilot would have used the chain guns' fully automatic fire to shred the doors. McCreery fired six shots—and the two big metal doors cooperatively collapsed, falling forward onto the ground to create convenient ramps.

McCreery landed the helicopter neatly at the foot of her newly created ramps and smiled back over her shoulder at David.

"Access granted, sir."

DAVID HIT the ground to the echoing thunder of a trio of explosions.

"What the hell was that?" he demanded on the command channel.

"Three SUVs with blacked-out rear compartments just tried to make a run for it," Klein reported. "They fought the LAWs and the LAWs won."

Light Anti-armor Weapons were one-shot anti-tank rockets. The SUVs might have been armored, but it wouldn't have mattered if the Warriors had hit them with the disposable missiles.

"I take it they aren't going anywhere?" David replied.

"And neither is anything else," the Warrior replied in a satisfied voice. "Parking entrance is debris, wreckage and fire. Nobody is getting out until we bring in a bulldozer."

"Good. Leave a few more of the rockets with a team to make sure of that, and then move on the main entrance. We'll meet you in the center."

"Is it soft and gooey?"

"That depends on how many explosives it takes to get there," David told the Warrior, shaking his head. Klein was very competent, but he was *not* a professional. Working with the Elfin was taking some getting used to.

"Sir, down!"

David's prescient threat sense flared even as his subordinate began shouting, dodging sideways as a machine gun opened fire. A stream of silver bullets flashed through where he'd been standing, but the big man was literally inhumanly fast.

By the time he hit the wall, his sidearm was out and a three-round burst of fifty-caliber silver rounds spat back at the machine gun. An ordinary human's wrist would have shattered under the impact of the caseless rounds firing, but David hadn't been ordinary in quite some time.

The machine gun fire stopped—and then a new gun opened fire much closer to David as Chris "Stone" Johnson, his team's heavy weapons expert, returned the favor. The tall shaven-headed Agent walked the fire from his magically stabilized M60 across the area the defenders had attacked from, shattering walls and crates alike.

Then a streak of blue flame blasted through the hole Stone had created and exploded as Kate Hellet, David's Mage, finished clearing the zone.

There was no more incoming fire, but the brief firefight had made a mess of the loading dock. Crates of food and the various supplies needed to run a casino were scattered around them, many of them shattered or thrown aside by the firefight. One wall was a burning wreck around a set of double doors, leading toward where David's augmented-reality helmet overlay said the vampire quarters should be.

"Control," he addressed Leitz. "Shouldn't there have been *some* kind of vehicle here? This kind of loading dock is almost never empty."

"Checking," she replied crisply. "Shit. There were four trucks parked there when we pulled the recon photos at sunset. They must have moved out overnight."

"Find them," David ordered, then holstered his pistol and drew his sword, a leaf-bladed weapon with a strange red tint. "Thirteen, on me. Let's go burn some vampires."

"Secret upper floor is a nightmare theme park," Mason reported on the radio. "There were about a dozen fangs up here—all neutralized—but it looks like it started life as the private party room. And then someone added the *lovely* stone blocks with the restraints and the blood channels."

The Mage sounded more than a little sick.

"They've been used recently, too," she concluded. "We're sweeping the area, but I think we've secured this floor. Thermal scans suggest prisoners—and secret walls hiding said prisoners. We'll find them, because Horned One give me strength, a mere *wall* is not stopping me from saving those people."

"Understood," David replied, his own suit's thermal scanners sweeping the backrooms. Vampires weren't quite room-temperature, but it was definitely easy to tell the difference between them and their prey via thermal scans.

It wasn't so easy to tell the difference between their prey and their blood-addicted minions, but that responsibility went with the job. By and large, you could draw the distinction by who was shooting at you.

His pair of subordinates trailed in his wake as he charged into the central hallway of the rear section of the casino, the demon-forged sword *Memoria* glowing red in his hand as the squad of Thralls waiting for him opened fire.

Assault rifles barked, the reports echoing in the enclosed space as

David dodged where the bullets were going to be, ducking under the gunfire as he blurred across the room.

Self-preservation won over the combination of addiction and mind control that made the men Thralls, and half of them threw down their weapons as the Empowered cop arrived in their midst. The others tried to open fire at point-blank range.

A blur of steel later and half a dozen men collapsed to the floor. Those who surrendered would live. So would some of the ones who hadn't, if they made it to a doctor in time.

"Put pressure on the bleeding," David snapped at the Thralls who'd thrown down their guns. He calmly wrecked each of the weapons in turn. "A follow-up team will be here momentarily. If you don't cause trouble, you'll only be arrested."

The three dead men on the floor were a mute answer to what would happen if they did cause trouble.

"No vampires here," Stone noted, catching up. He pointed his M60 at one of the Thralls. "The fangs. Where'd they go?"

"Down," the man said, his eyes crossing as he stared at the barrel of the gun. "They went downstairs. We were to hold while they got out."

"Where are the prisoners?" Hellet demanded, joining them.

"Upstairs," the Thrall said quickly.

"There are cells under here," David pointed out. "What was down there?"

"We use them for prisoners sometimes, but they'd kept everyone except the fangs themselves out of the underground for the last month." The man was starting to hyperventilate as Stone's gun, held in hands that had literally transformed to granite and had no give to them at all, sat motionlessly in his face. "I don't know anything."

"Stone," David said warningly. "He surrendered. Everything from here goes by the book."

The only reason the Thrall wasn't likely to be executed was that the process of weaning him off vampire blood was excruciating…and had a sixty percent likelihood of killing him before he ever went to trial.

"Thermals show this floor is clear," Hellet told David. "I guess we're going downstairs?"

"Klein, Mason," he said into the channel. "Back section is clear of vampires. I have prisoners; I'll need a security detail.

"We're going to hit the dungeon. Mason, I want ONSET Fifteen coming in right on our heels.

"We don't know what's down there."

[2]

UNDERGROUND PROBABLY WASN'T THE WORST POSSIBLE PLACE TO FIGHT vampires—that honor tended to go toward places with far larger crowds—but it was close enough that David White would prefer to never do it again.

So, of course, here he was, once more charging blithely into the dungeons of a vampire den. By now, he'd mostly accepted there were few as qualified for the job, but that didn't make it any less dangerous or any less terrifying.

If there were any lights in the basement of the Golden Twilight Casino, they'd been turned off when the vampires had retreated down there. Presumably, there was a link through to the underground parking lot, but they'd have realized by now there was no escape that way.

The only way out for what could easily be thirty more vampires was *through* David White and ONSET Thirteen.

Fortunately for him, he didn't need light any more than the vampires did these days. He turned off the thermal vision on his helmet visor, letting his own superhuman senses reach out into the darkness to find the enemy.

"We have no overhead thermal of the basement," Leitz warned

over the radio. "It's definitely shielded; they did not want anyone realizing anything strange was going on down there."

"Not much down here, either," Stone noted, the man's voice strangely high-pitched, the legacy of an ugly scar across his throat. "Thick walls, warm, humid air. Anyone bring AC?"

"No," David replied bluntly. He pointed. "That way, at least six people moving. Mason, Klein, where are we on numbers?"

"Fourteen vampires, eight prisoners, on the top floor," Mason replied instantly. "Vampires are dead, prisoners liberated. No Thralls up here, but it doesn't look like anyone was living or working up here, either."

"Unknown in the SUVs; at least three vamps at a guess," the Elfin replied. "Four vamps in the main hall along with a dozen Thralls. All down, no prisoners. We've got about a dozen Thralls and twice that in un-addicted civilian employees in cuffs, including the collection you left us."

"Call it twenty-one to twenty-four vampires down," David concluded. "Any guesses on what's left?"

"Anywhere between six and thirty," Leitz said grimly. "The Thrall thought his own bosses were downstairs, but they may have eaten Klein's rockets. I'd err on the high side, Commander."

"Wonderful." They were getting closer to the pocket of movement he'd heard, probably close enough that the vampires might be able to hear their whispered conversation even through his helmet.

Carefully waving Hellet and Stone back, he stepped lightly forward. Listening carefully, he moved as silently as he could...and then his prescience flared and he dropped to the ground as a bolt of white fire blasted through where his chest had been.

"At least one Mage," he snapped. "Hellet!"

"On it."

The darkness faded as the two Mages unleashed on each other, the vampire trying to take out the ONSET Mage and her companions, and Hellet simply keeping the vampire contained. Multicolored fire filled the hallway, and David managed to spot the vampires and their impromptu barricade at the other end.

Stone noticed them at the same time, the big tanned man diving out into the hallway and coming up into a perfect firing stance before the vampires opened fire. Their first few bullets ricocheted off the man's suddenly granite skin, and then he returned fire.

Neat bursts of silver bullets tore apart the tables the defenders had overturned, shattering a magical shield as the Mage was forced to split his attention. One vampire went down. Then another.

And then David arrived, bouncing off the wall to land in the middle of the vampires. *Memoria* flashed across the vampire Mage, shattering a desperate last-minute attempt at shielding, gutting the creature. Prescience warned him and the ONSET Commander dodged sideways as two vampires opened fire with assault rifles.

With him out the way, they hit each other and both went down. One of the last two crumpled to the ground as Stone's bullets found a lethal mark, and *Memoria* decapitated the last in a single blow.

"Clear," David snapped. "Moving forward. Mason, what's your status?"

"Coming down the stairs behind you," she replied. "Aboveground is secure. It's just digging out rats now."

David exhaled heavily and studied the wreckage of the vampires' barricade.

"These rats have teeth," he noted. "You have our location flagged. Take the other direction."

"On it."

Reaching the end of the hallway and passing into the main section of the basement, David realized just how applicable the description of Golden Twilight's basement as a dungeon had been. Literal cages lined the walls of an open space the original architect had probably intended as a storage room, though they were all empty today.

The equipment in the room didn't help with the impression, with medical gurneys modified with heavy cuffs and chains scattered around the space. Some had IV stands attached, a couple of empty bags leaking onto the floor with a medicinal scent David didn't know enough to identify.

"This looks like a horror movie's idea of an insane asylum," Hellet muttered. "And the complete lack of anybody doesn't help."

Despite the current darkness, there *were* lights in the room, though turned off, and David hit the switch after a few moments. The room didn't fit his expectations. All of the medical equipment was expensive and modern but matched with restraints that wouldn't have looked out of place in the dungeons of the Spanish Inquisition.

The cages also contained what looked like full-body restraints. David wasn't sure what the place *was*, but everything was consistent.

"They didn't need this for prisoners they were keeping for food," he said softly. "What *is* this place?"

"Vampire jail?" Stone suggested. "The fangs have things they lock their own up for, right? Wouldn't you need most of this to keep one of them prisoner?"

David shook his head. There were a multitude of reasons why ONSET's policy on vampires was *shoot on sight*, ranging from the infectious nature of the disease that created them to the difficulty of containing an adult vampire.

The vampires would only have to worry about the latter, he supposed, but it still didn't fit.

"It doesn't matter," he noted grimly. "There's no one here now, prisoner or jailer. Let's move."

Leaving the strange dungeon-like space behind, they proceeded to find an even more modern-looking medical clinic where, once again, everything was equipped with heavy leather cuffs and steel chains. Massive supply cabinets lined one wall, but all of them had been torn open and ransacked recently.

"Someone's trying to make a run for it with enough drugs to buy a small empire," Stone observed. "We didn't run into them, though, and only one exit from here."

"Cover me," David ordered as he reached the half-concealed side door. When it refused to open outward, blocked with something heavy, he simply ripped it off its hinges.

A big steel filing cabinet half-fell through the doorway once the door was removed. With a grunt and a wince, he embedded a gloved hand in it and yanked it through the door frame. The metal box crashed to the floor of the clinic, clearing the way through.

The other side of the door appeared to have been a records room, hence the heavy filing cabinet that had blocked the door. The exit was open, the door hanging from its hinges in mute testimony to where the vampires appeared to have fled.

David kept his senses peeled as he moved forward, but all he could hear were the inevitable mechanical noises of a properly operating underground ventilation system, nothing that could guide him to his enemies.

"Check the doors," he ordered as they moved down the hallway.

In response, Hellet gestured and every door swung open simultaneously, exposing storage rooms and simple quarters with rough cots. This was likely where the more junior vampires or Thralls had been stuffed, out of sight and out of mind of their superiors.

"Where did they all go?" he demanded.

"Floor plans say the end of the hall should link up to the parking lot," Leitz warned him over the radio. "If they've dug in anywhere else to hold, it'll be in there."

"Wonderful," David replied. "Makes sense. Anything I should be aware of?"

"We have no idea what these people have for gear, but they've demonstrated again and again they have gear they shouldn't," she pointed out. "And if I were keeping heavy weapons in a relatively public building…"

"They'd be in the private section of the parking lot," he agreed.

"Wait for Mason, sir," Leitz suggested. "There's no way they can get out."

"We put down one Mage," he told her. "There could be more. A Mage could make that whole debris fall disappear."

There was silence on the channel.

"Shit."

"We're going in."

THE HEAVY SET of double doors leading into the underground parking lot had been chained shut, but that didn't slow David down for more than a few seconds. *Memoria* slashed through the door, severing the chain, and then the stocky officer kicked the door open and charged through at full speed.

The shell that flashed through the doors missed him by at least a foot, but the shock wave of the artillery shell passing by threw him to the ground, the shell flying down the corridor to turn the records room into an earth-shaking fireball.

"*Holy shit!*" Stone cursed. "The *hell* is that?!"

David was already moving, registering the tracked vehicle sitting in the middle of the open parking garage, the barrel of the big artillery gun returning from recoil as its autoloader activated.

"Is that a *tank*?"

"Self-propelled artillery," Leitz pointed out over the radio. "Running the model, but you're probably talking a one-five-five cannon."

David barely registered the conversation, counting the seconds as the big gun loaded, skewing to try and follow him. A side-mounted lighter gun opened fire as well, machine gun rounds shattering the concrete as they chased him—but he moved faster than the gun could track and leapt, leaving the ground ten feet away from the mobile howitzer with *Memoria* flashing through the air to bisect the barrel of the main gun.

And, as it turned out, the second shell they tried to fire. The ensuing explosion flung him away from the vehicle, his armor somehow holding against the heat as he slammed into the concrete wall of the underground lot.

There was a stunned silence for several seconds, and then Stone's M60 opened up as the gunner started to pick out targets. The vampires rapidly responded, and David traced them by the sound of their weapons as he charged through the smoke.

His Sight warned him about the Mage just in time, allowing him to dodge sideways as a burst of wind ripped the clouds of smoke apart, trying to provide clear vision on the attacking ONSET agents. David's prescience allowed him to move *with* the smoke like an armored ghost, approaching to barely half a dozen feet from the Mage—lunging distance.

The vampire never even realized the ONSET Commander was there before *Memoria* stabbed into his throat, cutting off any spells he was planning on casting.

There were only a handful of vampires left, but they opened up on David with a will. Half a second's prescience and inhuman speed were enough for him to dodge bullets, but not enough for him to advance in the face of that hail of fire. He was forced to retreat to evade their bullets, but that wasn't enough to save the vampires.

As soon as he was clear, Kate Hellet went to work. A ball of blue witchfire whipped through the smoke, dropped into the middle of the vampires, and exploded into streams of plasma that burnt everything they touched to ash.

Hellet couldn't do that often, but it was enough for now. The pair of vampires that dodged her witchfire went down almost instantly to Stone's fire, leaving the room suddenly, finally still.

David crossed back to the still-smoldering artillery piece.

"Leitz?" he said slowly.

"M109A6," the analyst explained. "Mobile artillery piece, one hundred-fifty-five-millimeter gun-howitzer. Could have come from a dozen sources, but I'm guessing a National Guard unit. We'll have to see if there's any intact serial numbers to trace it."

"Any more surprises?"

"There shouldn't be," Leitz told him. "It looks like we've swept the building. You're secure, Commander."

[3]

The main hall of the Golden Twilight Casino reeked of blood, gunpowder, and burnt electronics. The ceiling lights were on now, though several of them flickered from damaged wiring and others were simply gone, and they illuminated the wreckage where Klein's Elfin Warriors had blasted their way in past a squad's worth of Thralls.

Now those same Warriors were laying white sheets over the dead defenders, waiting for a forensics team to come take on the unenviable task of cataloging the dead, human and vampire alike.

"Where are the prisoners?" David asked as he surveyed the wreckage.

"Ours or the vampires'?" Mason replied. The Mage had removed her helmet and let her long gold braid fall down over the black armored bodysuit that formed the core of ONSET's tactical armor.

"Both," he admitted. "Though I meant ours."

"The rescuees have been loaded onto a pair of Pendragons and are being shuttled straight to the Campus for medical exams," she told him crisply. "The prisoners are currently locked up in a storage room used for spare slot machines; Samuels is guarding them."

The Campus, located near Colorado Springs, was the hyper-classified headquarters of the Office of the National Supernatural Enforcement Teams. While other facilities hosted the offices of the various pieces of the Omicron Branch of the US Government that handled the supernatural, the ONSET Campus was slowly becoming the centerpiece of supernatural law enforcement.

The fact that it was fortified to withstand attack by anything short of multiple dragons had something to do with it.

"Control, what's the status on our forensics team?" David asked Leitz.

"They just left the Campus; ETA a bit more than an hour," she replied instantly. "Two teams and a portable lab setup; they were waiting for the all clear."

"Thank you," he said. He'd known what was being sent, but making sure all of the information was conveyed was still useful.

"Klein." He gestured the Warrior over to him. "How are your people holding up? We didn't lose anyone, right?"

"No losses," the battle Mage confirmed. Like Mason, he'd removed his helmet to reveal the dark skin and hair of his half-Chinese features. Despite having shared beers with the man, David had no idea what had led to a half-Chinese Mage becoming enough of a Tolkien fanatic to end up with the Elfin—or if the man's encyclopedic knowledge of the *Lord of the Rings* had come after joining the organization, as it did for many.

"We have a few wounded but nothing serious," he continued. "They're outside, being treated in the Pendragon."

"Any further warning signs or concerns?" David asked. "I'm sure the Reno PD would prefer to let people back into their homes sooner rather than later."

"Do we really want an audience yet?" Mason replied.

"Not really, but we'll keep the casino itself under lockdown," he told her. "Crime-scene tape, FBI jackets; we all know how it works. No one is going to question the black helicopters, even if it helps fuel a conspiracy theory or six."

"It always does," she agreed. "We've swept the upstairs again. Everything looks clean. Klein?"

"We're still picking through pieces, but I don't think we've any enemy combatants hiding in a broom closet anywhere," the Elfin told them. "This building is secure, at least until the gamblers show up and start asking where the dealers are."

Some of the slot machines and tables had survived the brief but intense firefight, but the staff was probably going to have to find new jobs.

"I'm relatively certain that even the stripe of gambler that shows up to a suburban Reno casino is going to notice the crime-scene tape," David replied. "I'll get in touch with the cops, let them know we're lifting the evac order.

"Keep an eye out regardless," he ordered. "I don't want surprises."

THE CONTRAST between the mundane gaudiness of the casino, with its slot machines and poker tables and bar, and the bodies of the vampires and their magically controlled minions was jarring. Several of the machines and tables had been shattered by fireballs or blades of force, not bullets, as the Mages among the Elfin Warriors had cleared the way for their compatriots.

The empty, abandoned state of the casino would have been disconcerting enough. The rows of bodies, combined with David's own ability to see the magic that had so recently torn through the air, only added to the feeling.

The oppressive feeling of death and decay leaking down from the concealed floor above them didn't help.

"You know, every so often, I wonder if we shouldn't try and negotiate with the Familias," Mason said softly. "And then I see places like the hellhole upstairs here and am reminded of why we shoot them on sight."

"There's no saving a vampire once they've turned," David agreed. "Though, as I understand, they don't *have* to drink human blood. Animal blood is fine, but they drink human blood to be *assholes*."

She shook her head.

"Don't go up there," she advised. "I had to, and the forensics people have to, and after that, I recommend we burn this whole place to the ground."

"That bad?"

"That bad." Mason shook her head. "It was bad enough for me, and my Sight isn't nearly as strong as yours. You should *definitely* not go up there."

David shivered. His Sight gave him many advantages: he could identify supernaturals at a glance, he could see several moments into the future, and he occasionally got glimpses of even further…but it came with a cost. He could See the horror, despair and sickness of a place like the upstairs club, and it was difficult, at best, to forget what he had Seen.

"If we have it secure, then I see no reason to go up there," he agreed. "Did you find anything to suggest what the hell was in the basement or where those trucks went?"

"There wasn't exactly a big book labeled EVIL VAMPIRE PLANS FOR THE CURRENT YEAR on the table," Mason replied. "The forensics team will rip their computers apart; that'll get us our answers."

David shook his head.

"I can't help feeling like it might be urgent," he admitted. "That weird clinic dungeon has my teeth on edge, like we're missing something."

"We're always missing something with the vampires," she pointed out. "We've basically been at war with them for as long as the Omicron Branch has existed; they haven't exactly given us tours of their homes and explained how their society works."

He chuckled.

"Leave it to the IT people, then," he agreed. "I'm going to give Charles a call, see if His Scaliness has any ideas."

"Enjoy," the other Commander said. "Tell him I said hi; I'm going to go check in on our outside patrol and make sure the Warriors aren't doing anything outrageously cover-blowing."

"They're not *that* bad."

"No," she agreed. "They just have no idea how to even act like federal agents, and the Reno PD has a decent idea of what Feds *should* look like."

"Well a nae, Commander, what would ye be looking to talk to little ol' mae about?" Charles brogued over the radio.

The discrepancy between the impression you got talking to Charles over the radio, where he spoke like a 1930s Irishman and broke computers like a 2010s hacktivist, and the fact that the being in question was an immense fire-breathing lizard was…severe.

"Charles," David said warningly. "I've just spent the last twenty-four hours with Klein. My tolerance for jokers is sorely pressed."

"The question stands," Charlies replied, his tone becoming more serious. "As soon as me minions arrive on scene with their Wi-Fi repeaters and hard drive cloners, the entire computer network of yer new toy will be mine to play wit'. So, what do ye need?"

"There were four trucks here last night," the Commander told him. "They weren't here this morning. At some point while we were waiting for the sun to rise, four eighteen-wheelers full of *something* left a major vampire den.

"Given that the basement was full of cages and top-notch medical equipment but uninhabited, I'm guessing whatever *left* had something to do with that—and I want to know what it was and where it went."

"Ye don't ask fer much, do ye?" the dragon said slowly. "It depends on how much they stored in their computers, Commander. They may not 'ave stored much of anything."

"We've got a few more arrows in our quiver," David replied. "But I have faith in you, Charles. You're my best hope."

"Flattery will get ye everything," Charles replied with a deep chuckle. "I'll talk to Leitz, see if we can nail down anything leaving Reno overnight. There cannae 'ave been that many convoys of four big trucks leaving together."

"I need to know where they went," the Commander told him. "We expected more vampires here, and I *don't* want to see a few dozen vampires showing up in a group somewhere."

"We'll find them, David," the dragon promised. "With the kind of starting point ye've handed us, they can't hide."

By noon, the forensics teams had arrived, bespectacled and lab-coated technicians who swarmed over everything remotely resembling paper files or electronics, attaching cables and taking pictures as they went. David understood what they were doing, to a point, but he also understood when the best thing he could do was get out of the way.

His Sight and training meant he wasn't a complete liability to this process, but the teams that ONSET had been holding on standby to clean up after this op were the best they had. He wasn't going to joggle their elbows.

Especially not when he had his own work to do. He spent most of his early afternoon fielding questions from a polite but persistent Reno PD Deputy Chief.

"We have been entirely cooperative with Homeland Security," the man told David, "but I think you understand, Mr. White, that we have a real and legitimate cause to understand just what was going on here."

David sighed.

"Deputy Chief Fiscella," he said firmly, "I have tried to be polite and subtle about this, but allow me to be blunt instead: everything involved in this operation is classified at some of the highest levels. We are dealing with one of the most insidious internal threats the USA has ever faced, and I am not authorized to even share that much information!"

"If my city is under threat…" Fiscella replied, trailing off.

"We will keep you informed of anything we discover that is relevant to the security or safety of Reno and its citizens," David told him. "Beyond that, I repeat, this whole affair is classified. I cannot tell you more and will not tell you more.

"You know how this works."

"I know how it works," the policeman replied, "but I've never had the Feds launch an airborne assault on a casino in my city before, either. Or been asked to evacuate a chunk of the city. What the hell was that about?"

The evacuation had been as much to allow ONSET to go in with full supernatural force without having to worry about witnesses as anything else.

"Chief, we knew the organization present here had access to military-grade weaponry," David explained patiently. "While we weren't worried about, say, weapons of mass destruction, it was quite possible that they had explosive stockpiles or poisonous agents sufficient to cause serious risk to the public."

For example, the artillery piece that had tried to kill him would have been perfectly capable of leveling a block a minute or so, given a chance. But that, again, wasn't something he could *tell* the police officer.

"It was safer to evac the area than risk civilian casualties," he continued. "I much prefer having been overcautious to having even one unnecessary death."

Fiscella shook his head.

"And that's all I'm getting, is it?" he asked.

"That's all you're getting," David agreed. "We appreciate the loan of the transport busses, Chief, and we'll have them back to you soon enough."

The Reno officer shook his head, clearly tempted to tell David to find his own damned prisoner transportation, but he just sighed in the end.

"They're on their way, Mr. White," he allowed. "They'll be here soon."

And with that, the overly long conversation was finally over, and David stepped away as his radio chimed, informing him of yet *another* crisis.

Sometimes, the battle was easier than the aftermath.

"Weel nae, we've got bad news and good news for ye, Commander," Charles told David as the Commander watched the sun begin to touch the Rocky Mountains to the west of him. He and Kate Mason were sitting on the decorative bench in front of the Golden Twilight Casino with the senior forensics man while the dragon filled them in by radio.

"It's almost nightfall," the Commander pointed out. "If those trucks are being driven by vampires, they're going to be on the road again soon. Unless you've found something amazing in the casino's computers, I hope you've found them."

"The bad news is that it looks like there were no electronic files associated with the clinic in the basement," the senior forensics agent, a white-haired and somewhat stooped man who David suspected was wearing tweed under his white lab coat, named Brian Rose. "My best guess is that everything was in the paper records room you passed through next to the clinic."

"The one that blew up," David concluded.

"I suspect that destroying the records was actually the intent of that shell," Rose told him. "While a hundred-and-fifty-five-millimeter shell could probably kill even you, the likelihood of hitting you is low."

David was a Class One Regenerator, capable of recovering from anything that didn't kill him in relatively short order—and supernaturally tough enough that "didn't kill him" was a very broad category. Nonetheless, he agreed with Rose's assessment. A fifteen-centimeter artillery shell would almost certainly spread what was left of him in a wide enough area that he would be very definitely and finally dead.

"What was in the records that they risked collapsing the building to destroy?" David wondered aloud. A 155mm shell could easily have collapsed enough of the foundations to bring the whole casino down. It was overkill for almost any single target, let alone one *inside* the building.

"The records room was both physically and magically reinforced," Rose replied. "If that shell had detonated two feet earlier, the shockwave would have killed your team. As it was, the same spells that would have stopped someone from blasting their way into the room kept the explosion contained.

"Unfortunately, that also means that everything in the room, from the paper files to the metal cabinetry, was utterly destroyed," the agent concluded. "We have no data on what was in the basement at all. We're doing some serial-number analysis of the medical equipment, but the Familias have always been good at covering their tracks."

"Damn," David said mildly. "What about the trucks?"

"There's no records that even say they were here, Commander," Charles told him. "The receiving and shipping databases say the last trucks that came through left around noon yesterday. Nothing in the computers, no paper files. It's like those four trucks in the satellite imagery don't exist."

"So, that's bad news and bad news," David concluded. "I thought you said there was good news as well, Charles."

"The *good* news, Commander, is that yer Leitz is very, very good at what she does," the dragon said. "We interlaced a few bits of surveillance footage and tracked the trucks' *arrival* back to the interstate and then several states over.

"To the last toll road they were on," he added, to be clear of what he'd found. "We matched the time slots, and I've got four toll transponders. Now, Nevada doesn't have toll roads, so we can't track them the way we could in, say, Massachusetts, but this *particular* transponder has a covert GPS included that Homeland Security would really prefer no one ever realized was there."

"You found them," David said sharply.

"They're together at a motel on the edge of the Fremont-Winema National Forest," the dragon explained. "Is very public, in the view of an entire small town. I presumed ye didn't want to make a show of this."

"We need to catch them, David," Mason pointed out. "But Charles is right. We can't go after a convoy of vampires in the middle of a town."

"Most likely, they're heading further north," Charles pointed out.

"We can ambush them on the road. It's not perfect, but we can make it work," David concluded. "We'll need to keep an ONSET team and half of Klein's people here to keep an eye on the casino, too."

"One of us stays, one of us goes," Mason agreed. "And we've got to move quickly. Helicopters or not, that's quite a way to go."

"Rock-paper-scissors you for it?" the broad-shouldered Commander suggested, but Mason shook her head.

"I am not playing rock-paper-scissors with a *Seer*," she replied. "Go! But you get Klein," she added with a wicked grin.

[4]

"This is Klein. Convoy has left the motel, is heading north towards the park," the Elfin Warrior reported. His Pendragon was holding a high surveillance course, wrapped in the veil of the battle Mage's concealment spells, above the highway the vampires appeared to be taking.

If there'd been any doubt that they were chasing vampires, the timing of the trucks' arrival and departure from the motel would have helped dispel it. According to the motel's computers, they'd checked in about twenty minutes before sunrise, paying cash, and they were leaving ten minutes after sunset.

"They picked up some friends somewhere along the way," Klein warned. "Four big Fords, red ones. Accelerate like they're stuck in mud, soo…"

"Armored," David concluded.

"Exactly. Pickup trucks, detachable covers. I'm guessing there's a reason for that and one we won't like."

Escorts. Likely armed escorts, from the sounds of the covers Klein described. Those could easily conceal machine guns or even an antiaircraft rocket launcher.

The vampires knew who would be hunting them, and with the

Golden Twilight Casino seized, they had to know they were being hunted.

"It is what it is," David concluded. "McCreery: I want those escorts dialed in. We'll give them one chance to surrender"—after all, they might *not* be vampires—"but the moment they try and shoot back, I want them to be fireballs, clear?"

"Gotcha."

"Klein, keep following them," he ordered. "Once we get going, I want you to drop in behind them. No retreat."

"They won't run far," the battle Mage promised. "But…aren't they going *forward*?"

David smiled grimly.

"Hellet and I will deal with that. We want those trucks intact, people. We need to know what the hell was so important they're escorting it with covert armored vehicles into the middle of nowhere."

"This whole operation has left us with more questions than answers," Klein pointed out. "I thought working for the government meant we'd know everything."

"Ha!" David chuckled. "The OSPI analysts are good, but we've been playing spy and counter-spy with the vampires for sixty years."

The Office of Supernatural Policing and Investigation had been the first of the Omicron agencies, created in the years between the World Wars to try and get a handle on the growing strangeness of the world—and to deal with the present and dangerous threat of North America's vampire population.

"They know our tricks and they've managed to keep their damned secrets. I think we're about to blow a few they'd prefer we didn't know wide open."

"And blow some fangs away in the process," Klein replied with relish. "Have I mentioned, Commander, that I *really* like that part of this arrangement?"

The Vampire Familias had made very few friends among the supernatural communities of the world. The Elfin might nominally be a social club, but the Warriors hadn't existed to protect it from *Omicron*.

"Let them get farther away from everyone," David ordered. "We're about to blow up a highway, let's *not* do it in front of witnesses."

DAVID DIDN'T EXPECT the vampires to surrender—if nothing else, Omicron's usual policy toward captured vampires was euthanasia—but the simple fact remained that his people were police and that left them with legal and moral obligations.

The exact moment to act was hard to pick, even for a man with the ability to see the future. His usual prescience was less than a second, deadly in combat but otherwise only minimally useful, but if he focused hard enough, he could tell something as predictable as "Are there cars coming the other way in the next few minutes?"

"Now," he ordered calmly, his sense of the future finally clear of witnesses—something that would never have happened on a busier stretch of highway or time of day.

"Go!"

The two helicopters screamed out of the night, concealment spells dropping as they swept in over the trucks and their escorts. David keyed his helmet mike, linking it to the Pendragon's external speakers.

"This is ONSET," he told the convoy. "Pull over now and surrender or we will stop you with lethal force."

The announcement would take some explaining if he was *wrong*, but on the other hand, no one innocent was going to be taking an escorted convoy down a deserted highway in the middle of the night.

He was completely unsurprised, however, when the response was for the four escorting pickup trucks to lose their covers, the plastic-and-canvas structures falling free almost instantly from vehicles moving at eighty miles an hour.

What he was *not* expecting was to be immediately pinged by military-grade tracking radar as four antiaircraft turrets, presumably liberated from some National Guard unit's stored air defense gear, revealed themselves and immediately spun to try and target the helicopters with their missile pods.

Unfortunately for the gunners, McCreery matched their superhuman reflexes and had already dialed them in. Hellfire air-to-surface missiles blasted free before the turrets even began to move. Only a single missile made it into the air before the turrets and their attached pickups disappeared in the detonations of the armor-piercing warheads—a missile McCreery intercepted with a shot from the helicopter's cannon that no mundane pilot could have matched.

The weapons were designed to take out tanks. It was *probably* overkill—but from the trucks' sluggish acceleration and clearly present armament, it might well not have been.

The lead eighteen-wheeler swerved, trying to avoid the burning wreckage that had been its forward escort. The convoy had been too close together, the escort less than twenty feet in front of the truck. The driver managed to avoid the fireball but not to avoid jackknifing the truck.

The big transport tumbled, falling over on its side and skidding along the road in a shower of sparks. The following trucks were barely luckier, two of them slamming headlong into the flipped truck and grinding to a halt.

The fourth truck managed to brake to a final halt…with the tractor grinding over half of the wreckage of one of the escort vehicles.

"Dropping now!" McCreery announced, stopping the helicopter a handful of inches off the ground to allow David and the rest of his team to jump out.

The Commander hit the ground heavily, his helmet's AR display warning him that Klein's people were deploying opposite.

"Sweep in and meet up with the Elfin," he ordered Hellet and Stone. "Secure the trucks, I don't want them disappearing on me."

"After that crash, they can't possibly be…"

Hellet trailed off as they approached the chaos they'd caused. Despite having jackknifed, crashed into each other, and driven over a burning pickup truck, all four trucks were basically intact. Armor could only allow a vehicle to survive so much—for that level of invulnerability, magic had to be involved.

And if the trucks had survived that well…

"Take cover!" David snapped. "I doubt the drivers are unarmed!"

His prescience flared a moment later as he rushed into the shadow of the jackknifed truck. A pair of submachine guns opened fire, the shooters trying to take down his companions.

Stone's machine gun answered, two short bursts that silenced the smaller weapons.

"Multiple hostiles," the big gunner reported. "Two down, but I've got movement. Watch your backs."

David ignored Stone's suggestion and vaulted onto the jackknifed truck, his own battle carbine swinging free from its quick-release harness as he landed on top of the disabled vehicle. Prescience flared a warning and he fired a burst of silver bullets at the same moment that one of the vampires popped up with an SMG.

He dodged the incoming bullets. The vampire didn't, sprawling backward as the silver short-circuited his inhuman healing factor.

Leaping down from the truck, he opened fire at a hint of movement, dropping a second vampire as the creature charged out of the shadows of another eighteen-wheeler with a combat shotgun in its hands.

"Sir, down!" Stone shouted as the occupants of the last two cabs emerged as a coordinated unit, automatic shotguns and submachine guns alternating as the gunfire forced David back behind the jackknifed truck.

Several bursts from the big man's M60 held the vampires up—and then a glittering blue blast of chain lighting smashed out of the sky, a fork of the bolt hitting each of the four vampires and incinerating them simultaneously.

"You're welcome!" Klein chirped over the radio, leaving David shaking his head.

There was a *reason* they kept the battle Mage around. It was good to be reminded of that occasionally, given how damned *annoying* the man could be.

Still shaking his head, he swept the scene with his Sight, searching for any sign of remaining defenders. Nothing moved in the night except the flickering flames as the last of the gasoline in the trucks burnt itself out.

When he looked at the containers on the back of the trucks, however, even his Sight drew a blank.

"We're secure on the ground," he told his people. "The trucks are sealed but shielded; I'm getting both lead plating and magical enchantment.

"Just what the hell were they carrying?"

"That's what we're here to answer, boss," Stone replied.

"Agreed. Klein, orbit at two thousand feet and link into orbital surveillance," David ordered. "Keep your eyes peeled; I want to know the moment anyone is heading our way down this damned road.

"Hellet, Stone, you're with me. Time to see what the vampires tried to hide."

APPROACHING the trailer on the jackknifed truck, David quickly realized that however ordinary the containers looked from the outside, they were something entirely outside the norm. There were no easily accessed handles or controls for the doors, and his Sight was picking up more and more spells wrapped around and into the metal.

"Kate, can you right this thing?" he asked.

"Of course," Hellet agreed.

Tendrils of magic reached out from his Mage, wrapping themselves around the bulk of the eighteen-wheeler—and then snapping like overstretched cheap string.

Hellet recoiled, breathing heavily as her entire body trembled.

"Kate?" David checked in on her.

"Security field," she explained after a moment. "Plus, the damn thing is heavier than I thought. I tried to tighten my grip and triggered a counterspell. Give me a minute, I need to regain my breath."

He nodded, stepping back to examine the truck while she recovered. Hellet was far from the most powerful Mage—Klein, for example, was stronger—but she was strong enough to be a senior member of an ONSET team.

Any spell that could completely shut her down like that was serious magic. It was quite a defense to layer into a truck.

"All right," she said after several minutes. "Now I know what the little fucker is going to try…let's see what we can do."

This time, the tendrils of magic wove across David's Sight to form a net around the trailer and the tractor cab, hovering ten inches away from the vehicle for several moments while Hellet assessed the situation...and then struck.

Both pieces of the multi-ton vehicle lifted into the air, rotating gently to drop back down on the wheels with a visible impact.

"There you go, sir. One truck, somehow still in working order."

All four trucks were still in working order. The vampires had invested a *lot* of money and resources into making sure these vehicles remained intact, from armed escort vehicles to an incredible amount of magic woven into the trucks themselves.

It was no more obvious the doors on the back of the truck opened now Hellet had lifted them than when they'd been sideways. Shaking his head, David mounted the step beneath the doors and found himself a grip.

"Stone, give me a hand here," he ordered.

Neither he nor Stone were particularly strong by the standards of supernaturals, but either could have won any strongman competition on the planet without trying. While the actual door controls appeared to be behind a locked and recessed panel, there were enough protruding parts on the door that they could get a grip.

"One. Two. *Three*."

Both men secured their grips as best they could and yanked, exerting enough force to rip the doors entirely off their hinges. After straining for several seconds, however, they had to relax, as the truck door hadn't even twitched.

David studied the metal balefully with his Sight. Even from this close, he could barely make out the spells woven through the metal. Shielding and silver and lead plating had rendered much of what had been done indistinguishable.

"I think it's here," he admitted aloud, tapping on what he *thought* was a recessed panel. "Stand back," he ordered Stone—and drew *Memoria*.

The sword had been forged by a demon from the souls of several brave men and women who'd tried to kill it. Its most notable ability was to impede regeneration, a thought that made David's shoulder, injured a month before by a blade with similar properties, twinge with mostly healed pain—but it had others as well.

What he needed right now was its edge, the one that could cut through magic and steel alike, and he applied it carefully. His first few attempts to gently cut open the compartment failed, however, and for a few moments, he thought that even *Memoria* was going to fail to get them into the truck.

Thankfully, when he applied more force behind the sword's impossibly sharp blade, spell and steel alike finally parted. Three slow and careful cuts later, he ripped the cover off the truck door, revealing a relatively standard-looking handle.

After everything it had taken to get to this point, he half-expected the handle to attack him when he gripped it, but instead, it smoothly turned, pulling the lock open and allowing him to swing the door open and look into the pitch-black interior of the cargo container.

He didn't need light as much as most humans did, and once the shield concealing the contents of the container was gone, the auras inside provided all the light his Sight needed to see the occupants.

The trailer had been heavily reinforced: beyond the silver-and-lead plating and the spells he already knew about, there was a several-inch-thick layer of steel armor on the interior of every surface. Anchors had drilled into the steel plating, supporting heavy chains identical to those in the dungeon-like clinic at the Golden Twilight Casino.

Each side of the truck held five ten-point tie-downs made with some of the heaviest chains he'd ever seen, wrapped around the wrists, ankles, throats and torsos of surprisingly ordinary-looking people. The ten occupants varied in age, ethnicity and gender, ranging from a Japanese man who had to be eighty to a blonde teenage girl who couldn't have been much over seventeen.

All of them were…ragged. Their clothes were dirty and torn, and their auras were *wrong*.

David stepped over to the closest, the ancient Japanese man, to check on him. As he approached, the man's eyes snapped open, and something in them sent atavistic shivers down the ONSET Commander's spine.

The man lunged forward, teeth flashing in the light from the fires outside as he tried to bite David, only to instantly come up against the limits of the chains with a horrendous sound of straining metal. Nonetheless, he continued to struggle, trying to somehow reach and sink his half-grown fangs into David's flesh.

The noise awoke the others, all of their eyes opening and focusing a feral hunger on David. Every instinct he had as both a human and a cop told him to get the hell out of there, and he was only half-conscious of his step backward.

He stopped himself before he fled the trailer, focusing his Sight, making sure he understood just *what* they had found. Their auras confirmed the only answer that made sense, the only answer that tied together the dungeon, the clinic and the heavily escorted trucks with deadly logic.

All ten of the truck's occupants were freshly turned vampires, feral with the mindless hunger of beings who understood nothing, comprehended nothing…except that they were hungry and blood smelled like food.

[5]

"Sir? Commander White?"

Stone voiced the concern clear on both of David's subordinates' faces as he half-stumbled out of the truck, his entire body trembling with nerves.

"Fledglings," he told them. "The trucks are full of just-turned fledglings. That's why the doctors, the medical care—but also the chains. Even vampires can't stop them trying to eat everything that comes near them."

"Son of a bitch," Stone replied. "That's... Fuck. So, we basically just shot up a convoy full of the vampires' version of nursemaids?"

"Nursemaids to feral, homicidal, people-eating 'kids'," Hellet noted. "We don't have the antivenom with us, sir, but we can probably get it air-lifted out..."

"Too late," David said grimly. "They're all too far gone to be brought back; they're vampires now. I just don't know what to do about them."

He looked around at the trucks. Assuming the other three were the same, he now had forty prisoners. Prisoners that couldn't be negotiated with, couldn't even be *spoken* to, and would try and eat anyone who came within ten feet of them.

"What do we *do*?" Hellet asked plaintively. The description of the convoy as "nursemaids" might have struck a chord with the ex-teacher, but David didn't have an answer for her.

He stepped farther away from the trucks, shaking his head.

"You know our standing orders," he said softly. The vampiric virus was highly infectious, deadly to well over half of those infected, and incurable past a certain stage of progression. A fledgling vampire was a mindless killing machine, and an adult vampire was a murderous, powerful supernatural.

Standing orders treated vampires of any stripe as literally rabid dogs, to be put down by any means necessary.

"I have to call it in," David concluded. "I...I can't just walk in there and shoot a bunch of chained-up people who don't even understand what's going on."

That was what the standing orders required of him, but he wasn't sure he had the stomach for it. Walking away from the wrecked convoy into the darkness, he tapped a series of commands on the controls for his helmet and reached out to Command.

"Warner here," a crisp female voice answered him after a moment. Major Traci Warner was the commander of the ONSET Campus and the overall second-in-command of ONSET. "What's going on, White? Is the convoy secure?"

"It's secure," he said grimly. "They had more military gear they shouldn't have had, antiaircraft missile pods. I didn't recognize the design, but I suspect it's not supposed to be mounted on a pickup truck."

"Any losses?"

"No. My team is fine; we have contained the situation and broken open the trucks. They were heavily protected and sealed."

He swallowed, trying to work out how to phrase the explanation.

"White," Warner said slowly. "You just scored an epic coup over the Familias Romanov, shattering one of their key remaining facilities and seizing whatever it was they tried to sneak away...but you sound like you just lost your dog."

"Ma'am...the convoy was carrying fledglings. Forty of them, chained up to make them safe for transport."

The radio channel was silent.

"That adds up, doesn't it?" she finally said. "The Golden Twilight would be where they concentrated the poor bastards they turned until they could transport them somewhere more remote. I'm told it takes a year for a fledgling to regain their mind."

"We don't know where they were going now, but, ma'am...what do we *do*?"

"What you have to, Commander," Warner said grimly. "They're an infection vector. Burn it out." She paused. "I know what I'm asking, White. I'd suggest using the helicopters to incinerate them from a distance, but if they're as protected as you say..."

"I'm not sure even the Hellfires would take these out," David admitted.

"We cannot allow *forty mindless vampires* loose, Commander," she told him. "We have no capacity to handle them, no process or procedure to cure them. There's only one mercy left you can give the poor bastards.

"Understand?"

"I understand, Major," he replied, swallowing hard. "I understand."

DAVID WALKED BACK to his people with a leaden step, shaking his head as Hellet looked at him questioningly.

"I'll need your spare clips for the Silver," he told her quietly. "Then you and Stone pull back to the helicopter."

He might hate this, but he sure as hell wasn't going to ask anyone else to do it for him. The caseless nature of the Omicron Silver sidearm meant that it carried more rounds than a fifty-caliber pistol had any right to, but that was still only nine rounds per clip, and he only had two spares.

He didn't even have enough *bullets* for the damned job.

His Mage looked like she was going to protest, then sighed and handed over her two spare clips. He dropped them in a pocket and shook his head.

"Go," he ordered. "This is a shitty enough part of the job; I'm not making you watch."

"Yes, sir."

His two subordinates retreated to where the Pendragon was waiting, probably with more speed than was appropriate—but he couldn't blame them. None of them had signed up for this job to shoot people who'd been chained to the side of a truck, not that letting the vampire fledglings go would exactly help the situation.

David's own approach to the already-open truck was nowhere near as enthusiastic. He understood what needed to be done and why, but that didn't mean he was okay with it, let alone okay with *doing* it.

"Commander," Klein's voice suddenly cut into his ear. "I understand what's going on and why, but you may want to get Hellet and Stone back. You have incoming."

"What?" David snapped, clicking back to reality at the Elfin Warrior's words. "What *kind* of incoming."

"Fast, black and expensive—and followed by a trio of Land Rovers," Klein replied. "And when I say *fast*, I mean the lead car just broke two hundred miles an hour and is maybe five minutes away from you.

"I'm not betting on them being random passers-by *or* friendly. Do you need me to rain fire from on high?"

"We don't know who they are," David replied, grateful for the distraction. "Veil your chopper; be ready to act on my command."

"Hellet." He turned back to his own team. "You do the same. Veil McCreery's chopper, then you and Stone take cover. I'll play greeter.

"Like Klein says, nobody does that speed in this kind of situation without a reason, but let's not assume that so hard, we start blowing things up without being certain."

THE CAR that came screaming out of the night looked like it belonged in a Batman movie. Unless David missed his guess, the black sports car probably cost more than he could ever afford...and the USA's supernatural cops were *very* well compensated.

It was still going well over a hundred miles an hour when he spotted it, before slamming on the brakes and turning, sliding into a perfect stop five feet in front of David. If he hadn't been prescient, the stunt would have been damned intimidating.

The arrival and the timing were strong suggestions as to just who the vehicle belonged to, but the windows, tinted far beyond any legal limit, were the final clue for him to be certain. Whoever was in the car was a vampire.

At a guess, a Very Important Vampire.

They hadn't actually tried to hit him, however, so he was willing to at least let them speak.

The driver's side door opened and a tall, gracefully athletic woman with shoulder-length black hair, clad in a black bodysuit similar to his own armor, emerged. Her aura *screamed* vampire at him, but she was unarmed, so he waited to see what she would do.

As he met her gaze, she bowed and stepped around to the other side of the car to open the passenger door.

David barely needed his Sight to feel the *Power* that radiated from the individual who stepped out. The stranger wore what looked like the robes of a Catholic prelate but in a far darker red than David had ever seen on the priests of his family's faith.

His head was shaved, his eyes glittered black in the headlights of the stopped truck and, like his escort, he was unarmed.

The stranger spread his hands as he faced David and bowed.

"Commander David White," he said softly in a thick, strange accent. "I will warn you now that the veils your Mages have raised are insufficient. I know where your people are hiding."

"Is that a threat?"

"No. I am not here to make threats," the vampire told him. "You may call the me the Arbiter."

"And why, Mr. 'Arbiter', are you here?" David asked.

"I am here to negotiate the release of my charges," the Arbiter replied, gesturing to the trucks. "The failures and sins of the Familias Romanov are many and known to me, but these *teknon* are innocent of their progenitors' crimes."

"They are also feral maneaters," the ONSET Commander noted. "A state you vampires don't seem to rise above very easily."

The vampire winced.

"My kind is very old and very bitter, Commander," he said, "but I will not argue their crimes. I will argue that the *teknon* in these trucks are innocent of them. Yes, some may have killed, but they do not understand what they have done."

The red-robed vampire shook his head.

"You have the concept of criminal insanity in law," he pointed out. "Any action these children have taken would fall under that state. They have lost their minds. It falls to me to bring them back."

"And then they would become Romanov foot soldiers. I cannot permit that," David told him.

"Commander, have no illusions," the Arbiter replied calmly. "You cannot defeat me. I don't believe I could kill you, either, but I could certainly leave you impotent while I wipe out your team, destroy your Pendragons and kill your Elfin allies."

"You would not be the first vampire to think I could not defeat them," David said quietly.

"I am far, *far* older than even Marcus Dresden. I *will* secure the safety of my charges, Commander, but I am sworn to nonviolence except in the defense of the *teknon*."

A pacifist vampire? If the Arbiter was telling the truth, he was something entirely outside of Omicron's understanding of vampire society. They'd understood Marcus Dresden to be the oldest and most powerful vampire in North America…but if this Arbiter was older…

"I am prepared to offer a compromise," the Arbiter continued. "I do not wish to fight you, but my oaths require me to secure the safety of the *teknon*. Your orders require you to murder them in cold blood, but you are a man of honor, I believe."

"Say your piece, vampire," David finally allowed.

"Allow me to take these fledglings, these *teknon*," the old vampire asked. "My Keepers and I are sworn to peace; we will harm no one. We will simply take the trucks and go.

"In exchange, these *teknon* will not rejoin the Familias Romanov.

They will be mine and join my Keepers, sworn to pacifism and to never touch human blood. They will harm no one; I swear it."

"You can't expect me to believe that," David replied. "There are no guarantees."

"I offer only one guarantee, Commander White: that if they break the oaths I lay upon them, I will destroy them myself.

"The Familias has brought enough bloodshed to our country, Commander," the Arbiter told him. "Let it end for tonight. I offer you my word, my sacred bond, my oath upon the Cross of our Savior.

"Whatever you will accept, I am prepared to swear," he continued, "but I am not leaving here without the *teknon*.

"I would prefer we all left here alive."

David didn't have the authority to accept the deal. He knew that. Per standing orders and Omicron policy, there was only one thing he could do with the fledglings—the *teknon*, as the Arbiter called them. That meant he would have to fight the Arbiter, a battle he suspected would be more even than the vampire seemed to think, and yet…

If he somehow managed to overcome a technically immortal being with centuries or more of experience on him, duty would then require him to walk into those trucks and shoot forty chained-up people in the head.

Chained-up people who hadn't *chosen* to become vampires. Who had no idea what was going on, who couldn't even conceive of the fate that they'd been handed.

Killing them was a mercy…and yet…

"There are no guarantees my superiors will accept," he told the vampire levelly. "No promises you could make, no oaths you could swear. They will never believe a vampire."

"So long as that is true, David White, then this war can only continue," the Arbiter told him. "I believe there can be peace, that vampires do not need to be predators in the night, hunted like rabid dogs.

"Let me make these men and women something *else*."

Three Land Rovers pulled up behind the sports car, the massive SUVs each disgorging four more vampires. These wore simple white robes that concealed their forms and could easily hide weapons, but none had visible guns.

They stood by their vehicles, waiting for David and their master to decide if there would be more bloodshed tonight.

"We'll back you, sir," Hellet's voice said softly in David's ear. "Fight him or let them go, we're behind you."

David *might* be able to kill the Arbiter, but he doubted his team would survive the fight. He'd lose Stone and Hellet and likely most of the Elfin as well. He'd add a slew more deaths to his conscience, and for what? To enable him to add cold-blooded murder as well?

He sighed and stepped to the side, gesturing the vampires to the trucks.

"If you betray me, I will hunt you and every one of these vampires down," he warned the Arbiter. "To the ends of the Earth and beyond all time. You will not be able to escape me."

"If I fail these *teknon* so greatly, you will not find me hard to catch," the vampire replied, gesturing his minions forward. "I swear to you, Commander, they will be better than the vampires you have known.

"Or I will destroy them myself."

[6]

THE WHITE-ROBED VAMPIRES MADE THEIR WAY FORWARD TO STUDY THE crash site. They seemed remarkably unbothered by the bodies and the wreckage that had been a Familias Romanov strike force an hour before, stepping around debris while they studied how best to move the trucks.

They seemed equally unbothered by the watching ONSET agents and hovering helicopters, a lack of concern somewhat validated when they realized the wreckage of the forward escort truck was going to stop them moving the tractor-trailers.

One of them, a young-looking woman who would have been stunningly attractive if David didn't know exactly what she was, gestured at the wreck. There was a pulse of power, as much felt as seen, even to his Sight, and the wreckage simply…disintegrated.

It was a twisted mass of metal, likely containing at least two and probably four or five bodies, one moment…and the next, it was faint white dust blowing away in the wind.

The vampire Mage's aura, however, revealed the truth. She might have made it look casual—these vampires were clearly trying to be impressive—but her aura flickered with an exhaustion she managed to not show as the spell completed.

"Show-off," Hellet murmured in David's ear. "Sure, if it's the only thing I'm planning on doing tonight, I can do that too."

"Behave," he replied, equally softly. Three of the white-clad vampires returned to their Land Rovers while the others piled into the trucks, one into each back section—something David wouldn't have been brave enough to do!—and one into each cab.

Then the trucks they'd spent so much effort to track and catch were on their way, the black sports car in the lead and the three Land Rovers falling into formation around it.

David watched them go, wondering if he'd done the right thing. As the sound faded away to silence, he tapped his communicator.

"Charles, it's White," he pinged the dragon. "Those trucks are in motion again. Track them."

"In motion?" the dragon asked. "I thought ye'd taken them."

"I had," the ONSET Commander confirmed. "A new player entered the game and I had to make a call. I want to know where that player takes those trucks, Charles. It's important."

"If this 'player' is remotely competent and knows we could track them, we won't be able to follow them far," the dragon warned.

"I don't expect them to go far, but I know," David replied. "We'll likely lose them."

"I'll track them," the dragon agreed slowly. "But...just what deal did ye make, Commander? I'm not sure ye had the authority to let those trucks go."

"I didn't," David told him. "But I wasn't going to shoot chained-up fledglings, either. Had to make a call."

"Aye," Charles said. "Ye're going to pay for that call, ye know that, right?"

"I know."

DAVID TOOK another turn around the perimeter of the battlefield, then sighed. It was time to face the music, if for no other reason than that Major Traci Warner controlled his cleanup teams.

"ONSET Thirteen Actual, reporting in," he said crisply on the main command channel. "Situation is resolved."

"'Resolved'," Warner echoed back at him. "What exactly does *that* mean, White? One moment, we're lighting up with reports of incoming vehicles, presumed hostile, and the next you go silent.

"What the *hell* happened, David?"

There wasn't much point beating around the bush, and David White didn't have much taste for that even if he thought he could escape the consequences of his choice.

"We had incoming vampires but not, as it turned out, incoming hostiles," he told her. "We met the vampire who was supposed to be taking in the fledglings, a very old, very powerful vampire named the Arbiter."

He paused.

"No one briefed me on any millennium-plus vampires in the continental United States," he said slowly, "so I'm guessing we didn't know he existed."

"There aren't supposed to be any millennium-plus vampires, period," Warner replied. "What did he want?"

"The fledglings," David explained. "He called them *teknon* or his charges. He didn't want a fight, but he was prepared to fight for them."

There was silence on the line.

"What did you do, Commander?"

"I let him take them," he said flatly. "He would have represented a fight my team was not ready for, was not prepared for, and would likely take brutal losses to win.

"I was not prepared to take those losses to allow us to murder forty people in cold blood."

His words hung in the night air like bombs.

"They aren't people, David," Warner replied quietly after several long seconds. "At that stage, they're mindless beasts—mindless beasts who have almost certainly killed."

"We can't just shoot every American citizen who gets infected," he snapped. "There has to be a better way—and maybe this Arbiter can give it to us."

"He's a vampire, David. He might be old and powerful and

perhaps he decided to talk today, but he feeds on humanity. We can't trust their kind!"

"He swore to me, to a *Seer*, that he would bind them to never touch human blood and that if they broke that oath, he would destroy them himself," David said flatly. "You know what I see of the souls of men and monster alike. He did not lie."

"You let them go."

"I let him take them. I chose to trust his word rather than commit an atrocity that would stain my soul," he half-whispered.

"That was a violation of both standing orders and my direct orders on this mission," Warner pointed out.

"I was the commander on the ground. It was my call. I will accept the consequences."

He heard the Major sigh.

"All that effort to track them, and you let them go," she repeated. "I have to report this, David. The Colonel will have to explain to the Committee why, after everything we went through to hit the Golden Twilight Casino and chase down those trucks, we let them get away."

The channel was silent.

"Ma'am, there has to be a line we can't cross," David reminded her. "Or we aren't police anymore. We're just thugs."

She sighed again.

"Cleanup teams are en route. Klein will be reassigned back to Mason. You and ONSET Thirteen are recalled to the campus.

"Try not to get in any more trouble on the way home."

"Yes, ma'am."

[7]

McCreery brought the Pendragon in to land amidst the Campus's set of squat office buildings with practiced skill. No one aboard the aircraft said a word, each of them studying the home of their agency in silence instead of speaking.

The Campus was a walled compound a bit over half a mile on a side, nestled in the mountains above Colorado Springs. Three office towers marked the central point, surrounded by a collection of small apartment buildings that housed the ONSET teams and their support staff.

Even with all of the buildings, most of the ONSET Campus was underground. In those cavernous facilities, the US government's Omicron Branch manufactured the strange mix of technology and magic that gave both OSPI and ONSET an edge over both mundane and supernatural opposition.

It was also the closest thing David White now had to a home. It was slowly starting to sink in as they landed that his choices tonight might take that from him. He'd disobeyed orders and potentially loosed dozens of vampires on the world.

It might cost him his career and his new life, and he'd regret it if it did…but he wouldn't change his choice. David simply didn't have it in him to kill men and women chained to a wall, especially not men and women who had no choice in what they'd become.

It was a lot easier to fulfill a standing shoot-on-sight order when every encounter with vampire fledglings involved their mindlessly attacking.

"David, it's Charles," the dragon's brogue murmured in his ear. "Yer back on Campus?"

"Just landing," he replied. "What's up?"

"I need ye to come by mae cave," Charles told him. "Soon. I don't know how long ye'll be on duty before, well… The Colonel is on the phone with the Committee and no one is happy."

The Committee of Thirteen was the Special Committee for Supernatural Affairs, the subset of Congress authorized to wield Congress's full powers in supernatural matters. To all intents and purposes, they were the government of the United States when it came to the supernatural, magical, and parahuman.

David wasn't going to question *how* Charles, an expert hacker and the being in charge of ONSET's communications security, knew that Colonel Ardent, ONSET's Commanding Officer, was talking to the Committee, but if the dragon said he was in trouble…

"I'll send my team to their quarters and be right down," he promised.

WHILE CHARLES'S nature wasn't exactly a secret, there was a significant portion of even the Campus's population that didn't know that "Charles St. Patrick," a name chosen with vindictive glee by the dragon, wasn't just a human IT administrator.

Since the Omicron Branch also couldn't allow the dragon to fly around where people could see him, Charles had massive, extremely comfortable quarters set up underneath the Campus. Even for those in the know, reaching the dragon's lair required trekking through tunnels that looked little different from the rest of the maintenance tunnels underneath the massive complex.

Reaching the lair, however, you passed through a hatch-like door that wasn't big enough for the dragon himself and entered a vast open space floored in the blue plush carpeting ubiquitous to Omicron facilities. Bookshelves stacked fifteen feet high covered one wall, and a dragon-sized kitchenette filled one corner.

The main feature of the space, however, was the massive computing setup with its floating-mount keyboard and trackball in front of the massive hybrid of a dog-bed and a sofa that Charles used as a working seat.

The dragon was currently curled into that bed, his thirty-foot length compressed into a loaf-like position any cat owner would be familiar with—if on a *completely* different scale.

"Welcome, Commander," Charles greeted him. "Still feeling like ye made the right call?"

David glared at the dragon.

"Is this a test?" he asked. "Because I'm starting to feel like this is a test."

"*Life* is a test, my very young friend," the dragon told him in his thick brogue. "I do not control fate, though, to be honest, I could not have written a better test of Omicron's commitment to its ideals if you gave me weeks to think of it."

"Our ideals? How is a set of forty chained-up vampires a test of our ideals?" David asked, settling with a sigh into one of the comfortable chairs the dragon kept for visitors.

"It has always been the intent of the Omicron Offices to apply the Constitution and laws of the United States of America to the supernatural population as completely as possible inside the limitations of keeping their existence secret," Charles pointed out. "There has always been a conflict between that and the perceived necessity of eliminating supernaturals judged to be inherently dangerous."

"The vampires didn't exactly give us much choice."

"Or did you not give them any?" the dragon asked. "The Omicron Offices inherited the prejudices of the old judges of the Omicron Circuit they replaced, and the policy of those elites was unofficially 'shoot it or recruit it.'"

The dragon shook his immense head.

"The vampires wouldn't play," he concluded. "The United States government has been at war with the vampires for longer than I have been awake this time around. Longer than any living member of the Omicron Offices has been alive.

"Do ye *truly* know how the war started?" Charles questioned. "Because, believe me, Commander, the *vampires* remember."

"Do you know?" David asked.

"No," the dragon admitted with a chuckle. "I was a rock formation on an Appalachian hill until the eighties, David. I was strange-looking granite for eight hundred years, only vaguely aware of even the passage of time."

David shivered. Human supernaturals were Mantled, touched by a spark of power that needed a host to manifest. Dragons were of a type known as Imbued or Awoken, otherwise inanimate material give life by a supernatural spirit.

"I thought you were from Ireland," the Commander said.

"A long time ago," Charles admitted. "I left Eire before the end of the first millennium, as we count such things now."

"Why the accent, then?" David asked, considering the dragon's thick Irish brogue.

"All I spoke when I was Awoken were languages of tribes and nations lost to the world," the dragon replied. "The most useful of those languages were Latin and Gaelic, neither of which I knew in a modern form.

"My first translator was an Irish immigrant, a brilliant man who enjoyed the life of an Appalachian miner...but had learned Irish Gaelic at his mother's knee. I was lucky he found me, or things might have gone far worse."

For everyone, David imagined. The negotiations to convince a thirty-foot-long, fire-breathing, magic-wielding, flying lizard to come live in a sealed armored cave must have been fraught enough *with* the ability to communicate with Charles.

"Why did you want me down here?" he finally asked. "Did you have anything on those trucks?"

"I did," Charles confirmed, "but I wanted to show ye before it went up the chain, so you didn't get ambushed with it."

That didn't sound good.

"Look at the screen," the dragon continued, tapping a series of commands. The massive display changed into a map of the United States, and then zoomed in on the border between Nevada and California. Four blue dots appeared on it.

They were clearly still moving and quite a distance apart from each other, neither of which David had expected.

"Those are the trucks," he said levelly.

"They are."

"It's daylight around there," David observed. "The drivers I saw were vampires, and the trucks weren't tinted enough for them to drive during the day."

"Plus, they were moving in convoy," the dragon agreed. "For them to have split and still be driving in daylight..."

"We're not tracking them anymore, are we?" the Commander said levelly.

"The transponder is on the cab, not the trailer," Charles explained. "If I had to guess, I'd say yer Arbiter friend pulled into a truck stop and handed four random owner-operators an envelope of cash and the keys to a very modern truck cab in exchange for their current vehicle.

"He and his minions pulled out with the fledglings with their new cabs, and their old cabs get driven all over the United States by completely innocent truckers."

"We'll need to validate that," David pointed out.

"I agree," the dragon said. "That will fall on OSPI at this point, though; there's no point in sending ONSET teams after them, and—"

A ringing sound cut Charles off in mid-sentence, and the dragon tapped a command on his keyboard to answer his telephone.

"Major, a pleasure. What do ye need?"

"You have White down there, don't you?" Major Warner's crisp voice said over the telephone.

"Yes, ma'am."

"Cut him off. He's off the Romanov case as of now," she said sharply. "He's off *every* case; he's been officially relieved of duty and his clearances suspended."

David winced.

"I know you can hear me, David," she continued. "I'm sorry. The

Committee has ordered a board to review your actions. I need you to come up to my office, ASAP."

"Yes, ma'am," he replied.

Warner was silent for several seconds, then sighed.

"Yeah. We'll talk in person. Get up here."

The program shut off with a click and Charles unfolded himself to look David levelly in the face, his black eyes unreadable.

"Ye should go, lad," he said gently. "Ye needed to know we'd lost them, but now ye need to focus on yerself."

"I know. What do you know about the Arbiter?" David asked quickly.

"Nothing," the dragon replied. "And I mean it, David; that's not because yer clearances are suspended—I don't care about Omicron's bullshit. I've never heard of the creature...which means the title, at least, is less than eight hundred years old...and isn't used anywhere on the Internet I can find."

GIVEN THAT BUILDING ONE, the central tower in the Campus, was inside the thirty-foot concrete walls and at the center of an open area patrolled by armed guards and under continual manual and automated surveillance, the security measures to actually enter the building were probably overkill.

The minigun and remote-controlled weapons behind concealed panels were almost *certainly* overkill, but the Campus's defenses had been designed by a group of professional paranoids.

David presented his ID to the armed guards and provided a thumbprint as requested. The guards were just as respectful as usual, and he wondered if the rumor mill had picked up his suspension from duty yet as he made his way up to Warner's third-floor office, passing through another checkpoint to get there.

The short and slim redheaded woman was waiting for him behind her desk when he arrived, backlit to his eyes with the aura of the painting behind her and its defensive spells.

Warner's own aura pulsed azure blue. She was a powerful Mage, though she hadn't taken the field while David had been a member of ONSET.

She gestured him wordlessly to the chair in front of her desk, one of the uncomfortable unpadded ones she kept on hand for when she was displeased with her officers, and waited for him to sit.

"Major," he finally said. "You wanted me to see you."

She sighed.

"I did. You don't deserve to hear this mess over a phone or a radio, even if it is of your own making," Warner told him.

"Personally, I don't think we needed to involve the Committee in this, but they've been watching our actions against the Familias very carefully of late," she continued. "The new President seems determined to ignore the fact that Omicron exists, which has left the Committee feeling they need to keep a more direct eye on us themselves.

"They knew something had happened and they asked Ardent for an explanation. He wasn't going to lie to them," she concluded. "They are…unimpressed with your decision, Commander White. I'm not certain they agree with your estimate of the threat level that this Arbiter represented."

She held up a hand before he could say anything.

"You and I understand how such things are assessed," she continued. "I trust you when you say how powerful he was. The Committee, however, are mundane to a man and woman. They *don't* understand.

"All they know is that an ONSET Commander, one of the people they have been told are among the most powerful supernaturals in North America, backed down and let forty vampires, beings we've told them are among the most *dangerous* supernaturals in North America, go.

"Can you see why that seems problematic to them?" she asked.

David nodded. When Warner didn't continue, he spoke aloud.

"Yes, ma'am."

"They're requiring us to hold a board of inquiry, which means you are relieved until I can assemble four ONSET Commanders who haven't worked with you to sit on it," she concluded. "Your actions stand at the nexus, Commander, of which is more important: the policies and standing orders of the Omicron Branch, or the independent authority of our team leaders in the field."

She sighed.

"On the record, the board can do anything up and including sending you to a maximum security supernatural penitentiary for twenty years," she told him. "Off the record, you're most likely looking at a fine and a formal censure on your record; do you understand?"

"Not entirely, ma'am," David admitted.

"I doubt half of our Commanders would have done any differently in your position," Warner admitted. "And even if half of our Commanders might have, the authority of the officer on the spot is not something we can afford to minimize—even if you did fuck up."

"Yes, ma'am."

She shook her head.

"I'll accept that you might not have been able to beat him, but damn it, David, forty vampires…"

"When the Arbiter promised to make them swear never to harm a human, he meant it," he pointed out. "That much I can be certain of. Who he truly is, where he took them…I don't know any of that."

"That he even *exists* tells me we don't know as much about our enemy as we should," Warner admitted. "But that's my problem now. You, Commander White, are on leave until the board can convene."

"What about my team?"

"Technically, they're still on duty, but we'll be placing them on leave as well, at least for now," she told him.

"Am I restricted to Campus?" he asked.

"I know you," she said with a laugh. "Don't leave the country, don't forget your phone. Otherwise, do what you want until we call you. You won't run—and it's not like we couldn't find you if you tried."

[8]

Even access to magic didn't seem to have accelerated the rumor mill, in David's experience. It certainly hadn't *slowed* it, though, so all three current members of ONSET Thirteen were waiting in the lobby of the two-story apartment building assigned to the team.

In better times, all eight suites in the building would have been occupied and ONSET Thirteen would be at full strength. With the losses taken the previous year in Operation Sun Net, none of the ONSET teams were over half-strength, hence using Elfin Warriors like Klein and his people to fill in their numbers.

At least this meant he only had to face three subordinates immediately, with Hellet, Stone and McCreery the only ones sitting in the small living room waiting for him.

"So," Stone greeted him, the man's voice soft and high-pitched, twisted by the scar on his throat. "Do we still have a boss?"

"Your confidence in my continued employment is heartening," David replied. "Yes, I'm still your boss. For now."

"For now?" Hellet repeated. "What's going on."

"I have been officially removed from active duty pending the convening of a board of inquiry to go over my decisions with regards to the Arbiter and the fledglings," he told them. "Depending on how long it takes, you've been placed on leave as well."

He shrugged.

"If it takes more than a week or two to pull together a board, I imagine you'll be sent back into the field under a different Commander, but until they make that call, I'm still officially Commander of ONSET Thirteen."

"After everything you've done, that's all it takes?" McCreery demanded. "You're a goddamn hero, sir."

"Thank you, Agent, but I know my record," David replied. "So does Major Warner. So do the Commanders who will sit on the board. It's not my record that's being called into question, Shevon. It's my judgment."

Hellet shivered.

"That Arbiter…he was *old*, sir. And powerful. A Mage and a vampire both—I've never seen an aura like his before. Maybe one of the stronger demons might have been similar, but…"

"No," David replied. "Ekhmez was…well, he wasn't *human*. The Arbiter is. Mantled and ancient, perhaps cursed…but still human."

The demon Ekhmez had been the architect of the disaster known as Operation Sun Net, having coopted enough minions on Earth to lead the Omicron Branch's police forces into a series of traps that had almost killed them all—before David and a handful of others had killed the creature in a desperate strike into the heart of the headquarters of ONSET's sister organization, the Office for Supernatural Policing and Investigation.

"Unfortunately, it also appears he is very smart," David admitted. "Charles says we lost track of the trucks, which means he and those fledglings are now lost to us."

"Damn. Do you think he'll keep his word?" Stone asked.

"He meant it when he said it," the Commander replied. "I could See that. He might change his mind, people do that, sadly, but when he promised to show them a different way, he meant it."

"So, what do we do now?" McCreery asked.

"We're on leave," David told her. "You can exercise, train, or you can head off and visit or whatever you normally do on leave."

"What about you, sir?"

"I'm going to hit the library here," he admitted. "There doesn't seem to be much in our computers, but we've got records going back to the early nineteenth century. It's possible *someone* encountered this Arbiter before…and if there's anything about him, anywhere, I want to know it."

IT WAS easy to say he had a plan for digging into information on the Arbiter while still riding the high of a mostly successful mission and before his relief had really sunk in.

Having been on the go for almost twenty hours, however, David had to sleep before he could execute any of his plans—and the whole situation looked *much* more intimidating in the cold light of a Colorado spring afternoon.

An unwillingness to murder men and women chained to a wall might cost him his job, which…didn't say particularly good things about the organization he worked for, did it?

That thought on its own kept him staring out the window of his apartment at the various buildings of the Campus until twilight had almost entirely fallen. If there'd been more than beer in his fridge, getting very, very drunk would have been tempting…but it was almost impossible for a Class One Regenerator to get drunk off beer.

The same supernatural healing that would bring him back from bullet wounds or third-degree burns laughed in the face of artificial intoxication. The only highs his body seemed truly able to get now were natural ones, from excitement like being shot at.

In the absence of the ability to get drunk, research sounded like as much fun as anything else he could do.

DAVID WASN'T sure where the United States Library of the Supernatural and Paranormal, often called simply the Omicron Archive, had resided before the ONSET Campus had been built. Now, however, it lived on the thirty-second through forty-fifth floors of Building Three, above the Campus's primary hospital.

Like so much else on the Campus, it also lived behind multiple layers of security, so he wasn't surprised to see one of the Archive's librarians rushing toward the main entrance as he made his way through the thirty-second-floor security checkpoint.

"Commander White," the bespectacled middle-aged woman greeted him. "It's been some time since you've graced the Library. I'm Sharon Williams; I don't know if you remember me."

"I was mostly here with my training squad, Miss Williams," David admitted. "I remember what we were supposed to be learning that day, not much else. Sages have an…interesting impact on memory."

Sages were supernaturals capable of instilling knowledge that would normally require years in weeks. There were only four employed by the US Government, and each of them was more precious than an Army division.

"They do," Williams agreed. "How can I assist you, Commander?" She paused, coughing hesitantly. "My records show your clearance is under partial suspension, so there are things I won't be able to show you."

David nodded.

"I'm mostly looking for deep-background research," he told her, "but some of it might be high-clearance. I'm hoping the suspension only applies to active files."

"It depends on how deep-background, I suppose," Williams told him. "Certainly, I can't show you anything active…not that we keep much in the Library that is truly active. What did you want to look at, Commander?"

He smiled. The conflict between a librarian's urge to be helpful to anyone who actually came to their library and an Omicron officer's need to maintain discretion and classification was clear on Williams's face.

"Ancient history," he reassured her. "Truly ancient, by Omicron standards. I want to look at what we have of the O-Circuit reports and case files."

Williams blinked and pushed her glasses up her nose.

"The Omicron Circuit?" she questioned. "Yeah, I guess I can show you that. All of that's seventy or more years cold."

The Omicron Circuit Judges and their deputized officers from the various branches of the US Army and police forces had been the old answer to supernatural occurrences. When it was rare for an entire state to see more than one likely supernatural incident a year, all the USA had needed were three or four "in-the-know" Judges and maybe two dozen Pinkertons, Federal Marshals and soldiers.

Forty people, operating under the direct authority of the US Supreme Court and the President himself, had been all that dealing with the supernatural had required in the USA for almost two hundred years.

"The Circuit Archive is on the top floor," she told him. "It's…not well organized. I mean, it's a hundred and eighty years of files, and only some of the Judges had good secretaries—and none of them wrote the reports themselves!"

"It was a different time," David agreed. "Do we have any kind of organization?"

"We had them all scanned to microfilm in the nineties, so you shouldn't need to go to the originals, and we've had a few people go through and set up a database with high-level topics for *most* of the files."

"So, if I wanted to find reports on vampire interactions, I should be able to find them?"

"I can't make guarantees, Commander," Williams warned, "but I'll show you the setup."

THE SETUP WAS INTIMIDATING. David was no stranger to reading or research, even if neither was high on his list of things he actually *enjoyed*, but the Omicron Circuit Archive was something else. A single ancient computer completely lacking in even a local network connection ran a database program that David wasn't sure was any newer than the machine.

The database program had a listing of every roll of microfilm in the collection, some twenty thousand rolls holding almost two million pages of reports, photographs and court files. It was a mind-boggling amount of data and a stockpile that Williams clearly had only slightly more idea what to do with than he did.

"So, what are you looking for, Commander?" she asked after running him through the system. "It's a pretty giant haystack, depending on what kind of needle you're looking for."

"Let's start at the beginning," David replied after a moment. "Can you help me find the very first reports we have on verified vampire encounters?"

"Well, that's one of the categories we were flagging, and the microfilms are *supposed* to have the date included." The librarian *hrm*ed to herself as she tapped on the keyboard for a few minutes with David watching over her shoulder.

"Yes, here we go," she concluded. "There might be something older, but it wasn't labeled. This is Justice Conrad Bitter's report on the St. Paul's Church incident in what is now the city of Augusta, Georgia, in 1795."

"Bitter was…one of the very first Omicron Circuit Judges, wasn't he?" David asked.

"George Washington supposedly had a 'special affairs' squad during the Revolution itself, but no records made it to our archives," Williams told him. "He appointed two Judges to deal with 'affairs of superstition and ungodliness,' men who took the secrecy of their work seriously and are otherwise forgotten to history: Conrad Bitter and Joseph Reginald."

She shook her head.

"By 1796, Reginald was already dead, his replacement not appointed for another year. For eighteen months, Conrad Bitter was *the* man who dealt with the supernatural inside the United States."

"A mundane," David observed. "That can't have ended well."

Most mundanes did not deal with continued exposure to the supernatural well. Mental and nervous breakdown became more and more likely as exposure levels increased. Someone like Williams, who only saw most of it secondhand in documentation, would likely be fine for decades of service.

A mundane Inspector, like those that made up the bulk of OSPI's numbers, could generally only handle about two years of field work before being benched. Anything more and the likelihood of losing them, one way or another, grew too high.

"Bitter swallowed his pistol in 1798," the librarian said quietly.

"I'm not surprised. Let's pull this film, and I'll see what I can find. No need to keep you up into the late hours, Miss Williams."

———

THE LIBRARIAN SHOWED him how to find both the roll of microfilm and the index entry referenced by the database.

"All right, I can take it from here," David told her as he carefully fed the roll into the projector.

"I'm on shift until midnight, sir," she pointed out. "And there isn't that much demand for my services in the late evening, even here."

"I'll be fine," he said with a chuckle. "And I read slowly enough that I *hate* having someone read over my shoulder."

"All right, Commander. The intercom by the door can reach me if you need me," Williams told him with an understanding nod. "I hope you find what you're looking for."

"So do I. Thank you, Miss Williams."

The librarian left him alone, and the burly ONSET Commander turned his attention to the projector screen now showing the relevant pages. It appeared more like a journal than any kind of formal report, with curt phrases written in a plain hand still legible after two-hundred-odd years of style shift.

David appreciated the long-dead Judge's careful hand. He hadn't been exaggerating by much why he hated having people around when he was reading.

JUNE 6.

Rumors of ghosts at St. Paul's Church at the ruins of Fort Cornwallis. Dead redcoats from war?

Have not met ghosts. Would be a first. Will investigate.

June 21
>*Not ghosts. Rumors and wind.*
>*Priest reports missing woodsman though. Will look since here.*

June 22
>*Found woodsman. Two others. All dead by exsanguination.*
>*Same as Joseph. Might be different beast. Might be same.*
>*Ordered my guard to load silver in their muskets and sleep armed.*

June 23
>*The beast is here. The priest is dead.*
>*We are being hunted.*

THE REST of the page was blank, marked with what David suspected might be bloodspots. A tap of the controls, however, brought up the next page of the journal, where Bitter continued writing.

June 25
>*It is over.*
>*Wilbur, Aaron and Cork are dead.*
>*The beast was fast and strong, but like most, silver wounded it.*
>*I will bring its remains to New York to study.*

THE NEXT FEW pages were more ordinary, and David wondered if he'd be able to find the autopsy. The report of Bitter's encounter with a vampire was…well, normal for a vampire encounter, from his understanding. A group of mortal men had fought a superhuman creature and killed it, losing most of their number in the process.

Nothing in this report really touched on Charles's concern about how the war started. David wasn't even sure this was part of the war, so much as a single vampire—but then, one of the questions he needed to understand was: at what point had it become a war?

It could easily have been when Joseph Reginald had met his first vampire and apparently died. Or it could have been much later, when the Familias took something closer to their modern form.

David looked back at the list of documents dealing with vampires on the computer.

This was going to take a while.

[9]

THREE DAYS OF RESEARCH BROUGHT DAVID UP TO ABOUT THE 1830s. THERE hadn't been a lot of vampire encounters in those early days, one every two or three years, few involving more than one vampire. It wasn't until the 1820s that someone sufficiently knowledgeable about European folklore got involved for them to even call them vampires.

Before that, they were simply "the beasts," the single most common type of creature those first monster hunters encountered. If any of the men whose journals and reports David was reading had tried to speak to the vampires they encountered—or if the vampires had tried to speak to them—it wasn't recorded in the documents he had.

The sinking realization that there may have never truly been a *start* to the war, just two groups so antithetical to each other that bloodshed had been the *only* option, led David to abandon the Archive on the third day.

He brought a stack of printouts from the microfilm, including the St Paul's report as well as the report on Joseph Reginald's death, with him when he retreated to his apartment. He dropped the papers on one side of his coffee table and a large bottle of bourbon on the other.

Pouring himself a glass of the bourbon, he pulled a report at random from the stack and glanced at the microfilm headers he'd attached to the printout.

There had to be some mistake. He'd done a search for the last few reports flagging Joseph Reginald, the first Omicron Circuit judge killed by vampires...but Justice Reginald had died in 1794. The report now sitting in his hands was dated 1832.

The author, however, was the same as the report he'd read on Justice Reginald's death. Oscar Nelson had been Reginald's secretary, though he'd become an Omicron Justice himself twenty years later.

MAY 5, 1832

I have seen what is both a miracle and an abomination against God.

I have seen Joseph Reginald again.

I saw my old teacher walking the streets of New Orleans last night. Unchanged, he looked as he did the day that vampire drained the life from his body.

It was not an illusion or a nightmare. I called out to him and he came to me. We spoke of things only we would remember, laughed at stories of old while his two companions sat with us and smiled silently.

I did not wish to question, but my oaths and my duty demanded it. I steeled myself with the strength of God and demanded of him how he still lived, long after a man's four score and ten years.

The vampire I had believed killed him did not. Even the ham-handed bungling of our surgeon's autopsy did not slay him, for he arose after his burial, alive once more by the power of Hell itself.

My mentor, my dearest teacher, had become a vampire.

I did not believe him until he proved it by showing me his fangs and those of his companions.

He offered me immortality, though he warned the risks were high.

Any truly God-fearing man would have struck down the monster my friend had become...I failed. I fled.

MAY 6

I have spent the day in prayer and consultation with my contacts here. I have gathered a group of men wise in the ways of light and darkness. We shall hunt.

THE NOTES in Nelson's hand ended. A final note was scrawled at the bottom of the page in someone else's handwriting.

THIS JOURNAL WILL BE RETURNED to Washington with Justice Nelson's body. He was found in gentle repose in the entryway to the St. Louis Cathedral.
Of the posse mentioned, we have found no survivors or bodies.

DAVID WINCED. The Omicron Justices had barely been qualified to understand vampires, let alone fight them. Three vampires? Likely with allies, to have been openly walking at night. Even if Nelson had gathered twenty or thirty men, he likely would have failed.

So, one of the first Omicron Justices had been turned into a vampire—a far riskier and less certain process in the eighteenth century, with the Seal of Solomon that blocked away magic strong. Even now, as he understood it, the vampires could intentionally turn someone only half the time.

The rest of the time, the intended transformee died. It was better odds than someone bitten without thought of transformation, who would die ninety-five percent of the time, but given that success could mean immortality...

He slugged back the glass of bourbon he'd half-ignored, feeling the burn as he swallowed it. That chance meeting between Nelson and Reginald appeared to have been the first peaceful meeting between a vampire and a member of the United States' guardians against the supernatural.

It was perhaps inevitable that Nelson, the son of a Protestant minister and militant guardian of humankind for his entire life, had reacted the way he had. With almost two centuries' more of low-level bloodshed between humanity and vampires behind him, however,

David couldn't help but wonder if the vampiric ex-Justice might have been a chance for a better way.

On the other hand, the vampires had turned one of the men charged with dealing with supernatural affairs into a vampire…and it wasn't like he'd tried to reach out to his old colleagues. It was hard to tell from the ink and pen of long-dead men what the likelihood of a compromise had been then.

It certainly didn't seem very likely now. David might have spared this particular set of fledglings, but the normal state of a fledgling vampire he encountered was charging at him. Survival alone would leave him no choice.

He filled the tumbler with bourbon again. David White knew his limitations. He preferred to leave these kinds of thoughts to wiser men and women—except that Omicron had written off the vampires as vermin to be destroyed years before.

And David White had talked to too many of them now to believe that compromise was impossible.

EVEN WITH HIS regeneration and the ridiculous metabolism that came with it, drinking bourbon by the tumbler was a less-than-advisable practice. David still made it through three drinks, almost half the bottle, before he began to feel any effects at all.

He was eyeing the bottle and empty glass speculatively when he heard a knock on his door. For several long seconds, he considered the possibility of ignoring whoever it was in favor of the bourbon, but then he sighed and rose to answer his door.

He was surprised to find Kate Mason on the other side of it. The blonde ONSET Commander had changed out of her armored bodysuit into a long black skirt and a tight red sweater, probably enough to stand off even the chill mountain spring air.

With half a bottle of hard liquor in him, it took David a moment to realize he was staring. He coughed in embarrassment and stood back to let her in.

"Come in. What brings you to my door this fine spring night? I thought you were still in Reno."

"You're not getting the updates anymore," Kate pointed out. "Reno is wrapped. The rescuees are in controlled-environment counseling, the bodies are bagged and tagged, the surviving Thralls are under OSPI's care for rehab and eventual prosecution."

"Of those who survive," David said quietly.

"Yeah," she agreed. "When no vampires showed up for this long, we figured we could pull the security detail. There's a team of OSPI cops with Elfin Warriors on hand for backup. If anything else goes up, the local team will handle it.

"ONSET Fifteen is officially on leave for fourteen days," Mason concluded. "I can't help but feel that's related to your situation. I think the Major and Colonel think burnout might have had something to do with you letting them go, so they looked at who else had been going as hard for as long…and top of the list was my team and O'Brien's."

Michael O'Brien's ONSET Nine had been the team both David and Mason had served in before gaining their own commands. The big werewolf had been in command of supernatural strike teams for longer than either of them had been alive, which made him an extremely valuable resource for everyone around him.

"I won't deny my people need the break," David told her, "but I will be *fucked* before I will attribute not shooting a bunch of chained-up prisoners to burnout."

His companion chuckled, stepping past him to take a seat in his living room. She eyed the bottle and shook her head.

"You're drunk, David," she said gently. "I figured that out when you were staring at my tits, but it's a damned good thing it's just me."

He flushed at her reminder of his moment of distraction but joined her on the couch.

"Join me?" he asked, gesturing at the bottle. "I've got more glasses somewhere."

"I'm not a bourbon girl, and I doubt you have anything resembling drinkable wine in your apartment," Mason told him. "I've never seen you touch anything more than beer."

"Beer didn't get me drunk *before* my body picked up whatever spark of magic fuels what I am now," he pointed out. "Bourbon can get me there, I kind of like it, and…" He shrugged. "I was being damned tempted to get drunk."

She reached over and squeezed his shoulder, turning him gently to look at her.

"How are you doing, David?" she asked. "I read the full report. I don't know if I'd have done anything differently, but…they were *vampires*."

Her hand drifted up from his shoulder to touch the two small scars on his neck where a vampire had bitten him, a long time before. A vampire *fledgling*, with no clue of what she was or what she was doing.

A fledgling that Kate Mason had killed.

"I might have shot them all," David admitted. "I sent my team away so they didn't have to, but I was going to. Then the Arbiter showed up…and all I could do was be grateful I didn't have to."

"And since then, you've spent your time doing research into ancient history around vampires," she noted. "What exactly *are* you looking for?"

"I'm not sure," he confessed. "It was something Charles said, about how OSPI and ONSET had inherited the Omicron Circuit's war without necessarily understanding how it had started. But if there's some secret, something we don't think to look for…" David shook his head. "Either it's not in our files or I missed it, I think."

"I don't think there's some dark secret, David," Mason said. "They killed people, we killed them, they killed us. So long as they were eating people, there was only one option available."

"True enough," he agreed. "That's what the Arbiter promised these vampires wouldn't do."

"You believe him?"

"Yes," he confirmed. "He might change…but he meant it when he promised it."

"Then you made the right call," Mason told him firmly. "And I guarantee the Commanders who sit on your board will agree."

"That's what the Major thought," David said. "I…just keep thinking we have to know something about this Arbiter. He can't have existed in our country for as long as we've *been* a country without us knowing anything."

"Yes, he could," she disagreed. "Our intelligence on the Vampire Familias sucks and always has. Even if I didn't think they could have hidden an entire section of their society from us—and I think they could have—it could just as easily be we know of him, but not by that name."

"There's got to be something somewhere."

"David, are you really the person to be hunting this up?" Mason asked gently.

He laughed.

"No, but I don't know who else to ask. Right now, I'm in a bit of trouble around here, after all. I can't call on Omicron resources for a case I'm not on."

"So, call on other resources," she told him. "Poke the Elfin. Hell, ask that hacker...what was her name, Majestic?"

"Loring," David corrected. "She gave up being Majestic when we gave her a pardon as a reward for saving our asses."

Vanessa Loring, AKA Majestic, had broken into ONSET's emergency communication channel during Operation Sun Net to warn them the whole affair was a trap. It hadn't saved everyone...but without her, their losses would probably have destroyed Omicron.

"I have a number for her," he confirmed. "I could ask."

"You should do that," Mason told him. "And then, my dearest stubborn brute of a friend, I am taking you on vacation."

"Vacation?" David asked.

"Somewhere *not* here," she said firmly. "I'm thinking Vegas. The Strip is about as opposite to the Campus as we can find, don't you agree?"

When he'd first met Kate Mason, she'd been described to him as the team's "tame whirlwind." It was an accurate description.

"I..."

"*You* need to be somewhere where you aren't staring at a mountain, brooding," Mason told him. "Vegas, Commander. I could probably even talk Warner into making it an order!"

"Vegas, then," he conceded.

[10]

When morning arrived, David was still somewhat bemused by Mason's decision to turn his suspension into a vacation. He knew she wouldn't push him if he decided he really didn't want to, but she was right.

Plus, they'd barely had any time to spend together as friends since their promotions. The body blow ONSET had taken the previous year had left the new Commanders scrambling to keep everyone's heads above water. The availability of the Elfin Warriors as backup was only slowly beginning to ease the pressure, as even now ONSET hesitated to send the deputized civilians in as a primary response team.

The chance to spend a few days with a friend, far away from the demands of their work, sounded good. And that was before taking into account that Kate Mason, while a good eight years younger than David, was a stunningly attractive young woman.

Before he could go on anything resembling vacation, though, there was work he was planning on getting done or at least setting into motion.

Sitting at the tiny table in his apartment's kitchenette, he dialed the number Loring had given him in one of their infrequent email exchanges. The ex-hacker preferred text communication so far as he could tell, but she'd given him the number in case he needed it.

"Good morning, you've reached White Majestic Security Services," a chipper female voice—*not* Vanessa Loring, David noted—answered the phone. "How may I assist you?"

"Good morning," he replied carefully. "I'm looking to speak to Vanessa Loring, please."

There was a measured pause.

"I'm afraid Miss Loring is booked up in meetings all day today," the secretary cheerfully told him, and David managed not to audibly chuckle at the lie. "If you'd like to leave a message, I can make sure she gets it."

It seemed that Loring had decided one of the benefits of going legit was having staff to answer her phone. But since she'd given David the number…

"Can you let her know that David White called?" he told the secretary. "It isn't official business."

"Mr. White?" the young woman queried. "Please hold a moment."

The phone clicked over to cheap easy-listening music. Unless David missed his guess, Loring had instructed the secretary to *always* say she was busy, but had also provided a list of names that would be connected through.

After about a minute, the music cut off.

"David," the hacker who'd saved his life greeted him. "I didn't actually expect you to *use* this number, you know."

"Some of us actually like talking to people, Vanessa," he pointed out. "White Majestic Security, huh?"

"Some people get it. Most don't. The ones who do are some of my best clients," she said sweetly. "Some of them were on the wrong side of the old me and wanted to be sure no one else managed the same thing I had."

"It's going well?"

"Six staff, two admins, four coders, one of them a brownie," she reeled off quickly. "We are now the preeminent computer security firm for supernatural and in-the-know businesses in the United States."

Loring chuckled.

"It's a list of two names, and the other one is a djinn programming out of a basement who uses illusions to fake an office when he needs it," she admitted. "I figure Abdul will be working for me within a year; he really doesn't like talking to people."

"You hired a brownie?" David asked.

"I managed to sneak past your enchanted security," she pointed out, "but it was the first I'd seen in years that stymied me. I'm good... but I'm limited to mortal gear and mortal tricks. So, I hired someone who wasn't."

"So, you're linked into the supernatural community now?"

"The in-the-know community more so," she admitted. "In many ways, it's smaller than the actual supernatural community, but it seems to be a necessary interface. And a lucrative one."

"Good. I...need a favor," he told her.

"I figured. I charge for those, you know."

"I can afford it."

ONSET Commanders were *very* well compensated.

"You probably could," she agreed. "But we both know I'm not going to charge you. What do you need?"

"Information. The supernatural and in-the-know community might be the only place to find it, but I'm looking for data on someone who's slipped entirely under Omicron's radar: a vampire known as the Arbiter."

Loring whistled softly.

"Slipping under Omicron's radar is not easy, David," she pointed out. "I've received at least four offers for a *lot* of money if I could work out a way to sneak around your Echelon systems."

"Let's...both realize I have no idea what you mean," David confessed, and the hacker laughed at him.

"Fair. Let's just say I fundamentally disagree with its existence but I understand why *you* guys use it," she replied. "Completely under your radar, huh?"

"I suspect at least partially because he has no interest in fighting us," he said. "But I need to know what he is, who he is, and what the hell he's been up to."

"A challenge. I like those; they're more common on this side of the fence than I thought but still not common enough to keep me happy," Loring said. "I'll take a look, David. Usual email? You'll forgive me if I don't call you."

"That'll be fine, Vanessa. Thank you."

DAVID HAD MOST of his civilian clothes spread across his bed and was debating what to do with *Memoria* when Mason breezed into his apartment, knocking twice but barely slowing down before opening the door and coming in.

"Are you ready to go?" she asked. "I've got one of the cars standing by, and our flight to Vegas is in a few hours."

"Already all arranged, huh?" he replied, shaking his head. "I wasn't expecting to go anywhere; my stuff is in some disarray."

Mason glanced over the clothes on the bed, located his suitcase, and then gestured. Power flared along her hands and wrapped itself around David's possessions. They took to the air, neatly folding themselves as they flew into the suitcase.

In ten seconds, his suitcase was fully packed, more organized than it ever was when David packed it himself.

"Remember, we're traveling civilian," she told him. "Do you have a travel case for your gun?"

Technically, their badges should allow them to carry anything they wanted as carry-on. In practice, doing so would draw far more attention to them than Omicron preferred, so they were encouraged to check weapons—especially weapons that would draw attention all on their own.

Like *Memoria*.

"I have one for my gun, yes," he confirmed, gesturing to where it sat on the bedside table. "Already locked up."

"Good." With another airy gesture, the black box with the heavy caseless pistol and its ammunition blocks landed in his case, the clothes rearranging themselves to cover it.

"Still not sure what to do with the sword," David admitted.

Enough people had died to create *Memoria* that he didn't like to let it out of his sight.

"You can't carry it on and *nobody* is going to be comfortable with you checking it, including you," she told him. "Goddess knows I wouldn't leave it anywhere, but locking it up here is probably the best plan."

David considered it for a long moment, then sighed.

"As usual, you're right. I just don't like letting it out of my sight."

There was a heavy steel safe in his closet, magically and physically attached to the building's concrete frame. It already held the core components of his augmented reality wargear and his M4 Omicron carbine, and the harness hung up inside had a clip for *Memoria*'s scabbard.

"All right. Let's go."

THE FLIGHT WAS SURPRISINGLY NORMAL. It had been over six months since David had taken anything resembling civilian transport, most of his travel being via Pendragon on his way to one crisis or another. The crowded mundane urgency of the airport was almost soothing, though he doubted most of his fellow travelers would have understood the joke.

Most of them were distracted by Mason, anyway. She'd decided to glory in being out of uniform, with a long but surprisingly tight flower-print skirt and a similarly theoretically conservative high-necked sleeveless blouse that clung to her athletic frame.

David only barely managed to not be distracted by his companion, and he was used to her. He was relatively sure he saw at least one man walk into a wall, staring at her.

Despite his weapons-grade feminine companion, they made it into McCarran Airport without incident and grabbed a taxi to the Strip.

There, unfortunately, David was reminded of one of the downsides of having superhuman senses. Accessing the hotel check-in desk took them past the casino floor, where it seemed that *everyone* was smoking.

David might not be in any danger from secondhand—or even firsthand—cigarette smoke, but his sense of smell was as enhanced as the rest of his senses. The smoke wafting out from the casino floor hit him with physical force until he could consciously dampen down his nose.

While he was doing so, he basically followed Kate in a bit of a daze, missing her entire conversation with the check-in staff beyond his being asked for ID and a credit card.

"You okay?" she asked after almost physically dragging him toward the elevators.

"Yeah, just had to dial back," he whispered. "You *know* what my senses are like and…" He trailed off, waving at the smoke drifting around them.

"Fair," she allowed. "Didn't think of that. You can handle it?"

"Yeah. Just takes some conscious effort not to be able to tell you which brand of cigarette the dude at the seventh machine over, two rows back, is smoking," he told her, half-forcing a smile. "Sorry, did you get the room sorted?"

"*Rooms*," she emphasized. "Unless I got the completely wrong impression about this trip," she added with a lascivious wink.

He laughed, realizing that part of his mind had been thinking *just* that—and knowing just how bad of an idea anything of the sort would be.

"No, sorry," he admitted. "Just struggling with brain fog."

"Good," Mason said, her eyes flickering aside in an unreadable moment. Normally, David's Sight would have given him a clue as to what she was thinking, but Mason—like most Mages—had long before learned to shield her emotions.

"Here's your room key. I suggest we go shower off the flight and change into something more suitable for Vegas heat. Then let's hit the Strip and see the sights!"

[11]

Vegas was its own unique thing.

David had never been before, and the buffeting crowds as they made their way down the Strip, past gaudy hotels and a replica Eiffel Tower and brilliantly colored fake castles were an uncomfortable experience for him. He'd spent too long on duty, he realized, and he spent the entire walk, intended to get them out for air and to see the area, watching for threats.

"You can *breathe*, you know," Mason pointed out as they dodged out of the crowds into a Starbucks. "No one is going to swarm out of the crowd, guns blazing."

David turned a level gaze on her, noting that despite the light fabric of her skirt and tank top, the other ONSET Commander wore a short-sleeved blue jacket.

"And you don't have a gun under that jacket, do you?" he asked.

"Guilty," she admitted, flipping the loosely tied garment slightly further open to show the grip of a small revolver before tightening it again to cover the weapon. "*Some* paranoia is allowed, David, but you don't have to watch *everyone*. Let's go...I don't know, we're in Vegas. Let's go hit the slots."

"You know I can't," David pointed out. "It's not like I can turn it off, Kate, and we're not allowed to be obviously supernatural."

"It" in this case was his ability to see the future. For something as fixed as the "random" result of the next pull of a slot machine, he could know what it was well into the future. Certainly far enough to know whether or not to use a given slot machine.

He hadn't played cards much since his Mantle had fully taken hold, but he'd played enough to know that unless the deck was being continually reshuffled, blackjack was easy. His ability to read auras and emotions made poker a joke.

"You could lose intentionally," Mason suggested, but she was nodding as she said it. "Fine, let me grab some iced coffees and we can continue the walk. There's plenty to look at, if nothing else!"

That was true, at least, and David mostly managed to relax as they walked. He spotted signs and identifiers he never would have before as they went, though, picking out the one club owned by the Elfin and several advertisements for shops just off the Strip that, if he read between the lines correctly, concealed spaces intended for the supernatural tourists.

There wasn't much, though, which wasn't a surprise. The best estimate he'd seen was that there were roughly eighty thousand supernaturals in the United States, with about half again that number in humans who knew at least most of the truth. Even with tourism, there were unlikely to be more than a thousand or so of those people in Las Vegas at any given point in time.

"Let's get off the street," Mason finally said, something clearly bothering her. "The Elfin had a club, right? That should have a private space we can just…be."

THE NEATLY DRESSED MAÎTRE D' at the club wore a silver oak leaf on his lapel and bowed slightly as they approached.

"How may I assist you, miss, sir?" he asked.

"We're looking for the Tolkien room," Mason told him.

The man looked past her, making sure they were clear, then met her gaze and cleared his throat.

"You have no idea what the sign is, do you, Commander?" he asked.

"Nope," Mason agreed cheerfully. "But you recognized us the moment we walked in."

"Commander White has some renown," the Elfin maître d' replied calmly, gesturing at David. "For both of your information, you were closer than you thought. At one of our facilities, you should always ask for Rivendell."

"I'll keep that in mind," Mason promised. "So, sir, may we see Rivendell?"

"I'll have one of my people show you the way."

ANOTHER SUITED YOUNG man with a silver oak leaf pin materialized at a gesture, leading them through the club to what David suspected most of the patrons assumed was merely a decorative accent, a rip-off from the *Lord of the Rings* movies: a painting of the door into Moria, with its Sindarin runes spelling out SPEAK FRIEND, AND ENTER.

At a murmured phrase from their escort, the door shone with magic that mundane eyes couldn't see, and the young man simply stepped through the wall.

Familiar by now with the drama and jokes that went hand in hand with the Elfin, David and Mason followed him, stepping through the seemingly solid wall and passing into another lounge area, little different from the one outside.

"Welcome to Rivendell, Las Vegas, Commander White, Commander Mason," the young man told them with a bow. "I am instructed to inform you that Lord Riley has established a tab here to cover any reasonable costs. The Elfin recognize the debt we owe Commander White, in particular, and a few free drinks are hardly a payment on it."

"Thank you," David told him. "Are there any rules we should be aware of?"

"You'll note there are no slot machines or anything like that back here," the young Elfin said carefully. "There are poker tables, but the House does not become involved in gambling here except as referee. You gamble at your own risk, but note that the tables are enchanted to prevent aura-reading and prescience."

"Sensible," David murmured. "Thank you."

"Let's grab those drinks," Mason told him, leading the way toward a quiet corner table. "Here, at least, we can talk honestly." She shook her head. "I forgot just how much trying to dance around work affairs wore on me."

"I thought your religion gave you some scope for that," he said. The silver pentacle the Mage always wore was on a long-enough chain that it was currently hiding inside her shirt, but he was aware of her Wiccan faith...even if he freely admitted he had roughly zero clue what any of it meant.

"Some," she agreed. "Not much. There's a vast gulf between wearing crystals that should bring me wealth and luck and, well, flinging fireballs at vampires." The blonde shook her head. "Hell, I can weave spells to shatter stone and build bridges, and even *I'm* not sure if the crystal stuff is bunk or not."

A waiter came by and took their drink orders, and Mason slumped back into her seat, suddenly morose.

David studied her for several seconds, noting the degree of shielding locked into her aura, and sighed.

"What didn't you tell me before?" he asked gently. "You didn't drag me to Las Vegas just to get *my* mind off things, did you?"

"I was kind of hoping it would work a bit better for me, too," she admitted. "You aren't getting the updates on Golden Twilight, so I... didn't mention some stuff. You're not really cleared right now."

"I know," David said. "But it's eating you up."

Mason sighed.

"Romanov hit us the second night," she confessed. "Hard. Like... led by Tatiana Romanov's son, the last scion of the Romanov core family, hard."

"How bad?" David asked.

"Grigori was less dangerous than his mother, but more than bad enough when backed by half a dozen of the Familias's less...central Elders. And fucking tanks."

"*Tanks?*"

"Somebody in the Nevada National Guard is going to be having some extremely unpleasant discussions with OSPI investigators," Mason confirmed. "They had a tank *platoon*. Four of the damn things. Unfortunately for them, we still had Pendragons and two battle Mages."

She shook her head.

"It was late enough and things were over fast enough that we don't have too much to cover up with civilians, but damn. They went all out."

"Your team?"

"Samuels and Tsimote were both hit badly, but everybody lived. They and several of Klein's people were medevacked... we were lucky and better prepared than the Romanovs expected, and we suspect that may have been basically everything they had left."

"You weren't on leave to avoid burnout," he noted.

"No. My team is on leave because half of my people were in the Campus hospital for over a day and are on strict bed rest." She chuckled. "My being somewhere else is probably good for their recovery. No need to try and look good for the boss when the boss isn't there."

"It sucks," David agreed, laying his hand on hers and squeezing. "Losing Pell was...bad. Took a while to sink in, given how busy the aftermath was, but it was bad."

Pell had been his first pilot, killed in another attack by Romanov vampires.

"The good news is that we may well have broken the Familias Romanov forever," Mason replied. "The bad news is that Petrov Romanov is still alive...and, so far as we know, breaking the Romanovs will only allow Dresden to secure control."

"If the Romanovs are done, then the vampire civil war may be over," he agreed. "Toss-up whether that's a good thing for us or not."

The Familias Dresden had been the source of much of Omicron's intelligence on the Familias Romanov, one side of the vampire civil war intentionally pointing Omicron at their enemy. Even knowing they were being used, the Omicron Branch couldn't *not* execute on the intelligence they'd been given.

"Vampires killing each other was handy," Mason replied. "But too many people were getting caught in the crossfire, and *we* were being distracted from the demons. It's a damn mess, David, and I'll be glad to get back to killing things that wander through from next door *without* taking over innocent bodies."

"I hear you."

[12]

THEY RETURNED TO THEIR OWN HOTEL FOR DINNER AND WERE LOOKING over potential shows to see in the evening when David's phone chimed with a new email.

From Loring, it had a four-word subject line:

Fuck it. Call me.

Somehow, David wasn't surprised the body of the email was blank.

"I'll call her from my room," he told Kate. "I'll swing by yours when I'm done?"

"All right," she replied. "I'll pick a concert for us and be dressed in a bit. Find some nice clothes while you're at it; I know I packed some you'd laid out!"

He chuckled.

"All right, boss. I'll see what I can do."

The elevators delivered him back to his room and he dialed the number Loring gave him.

This time, she answered herself.

"Every time I think I've learned everything there is to know about what's behind the damn curtain, another fucking surprise pops up," she snapped before he even said a word. "Do you even have a *clue* how irritating you are to a professional knowledge sponge?"

"Um. No?" he admitted.

"Shocking," she said dryly. "What do you know about the Delphic Oracle?"

"Um. Greek myth, everyone asked her questions, generally phrased her answers such that she could adjust the meaning after the fact?" he reeled off.

"Give or take a few tons of salt, yeah, about that," Loring agreed. "Enough was dug up around her temple and so forth that even now, I wonder if there was really anything supernatural going on...but I wouldn't bet it against it."

"Well, there's a guy—or a girl, it's not like they generally deal in genders instead of cute emoticons online—who calls themselves the Tahoe Oracle. Why, I'm not sure, because I *guaran-fucking-tee* you that if they actually lived anywhere near Lake Tahoe, someone would have dug them out of their hole by now.

"That said, they were only a vague rumor in my old life, but these days, the in-the-know community knows a bit more," Loring continued. "There's an email address; it's relatively common knowledge. You ping it, you tell the Tahoe Oracle who you are and where they can find you.

"They send you a price, you pay it in bitcoin."

"Then they answer your question," David presumed.

"Fuck, no," Loring said bluntly. "That price, seven figures or so at minimum from rumor, is just to be able to *ask* your question. They find you, usually when you least expect it, you ask your question.

"They quote you another number. I've heard as low as six figures and as high as *nine* for that one. You pay that, cash or similarly untraceable currency, at a later date you arrange. They answer your question—in detail.

"They won't predict the future, but if you'll pay their price, they'll tell you anything you want to know about the present or the past," she concluded. "And if you tell *anyone* anything about the Oracle themselves before you pay them, you don't get your answer. If you tell anyone afterwards, they won't talk to you again...and rumor, again, has it they've ruined more than a few people who've talked too much."

"You're saying this person may know who the Arbiter is?" David asked.

"If anyone does, the Oracle does," Loring agreed. "So, I reached out. Told them who I was, who I was asking for, and where I could be found.

"Got a note back in under ten minutes, telling me they'd find you. That was it. No price. No asking where you were. Just...'the Commander will hear from the Oracle.'

"I don't think they're charging you for the meeting, David, which means you may not want to know what they're going to ask for the information."

"This isn't exactly official business, Vanessa," he warned her. "What if I can't make their bill?"

"I don't know," she admitted. "But I don't get the impression that wasting the Oracle's time is...healthy."

"Wonderful. Thank you, Vanessa," David told her. "If nothing else, it sounds like this person might be our only chance of finding this guy."

"Good luck," she said. "And...fuck. I want to ask you to tell me everything, but that's against the rules of this shit. I love this world I found, David, but fucked if I don't hate the whole mystical bullshit sometimes!"

MASON LOOKED at him like he was crazy.

"She said the Tahoe Oracle?" she asked.

"That was the name she gave, yeah. Sounded like a big deal, if what she was saying was true," David explained.

"I've heard of the Tahoe Oracle," Mason told him. "It's a...joke, an urban legend among the supernatural community, not someone real. Someone's fed Loring a crock of shit."

"Do you really believe that *Majestic* bought someone's crock of shit?" he asked. "This is the woman who managed to get into *our* systems, after all."

"Fair," the Mage allowed, letting the conversation die to silence as they exited the elevator, heading toward their cab. "But still," she murmured after a few moments, "even *I* find the idea of a functioning Oracle laughable, and I can conjure beings of pure energy to do my chores."

"I think we who live what others call superstition are perhaps a little to quick to dismiss what falls into that category but outside our own experience," David told her as they flagged a cab. "Which show were we going to, again?"

"It's a surprise," Mason replied, giving the driver the hotel.

Sitting in the back seat of the taxi, they let the driver babble at them about the show his brother was arranging at one of the hotels. There wasn't enough privacy for them to talk about anything related to work or the non-mundane.

Arriving at the hotel, it appeared that David was being taken to one of the many Cirque du Soleil shows. There were definitely worse fates in life, so he followed Mason willingly enough into the hotel.

Halfway across the casino floor, however, a neatly dressed man in a conservative suit fell into step with them, letting David's questioning glare slough off him like water off a duck.

"I speak for the Oracle," the man said calmly, his voice pitched just loudly enough that both David and Mason could hear him. "Your deeds, David White, have earned a free question—but not a free answer.

"Speak, that we may know what knowledge you seek."

David half-stumbled in shock, recovering quickly enough to catch Mason, who *did* stumble.

The stranger continued to smile calmly and keep step with them, and David's Sight revealed "his" true nature—the man was a construct, an assembly of energy and power conjured by a Mage or other powerful being…but a *far* more detailed one than he had ever encountered before.

"The vampire known as the Arbiter," he finally said as they neared the door to the concert hall and slowed, delaying joining the line to see what their new companion said. "I want to know who he is, where he came from and where he lairs."

"Ah," the stranger said in a hissing, almost serpentine exhale. "We suspected it might be him. A dangerous foe you seek, Commander...or perhaps an even more dangerous ally."

"Can you provide that information?" David asked. He didn't need the strange construct—or whatever the *hell* was behind it—judging his choices.

"We can." The construct produced a plain white card, which it passed to David. "The email address on the card will work once. Send us a location and a time, at least twenty-four hours from now. Meet us there with ten million dollars, cash or equivalents."

David choked.

"Ten million dollars isn't easily transported," he pointed out. "What kind of equivalent are you talking?"

"This is Las Vegas, Commander White. Half of these casinos have hundred-thousand-dollar chips. I'm certain a man of your...talents will have a way to acquire them.

"We have ways to acquire your information. Email us when you have the money."

With that, the stranger calmly turned and walked away, leaving David and Mason staring after him in shock until he disappeared into the crowd.

"An urban legend, huh?" David asked softly.

"Just what have you found, David?" Mason asked.

"I have no idea," he replied. "Nor do I have a clue how I'm raising ten million dollars in twenty-four hours without breaking my contract with ONSET."

"You have the whole show to think about it," she told him. "Let's not get distracted right away!"

———

THE SHOW, while spectacular, didn't provide David with an answer to the question of the moment. He and Mason both stewed over it until they got back to their hotel, at which point she walked into his hotel room with him and grabbed the chair at the desk, leaving him to either stand or sit on the bed.

He chose to stand, walking past her to look out over the Las Vegas skyline.

"I'm not seeing a lot of options," he admitted. "I can call it in, see if we can get the funds from Command. I'm not sure even ONSET's resources stretch to ten million of petty cash, however."

"And you're not on this case," Mason pointed out quietly. "We can bump it up the chain, but neither of us is supposed to be involved in this at all. This kind of intelligence coup is…rare enough you'd probably get the money, but…"

"Not quickly," David replied.

"Yeah. And while he didn't put an end time on his timeline, I can't imagine the offer's open forever."

"Or that the Arbiter won't learn people were asking about him," he said. "While I imagine he was expecting it, he strikes me as the type to protect his secrets. Thoroughly, if not necessarily violently."

"That's rapidly leaving us with only one option," Mason concluded. "And I'll admit, that option kind of sounds like fun."

"It also sounds like something that's going to screw me in front of the board of inquiry," he replied. "I can't imagine it's going to *help* my case if they find out I went and broke my contracts and oaths by abusing my powers to gamble."

"David, are we really going to do anything with this intel except turn it right back over to ONSET?" Mason asked. "We're just expediting affairs and making sure the deal is closed."

He shook his head.

"I can just see that going on my tombstone."

"Come on, David," she said with a bright grin. "Sleep on it, but you know I'm right—and you know it'll be fun."

[13]

Having conceded Kate Mason's point, at least in his own head, David dressed carefully the following morning. Professional clothes made him look less like someone who'd be trying to cheat the casino, at least in his own head, and he left the gun behind.

His FBI Division O credentials, always a useful fiction, went into the inside pocket of a light linen blazer. In the worst case, he suspected "I'm a Federal Agent" would work as a decent "get out of jail free" card.

Finally, he stepped outside and knocked on Mason's door. The rooms she'd booked were right next door to each other.

When she answered the door, he saw that she'd clearly been thinking along the same lines as he had…plus a certain degree of weaponized sexuality as a distraction. The tall blonde had produced a skintight sheath dress in a stunning turquoise that left little of her frame to the imagination despite covering her from halfway up her neck down to her ankles.

He exhaled sharply in surprise. He'd seen Kate Mason weaponize before, but never to quite this scale.

"Wow."

"You clean up nicely yourself," she told him with a wicked smile, stepping back into her room and gesturing him in so they could speak in private. "I take it we're on the same page?"

"We're in Las Vegas," David replied. "It seems…unpopular not to gamble."

"We certainly aren't paying the Oracle's price from *our* resources," she said. ONSET Commanders made good money, but not enough for the pair of them to even have a million dollars to hand, let alone ten.

"Exactly. So, let's go see what Vegas has to offer, shall we?"

"Do we have a plan?" Mason asked.

"Slots to build up a base, then either roulette or high-stakes blackjack," he told her.

"Some of the slot machines could cover the price in one win," she pointed out. "Wouldn't that be easier and draw somewhat less suspicion?"

"First," he held up a finger, "that would require us to *find* a slot machine that will win on its next pull. I can't change the odds, Kate; I just know what the next result is.

"Second, a big slot win is a big deal. Lots of attention. Big vanity checks. IRS agents and paperwork *right away*…and perhaps most importantly right now, they don't pay out in casino chips."

"And if we run the cash through our own accounts, that's asking for trouble," she agreed. "So, what do you plan?"

"Honestly, if I thought we'd get the cash fast enough, a big slot win would be easiest, but I'm betting that takes *days* to process," David replied. "I could deal with taxes and headaches, if nothing else; once we turn the data over, I'm pretty sure I can get Omicron to talk to the IRS for me.

"But I'm guessing we need to pay the Oracle by tomorrow," he concluded. "So, like I said, slots to start, build up a base of funds, then cash those in as chips and see where we go."

"I'm with you," Mason promised. "I'll see about keeping everyone around you distracted."

"That, Commander Mason, you are going to do without even *trying*."

FIVE HUNDRED DOLLARS from the cash machine wouldn't take most people very far in the slot machines at a Vegas casino.

David White was not most people.

His prescience ran about a third of a second into the future in combat, but combat was the one of the most chaotic environments possible, with people adjusting and changing their minds from moment to moment.

Things that were more predictable, he could see further. A slot machine ran on a random seed, a computer algorithm that produced a new number each time...but the seed was already set, and the number it produced would always be the same.

Stopping at the first machine, David focused on the idea of putting money in the machine and pulling the lever, stretching his Sight in a way that was...profoundly uncomfortable.

He managed to get an image of the symbols that would appear on the screen. He'd lose...but he needed to test it. The first set of bills went into the machine and he pulled the lever.

The screen lit up, "spun" its symbols...and spat out the exact combination he'd been expecting. He exhaled in relief, hoping anyone around him thought it was disappointment. It seemed this might just work.

With Kate Mason leaning against the machine next to him, watching, he repeated the stretch into the future. The next spin on this machine would be a small prize, fifty dollars.

He paid and spun. The machine chimed cheerfully and spat out a paper slip, instructing him to take it to the cashier to claim his prize.

"Yes!" he exclaimed, looking up at Mason, who grinned widely back at him.

"Good start to the day," she told him.

"Let's see if the luck holds," he replied, mostly for the benefit of those around him. "Let's try some more machines."

They wandered down the line of slot machines, with David touching each one in passing, doing his best to make it look like a ritual superstition. He intentionally lost on the next two machines, but the fourth machine he picked for its imminent seven-hundred-dollar payout.

Another paper chit. He passed them back to Kate who, in a gesture that probably distracted everyone in a ten-foot radius, folded them up and slid them into her bra from the side of her sleeveless dress.

"I'll keep them safe for you," she promised with a wink.

Shaking his head, David intentionally picked the next machine at random, pretending to be distracted by Kate, and lost. He'd started with enough for a hundred plays on the machines, and he needed to lose often enough for it to look like a statistical fluke that he was successful—while also keeping the wins under the threshold that would bring staff out to check on the machine.

One of the machines they passed was about to spit out a six-million-dollar jackpot, a temptation that held David in place for several moments before ruling it out and moving on, accepting three one-thousand-dollar wins on the next few machines as a scheme settled into his mind.

"Kate," he murmured to his companion as he passed her the chits. "Sixth machine back, the green one, see it?"

"Yeah?" she replied questioningly.

"It's about to spit out a jackpot and gather *everyone's* attention. I need someone to pull it in a few minutes. Can you manage something?"

"I can't manage mind control," she pointed out under her breath. "What were you thinking?"

"I don't know; suggest that it looks lucky to one of the regular gamblers? Try the voice-of-God trick."

That got a chuckle from her.

"That might work," she admitted, "if we don't send someone to the insane asylum by accident. Looking for a distraction?"

"I'm going to go for a string of small wins and then try and cash in fifty thousand dollars of chits for casino chips," he told her very quietly. "I want everyone looking somewhere *else* while I do it."

One of the gamblers, a tired-looking old woman who looked like she'd given up on, well, *everything*, suddenly looked up from her machine, confused. Her gaze settled on the machine that David had indicated and confusion switched for thoughtfulness.

She walked over to it, plugged in her five dollars, and pulled the lever.

The massive light display above the slot machines went crazy, noise and lights drawing attention to the woman as her exhausted smile gave way to the biggest grin David had ever seen on anyone in his life.

A crowd rapidly gathered around, congratulating her as a casino technician came out to check on the machine.

Taking advantage of the distraction, David quickly ran through his last twenty games, carefully selecting machines that would win him a thousand dollars each. Gesturing Mason over to him, he handed her the chits.

"What are we at?" he asked.

"Sixty-three thousand, two hundred," she told him. "Everyone's going to be distracted for a bit—apparently, our lucky friend over there has cancer but couldn't afford the treatment. She'd figured she was dead, so she was going to go out trying to win enough to live."

"Happy sob story," David agreed. "That'll keep everyone tied up *and* makes me feel better about this whole stunt."

"That's what I was thinking on both counts, once I saw the cancer in her aura," Mason murmured in his ear, her breath warm and distracting on his skin. "Make the world a tiny bit better of a place."

It was small and silly and idealistic...but David couldn't bring himself to disagree, either.

THE GIRL behind the cashier counter couldn't seem to decide which was more distracting: Kate Mason's frankly outlined form, the growing hubbub around the cancer patient winning the millions, or David's own unusually broad shoulders.

Most certainly, the young lady was *not* paying much attention to what she was actually doing, which was totalling up David's slot machine chits.

"We have some tax paperwork we'll need you to fill out," she said slowly, her gaze flickering back to Mason's chest, then rigidly to David's face while she flushed.

"Can I just get everything paid out in casino chips?" he asked. "I'm on a lucky streak and I'd like to take it to the tables. No point in filling out the tax paperwork when the number might get bigger, right?"

Or smaller. In truth, for anyone else, the number would inevitably get smaller. David was sure there was still supposed to be some kind of interim paperwork or changeover, but the clerk just sighed and nodded.

"Yes, sir; of course, sir," she assured him, and plugged the number absently into her machines, her eyes drifting to where an employee of the casino was bringing out an oversized vanity check for the big winner.

The machine chimed and happily spat out sixty thousand-dollar chips and thirty-odd hundred-dollar chips. The girl looked down at them and seemed to finally process the amount that David had turned in and was apparently planning on taking back out to gamble with.

He could *watch* her mental gears shift as she activated a mental script for sale of chips.

"If sir would like," she chirped brightly, "we keep the higher-limit tables in a private lounge. I can arrange for one of the floor managers to take you up."

David smiled. He'd been hoping for an invitation of that sort, but he'd figured he'd need to win and lose ten thousand or more dollars a couple of times to get there.

"That would be perfect, miss," he told her.

THE CASHIER MANAGED to conjure another, somewhat older woman in a dress that almost matched Mason's in its frankness. The floor manager lacked much of the ONSET Commander's height and statuesque frame, at least to David's eyes, and seemed somewhat perturbed by the comparison.

"If you and your companion will follow me, sir," she told David, scooping his collection of chips into a metal-framed carrying case. "I will show you to the Black Lounge."

"Thank you," David told her, falling into step as instructed. If nothing else, the woman was holding sixty thousand dollars of his money. Though, of course, if he tried to actually *use* it for himself, he'd find himself out of a job very quickly.

The manager led them through a set of doors tucked next to the main entrance to the casino and up a flight of stairs carpeted in what looked like black velvet, into a second-floor lounge that overlooked the main casino floor through a one-way mirror.

The music was quieter up here and there were no slot machines, just a trio of roulette wheels and tables for craps, poker and blackjack.

"The drinks at the bar are complimentary," their guide told them as she handed David the case of casino chips. "The minimum bet at all tables is one thousand dollars. Good luck, sir, miss."

She disappeared back down the stairs as rapidly as she'd appeared, leaving David and Mason to study the tables and bars for several moments.

"What are you thinking?" she asked him.

"You go grab us drinks," he told her. "I'm going to go lose to start things off."

Mason laughed and gestured him toward the tables.

He walked up the roulette table first, joining a collection of men and women, mostly in suits and dresses similar to what he and Mason were wearing—if likely more expensive.

"What would you like to bet on?" the croupier asked him as he joined the crowd.

"I've been lucky so far today," David told him, and dropped five one-thousand-dollar chips onto red. "Let's see what happens."

Roulette was outside his normal "range" for prediction, the wheel spinning for easily ten seconds. He still knew well before the wheel stopped spinning that he'd lost, but he was testing to see if he could push it. He could expand his funds rapidly using blackjack, but he could only win so much before the casino would start to question it.

He'd be better off with a few big-ticket wins at roulette than a steady progression at blackjack, especially since he still needed an almost two-hundred-fold increase.

The wheel ended on the black twenty, and the casino employee scooped the losing bids, including David's, into a basket—and paid out the rest, including several gold-and-black chips David realized were the hundred-thousand-dollar chips he needed for the Oracle.

"Again," David ordered aloud, dropping another five thousand dollars onto red. It was a good thing he wasn't regarding this as his money, or he wasn't sure he'd be able to do this. A man who could see the future wasn't the type to gamble for real.

This time, he focused hard and got what he *thought* was a hint... and left his bet on red. When the spin finished, he was right. He made up his losses from the first spin, then bet another five thousand on odd...which the hint *this* time suggested would lose.

The wheel hit the green zero, and David lost his money again—but he was smiling as Mason rejoined him, the other Commander pressing a tall drink into his hand and herself against his side.

"Ah, my good-luck charm," he told her. "I should have known better than to play without you here!"

He took a sip of the drink and coughed. He wasn't certain what the mixed drink was—he hadn't asked her for anything specific—but it was mixed strongly enough to hit even him.

With Mason back, his claimed "lucky charm", he threw ten thousand dollars onto the sixteen-seventeen-eighteen set and another ten thousand on odds. He felt her tense against him and smiled at her again. Mason *knew* the limits of his Sight, but the wheel was sufficiently carefully balanced that he could, just barely, read the result.

The wheel spun...and landed on eighteen. Mason audibly squeaked, pressing harder into his side as she swallowed half her drink.

The losing bets swept off, David accepted seventeen ten-thousand-dollar chips from the croupier with a broad grin.

"See, I said she was my good-luck charm!" he told everyone. "Let's go try the blackjack tables," he told Mason. "Let's see if your luck carries over!"

Knowing what card was going to be drawn wasn't enough of an edge to win every game of blackjack, and David didn't *want* to win every game. It was enough of an edge that, despite the continuing stream of complimentary drinks and food for him and Mason, he managed to turn just over two hundred thousand dollars into half a million over the course of two hours.

Hitting that mark, he could tell that the dealers were starting to get twitchy with his run of luck, so he thanked the three dealers, tipped them with everything he'd accumulated over the even half-million mark, and took a few moments to eat a burger and let his metabolism handle the alcohol.

Despite not currently needing a distraction, Mason remained well inside what would normally be either of their personal space bubbles, her leg touching his as they ate. It wasn't *unwelcome*, but he was concerned about how much alcohol she'd had—he'd tipped past "buzzed" a few times, but she didn't have his advantages.

"Are you doing okay?" he asked softly. "That's a lot of alcohol they've been feeding us."

"They know what they're doing," Mason confirmed, leaning on his shoulder to whisper into his ear. "And so do I. Running a sober-up spell pretty constantly, but acting the drunk lush certainly helps the distraction factor."

"That it does," he confirmed, controlling a shiver from her breath on his skin. "Looks like something's going on at the roulette table, and we need to wrap this up with a big win at this point. Let's check it out."

The was more than one roulette table in the Black Lounge, but there was no question which one he was referring to. A crowd was gathering around the central one, as several young men appeared to be egging each other on to larger and larger bets.

Two of them were dressed in designer suits, the third in jeans and a T-shirt, but all three had arrived with a stack of the black-and-gold hundred-thousand-dollar chips in tow.

"Any other bets?" the roulette croupier asked as David slid into the crowd, glancing at David specifically. All of the staff had earpieces for radios and he was sure his streak at the blackjack tables had been communicated around.

"Sure," David said cheerfully, stepping up to look over the table.

Between the three men, there was eight hundred thousand dollars on the table. Everyone else, it seemed, was simply watching.

"Let's make it a round million, shall we?" the cop said aloud, stretching into the future to try and judge the spin. He dropped two hundred thousand dollars, in the fifty-thousand-dollar chips the blackjack tables had given him, onto evens.

The wheel spun. David lost, as he'd known he would. So did both of the men in designer suits—but the jeans and T-shirt-clad millionaire won his line bet, collecting a million dollars in hundred-thousand-dollar chips as the rest of the chips went off the table.

The man smirked at David and the other two who'd been gambling, and his gaze fell on Kate Mason.

"My dear, it seems the good luck is shifting around," he told her with a not-quite-leer of a grin. "Why don't you come sit with me? I *guarantee* you'll have a better time than with him." He gestured toward David with his chin.

The provocation worked perfectly for what David needed, but it *also* made him want to remove parts of the younger man's skeleton, preferably slowly. He ground the flash of anger—and jealousy?!—under and smiled coldly at the man.

"She's with me," he said flatly. "Let's see who's lucky, shall we?"

With a momentary glance into the future, he slammed three hundred thousand dollars, all of his remaining chips, on the green zero while holding the other man's gaze.

"Well?" he demanded.

The youth grinned.

"You're on. A million on red, my good man," he told the croupier, "and five hundred thousand on...let's say twenty-six. I like twenty-six."

The other two millionaires threw their own bets in and a silence spread across the room as the crowd realized there was over *three million dollars* in bets on the roulette board.

David held his breath as the spin started. They'd delayed long enough that he wasn't *entirely* confident in his foresight, but as the wheel spun, his Sight answered him. He didn't let it show on his face as he held the younger and richer man's gaze for the entire spin…until it clattered to a halt.

"Zero," the croupier announced. "I have a win on the five-number bet…and on the zero."

"Yes!" Mason exclaimed next to David, suddenly wrapping herself around him and kissing him, hard.

For several seconds, his entire world shrank down to the fact that a stunningly attractive leggy blonde was attached to him, and then the croupier cleared his throat.

"Would you like your chips, sir?" he said, to a chorus of laughter.

"Yes," Mason said throatily. "In the case; we'll take them with us. I think I need to drag this young man upstairs!"

The chuckles of understanding laughter covered their packing over ten million dollars in hundred-thousand-dollar chips into the metal carrying case and retreating from the room to a chorus of applause. Even the younger man who'd "provoked" David into the bet could only muster a halfhearted glare that turned into a cheerful salute as Mason all but dragged David from the room.

[14]

Getting from the Black Lounge to the elevator took several minutes. Several minutes David spent convincing his extremely enthusiastic lizard brain that the kiss and ensuing limpet-like attachment of his coworker were an act, a useful distraction to keep everyone focused on the fact that they were clearly focused on jumping each other's bones…not sneaking ten million dollars in chips out of the casino.

That comfortable illusion lasted about five seconds after the doors to the elevator closed. That was how long it took for Kate to detach herself from his side, get a careful hold on the case of chips, and then pin him against the elevator wall to resume kissing him.

Thoroughly.

David's arms came up around her almost of their own volition, holding her tightly while returning the kiss fiercely. There were a thousand reasons this was a bad idea, but it was hard to remember them when a leggy blonde with a heart of gold was pressed against him with her tongue in his mouth.

The elevator came to their floor with a soft ding and Kate withdrew slightly, still inside David's arms and still with her own hands on him.

"I am not drunk," she said softly but firmly. "I am entirely aware of every reason this is a bad idea. That said, I *really* think you need to take me to bed. Now."

Those reasons flashed through David's own mind. ONSET wasn't technically a military organization, and its rules on fraternization were loose…but his own small-team leadership experience prior to entering ONSET meant he ended up leading multi-team forces. Kate had ended up under his command before and likely would again.

Even if she didn't, they were courting a level of emotional entanglement that could only make their jobs harder.

And he didn't care. At all.

Kate was holding the case full of casino chips, so he scooped her up in his arms, lifting her off the ground into his arms. She leaned into his chest with a throaty purr and he headed down the corridor, back to their rooms.

AFTERWARD, lying in the chaotic mess of blankets and sheets they'd turned Kate's bed into, David clung to her tightly. Part of him felt like she'd disappear if he let go…and from the way she returned his embrace, he suspected she felt much the same.

"So, it seems there is a heavy enough brick I can hit you with," she told him softly, leaning her head on his shoulder, careful to avoid the still-aching scar from the elf-blade wound. "Though, to be fair, I wasn't *certain* you were worth my time for a while."

"Oh?" he asked. "What changed your mind?"

"When a certain *idiot* decided that the best way to win the day was to get *stabbed*," Kate told him. "It was brave. And then I saw you in the hospital, recovering, and realized how upset I'd have been if I lost you."

"Sorry," he muttered.

"Don't be," she said fondly. "I wouldn't like you nearly as much if you didn't rank your own safety somewhere around priority six or seven."

"I didn't know I wouldn't be able to heal from the stab," David pointed out. "It's easy to deprioritize my own safety when most things can't actually hurt me for long."

"'For long', he says." Kate shook her head. "So far as I know, it still *hurts*."

"Yes," he said quietly, shivering at the memory of the elf-blade, a magical sword enchanted so its wounds *couldn't* be regenerated by someone like him, stabbing into his skin. "It still hurts. With the elf-blade...it never really stopped."

Very, very gently, she pressed a kiss to the scar on his shoulder.

"You brave, silly, man," she told him, then kissed him again.

"You know this was a terrible idea," David reminded her, still holding her against him.

"I know," she admitted. "But *I* don't have forever, and you seem determined to get yourself killed before you can discover if you do.

"So, today is all I know we have. And I'm not going to give it up; do you understand me, David White?"

"I do," he agreed, then kissed her. "But the problems remain, Kate."

"I know," she sighed. "We can't... We can't let this come back to work with us. But we *can* make sure we take leave together when we can. Steal what we can get for ourselves, because Goddess knows we're both giving everything we can to others."

"That...will have to work," David said. It was probably a terrible idea, one that could easily get them in trouble...but ONSET didn't actually have rules against fraternization.

"And speaking of work, you should email the Oracle," Kate told him, slowly unwrapping her naked form from around him. "And once you've done that, Commander David White, I can think of something *else* I need you to do."

[15]

LATER, SHOWERED AND DRESSED FOR THE CHILLIER AIR OF A VEGAS SPRING evening, they took stock of their assets. Both of them were clad in conservative black suits, the age-old standby of the federal agent for the very simple reason that the suits easily covered a concealed shoulder holster.

Kate carried the same small revolver she'd had on her the previous day, where David had the bulk for his jacket to cover the large, boxy shape of the Omicron Silver caseless automatic. He felt somewhat under-armed without the hilt and extradimensional scabbard of *Memoria*, but while he'd check the government-issued sidearm into a plane's cargo hold, he *wasn't* checking a demon-forged blade containing the souls of comrades and friends.

"I'm pretty sure those chips aren't supposed to leave the casino," he told his companion, studying the open case with its hundred-odd black-and-gold chips. "Want to bet they're tagged and an alarm of some kind will go off if we walk through the front door?"

"Mmm. Sixty-forty," Kate replied. "I don't see a reason to take a chance, though. My purse is an extradimensional space, similar to your scabbard. I figure we stick the chips in there, it will block any signal, and we walk right out of here without even a blip to make anyone suspicious."

"The Oracle will need to get them back in here," David pointed out, then shrugged. "Somehow, I don't think they'll have a problem."

"No," she agreed. "I've never seen a construct with as much fidelity as the one they sent. I don't know what the Oracle *is*, but I have no desire to screw with them nor any inclination to assume they can't do whatever they need to."

"Agreed," David said. "I have my suspicions, but the likelihood is that I'm completely wrong."

Kate laughed.

"Yeah, that's pretty normal if you want to make guesses in this job," she agreed. "Anything else we need?"

"Guns, ten million dollars, cellphones; check on all three," he told her with a grin. "I think we're good."

"All right." She leaned in for a lingering kiss, then broke free to grab the hotel phone. "I'll have the hotel get us a cab. Where were we meeting the Oracle?"

"I picked a five-star restaurant off-Strip, basically at random," he admitted. "I figured no one was going to blink at us celebrating our big win."

"Makes sense," Kate agreed, then glanced back at the still-open chip case. "What are we doing with the last half-million?"

"Cashing it out and disclosing it to Omicron," he replied. "I figure they'll make me surrender it, but hey, they might let me keep it!"

And since he lived in an Omicron-provided apartment and earned a generous salary, it wasn't like he *needed* the money.

When their taxi arrived at the restaurant, a pair of elegantly dressed young women immediately walked over to greet them. They were a matched set of curvy brunettes, clearly not twins but dressed identically in short and tight black dresses and holding hands.

"Mr. White, Ms. Mason," the taller one greeted them. "We speak for the Oracle. We made a reservation for the four of us."

David wasn't surprised to realize that both women were constructs. He was wondering if the Oracle actually *had* a physical body as humans understood it, or if it could only interact with the world through constructs. It was equally likely, though, that the Oracle simply chose to hide behind the constructs as a form of security.

"What should we call you?" Kate asked as they followed the constructs into the restaurant.

The shorter one of the pair smiled back over her shoulder.

"She is Amber. I am Beverly," she told them. "We're known here."

The front host looked up with a smile as she was speaking.

"Ah, Mrs. and Mrs. Tahoe. I thought I spotted your lovely names on the reservation list. I've set aside your usual private space."

"Thank you, George," Amber replied. "Have a bottle of wine brought to our table, please. The house Grigio; you know the one."

"I do indeed, Mrs. Tahoe," George replied. "This way, please."

The host led them to the back of the restaurant, to a small table tucked away in an elevated corner with a decorative lattice screening them from the rest of the room. It was more private than David had been expecting—and a waitress was already waiting with the bottle of wine the construct had suggested.

She poured four glasses, then retreated.

"The wine is excellent," Beverly told them. "Try it."

"Not to be rude," David said delicately, "but can you even taste it?"

The construct laughed, a silvery giggle that would probably have had unfortunate effects on him if that portion of his lizard brain wasn't thoroughly overloaded today.

"You and Ms. Mason both have the Sight, to different degrees," she confirmed. "We are...recurring constructs, with sustained memories and intellects. Extensions of the Oracle, we both remember our own experiences—such as the wine—and pass on all that we see, taste, and sense to it."

"So, Amber and Beverly Tahoe?"

"Exist, have driver's licenses, own property, and pay taxes," Amber told him. "Thanks to a confusing network of trust funds and numbered companies, it isn't necessarily obvious that we only exist part of the time and don't actually own a *home*."

The pair grinned, a matching wicked smile.

"We even got married in California in 2008, before they passed Proposition 8," Beverly noted. "The Oracle…is very unimpressed with humanity's current attitude towards sex and marriage."

That gave them two bits of information about the Oracle: one, that it *wasn't* human; and two, that it had been around for a long time.

"We recommend the steak," Amber told them. "The wait staff here is discreet, but we're best off waiting until our food has arrived to discuss business."

"I picked this restaurant at random," David said. "How did we end up at one that you are known at?"

"Had you picked a different restaurant, depending on the one, you might have met with different representatives," Beverly explained. "Anywhere on the Strip, it would have been us, but each of the representatives has cultivated different areas of the city."

"If you feel out of your depth, Mr. White, remember that we have been doing this for a long time, and are very, very careful," Amber told him. "So long as you are with us, your safety is guaranteed."

"We cannot, of course, speak for your safety after this meeting," Beverly warned. "For now, however, the waitress will be back in a couple of minutes. I suggest you consult the menu."

DAVID FOLLOWED THE CONSTRUCTS' suggestion and ordered the steak, as did Kate. The conversation stayed noncommittal until the steaks arrived, the Oracle's representatives teasing out the two ONSET agents' opinions of Vegas.

Once the food arrived, the waitress dropped off a second bottle of wine, making sure everyone's glass was full before she disappeared.

A curtain that David hadn't noticed before swung shut behind her, closing off the corner table from the rest of the restaurant. From the smiles on the two constructs' faces, they'd been expecting this.

For all that Amber and Beverly were manufactured entities, beings created of energy and someone else's will, they were charming, witty young women who clearly had distinct personalities from each other and, presumably, the Oracle itself.

It was a strange sensation, interacting with them, and the pair clearly understood *exactly* how David and Kate were feeling.

"Now, you should have a certain amount of money for us," Amber told them.

"We heard you had an *extraordinary* day at the Black Lounge," Beverly added. "Well covered-for, too. Well done."

"Thank you," David said somewhat awkwardly, gesturing for Kate to produce the chips.

The other Commander carefully counted out one hundred of the black-and-gold chips, sliding them across the table past her plate in stacks of ten. Beverly took each stack, running her hand over them like some kind of scanner, and nodded with each stack.

"One hundred Black Lounge gold chips," she confirmed, sliding the tokens into her cleavage. Presumably, they were either teleporting elsewhere or entering an extradimensional pocket like Kate's purse, as they certainly weren't *staying* inside her shirt. "Value, one hundred thousand dollars apiece, totaling ten million dollars.

"Exactly as agreed."

"And we were promised information," David reminded them.

"Yes," Amber agreed. "Everything we know on the Arbiter." She reached into her own cleavage and produced a black metal USB stick and slid it across the table. David took it, eyeing the data storage device carefully.

"Everything we know is on here, but I'll give you the summary," she concluded.

"The vampire you call the Arbiter was born as Anaxis in the city state of Athens," she began. "We're not sure exactly when; our methods get less reliable looking that far into the past. We do know that Anaxis commanded a hoplite formation under Aléxandros ho Mégas—who history recalls as Alexander the Great.

"Anaxis followed Aléxandros to war in Persia. At some point during those battles, Anaxis was turned and became a vampire," she explained. "Assuming he was in his twenties when he went to war, he is somewhere in the region of twenty-three hundred and seventy years old, one of the oldest vampires alive."

David inhaled sharply. He'd fought the previous ruler of the Vampire Familias, Marcus Dresden, a powerful and deadly opponent at a "mere" five centuries old.

"I thought Marcus Dresden was the oldest vampire in America," he pointed out.

"Marcus Dresden was the oldest *politically active* vampire in America," Beverly corrected him. "Vampires like the Arbiter have forsworn power to avoid the conflicts of their younger kin. He was never a member of the Vampire Familias here; he always stood separate from them."

"He came from France," Amber explained. "We're not certain at what point he became a Keeper, but he was the guardian of the Crèche in Paris when the Revolution began there. His associations made him vulnerable and he saw the Reign of Terror coming. He fled to America.

"Without his protection, however, the Parisian Crèche was destroyed."

David held up a hand to slow the spiel.

"Am I allowed to ask for explanations of phrases I don't understand?" he said carefully. Given that their one question had cost them ten million dollars, he wasn't sure just what was included in his answer.

"Yes," Beverly confirmed. "Detailed explanations of most of this is on the USB stick, but I am guessing you are questioning the Keepers and the Crèche?"

"Exactly," he admitted.

"You know, Mr. White, that a vampire is basically feral once first turned," Beverly noted. "A fledgling is extraordinarily dangerous and retains most of their intelligence but has no real concept of self or society, only of their own hunger.

"Have you ever wondered how the Familias deal with such an issue?"

"Yes, but I've never found an answer beyond four trucks of fledglings with an unknown destination," David replied.

"The answer is the Crèches," Amber said, taking over from Beverly in perfect turn. "With centuries of practice behind them, they have learned how best to contain and calm their children. If everything is done right, they can bring a fledgling back to themselves, with most of their pre-vampire memories intact, in about a year.

"If they screw it up, it can take two to three years and they remember nothing. The ancient vampires literally loosed their fledglings into the wilderness and watched for them to return when they were 'awake' again."

David nodded his understanding. That, if nothing else, explained where the four trucks of freshly turned vampires had been going.

"And the Arbiter runs one of these crèches?" he asked.

"The Arbiter is a Keeper," Beverly told him. "One of the vampires responsible for maintaining the crèches. They learned early on that having the scent of human blood aggravated the fledglings, easily costing them days or weeks of progress, so the Keepers had to swear off it.

"This transformed into foreswearing violence entirely by about the twelfth century. They regarded the oath as allowing them to defend their charges, but no more."

"You mean to tell me there's an entire group of vampires that don't touch human blood and are sworn to pacifism?" Kate asked. "I find that hard to believe."

"Mr. White met the Arbiter, one of the most powerful vampires alive, and breathes still," Amber replied. "He will not make himself your enemy, but he will destroy you if you make yourselves his."

David shivered, remembering the old vampire's gaze.

"So, he stands aside from politics and the Familias?" he said, trying to bring them back onto topic. "If he was a Keeper when he came to America, he has always stood aside here?"

"Exactly," Beverly agreed. "He arrived here and joined the one Crèche in North America, but then learned of the fate of the Parisian Crèche.

"Seven Keepers and fourteen fledglings died because he wasn't there to protect them," she continued. "The Seal was far stronger then than now, and those fourteen fledglings represented every vampire 'born' in Europe for two years—and an unusually fruitful two years, at that. The Crèche normally had a Keeper per fledgling."

"He arrived in America as Adam Waters and then learned of his failure," Amber took over. "He then bought a rural property far from anywhere, abandoned the New York Crèche, and went into a self-imposed exile for fifty years.

"The Familias sought him out in the late nineteenth century after the Familias Morgan attacked and burnt out the New York Crèche during the Civil War.

"Dresden had destroyed Morgan and his Familias, but he feared that maintaining the Crèche under his control risked the very problem that had caused the destruction of the New York Crèche. He asked Anaxis to take over the remaining Keepers and establish a completely neutral Crèche, truly outside Familias politics."

"He took the title Arbiter at that time," Beverly concluded, "and rejoined American vampire society as the ultimate babysitter. He knew raising fledglings better than any of the Keepers they had left, and none of the patriarchs intimidated him at all.

"He turned his ranch into a Crèche initially and has relocated it several times since, especially as the number of fledglings has dramatically increased in recent decades," she said. "He now runs it out of an underground facility that used to be a nuclear missile silo. He bought it at auction and has been expanding the underground tunnels since."

"The Mountain, as it is now called, is operating at a seven-to-one ratio of fledglings to Keepers," Amber noted. "Only the Arbiter's near-millennium of experience allows them to handle the influx."

"Where is this Mountain?" David asked.

"The details are on the chip," Beverly told him. "The facility has limited defenses beyond the Arbiter and his Keepers, but every Familias in North America will fight for it."

"Thank you," he told the two women. "And thank the Oracle for me."

"All we have seen, the Oracle has seen," Amber replied. "You have thanked the Oracle. The money serves that purpose as well." She inclined her head. "We have already arranged payment for the meal."

"Then I believe our business is done," David told her. He'd barely even registered the steak he'd eaten as the two constructs had detailed the life story of the man he was probably going to have to kill. Destroying the Mountain would undermine the vampires in the United States, possibly finally giving Omicron the edge to end the war.

"It is, but we have a final warning for you," Beverly said. "Your enemies are aware of your presence in Las Vegas and they believe you are vulnerable here. The noose tightens around you, Mr. White, Ms. Mason. You should leave the city of sin sooner rather than later—or you may never leave."

[16]

When the Tahoe Oracle gave a free warning, it turned out that one should listen. Immediately.

The restaurant was far enough from their Strip hotel that David and Kate let themselves relax on the taxi ride. They didn't relax quite so far as to start making out in the back seat, but the silent glances Kate was sending him left David quite certain what the plans for back in their room were.

He was distracted enough that he didn't realize the taxi was going the wrong way until his threat sense started tingling and he shook his head, focusing outside the vehicle and realizing they were a *long* way from the glitz and glamour of the Strip.

They were somewhere in an unfamiliar, industrial-looking district, well away from what the tourists were supposed to see, and surrounded by a seemingly infinite array of low-slung gray warehouses.

"Hey, driver," David called forward. "This isn't where we asked to go, what's going on?"

Even as he spoke, one hand slipped inside his coat and removed the clip on his gun.

"It's a shortcut," the man said crisply. "Saves us both time and you money, trust me!"

"Son, we've already been driving longer than it took to get to the restaurant," David pointed out. "What the *fuck* is going on?"

"It's Vegas, sir; you can't just take the same route back without going into one-way traffic," the driver replied. "Trust me!"

"I don't," David said flatly. "Pull the car over."

"What?"

"Pull the car over and let us out," he told the driver. He was more confident with just him and Kate in the middle of the worst of neighborhoods than he was in the back seat of a car he didn't know the destination of.

"I can't do that, sir," the driver told him.

David drew his gun. He didn't point it at the man, but he held it where it was clearly visible in the mirror.

"I am a Federal agent," he said calmly. "If you don't stop this car *right now*, there is going to be hell to pay."

His prescience flared and he twisted his body to balance as the driver slammed on the brakes, twisting the car into a wide turn more fitting a street racer than a taxi car, trying to throw David off as he threw the vehicle into a darkened building. He heard Kate slam against the side of the car, but he focused on the driver.

He swung the pistol up to aim at the man, only for the taxi to come to a crushing halt that crushed him into his seatbelt even as he braced himself.

"See? Stopped!" the driver announced—and then the windshield shattered and the man's head exploded, the sniper bullet smashing past David into the backseat of the taxi.

"Move!" he snapped at Kate, but she was already in motion. The door was open and she dove out, weaving an invisible shield that deflected the second and third shots.

They took cover behind the taxi for a moment, *feeling* the heavy metal chassis move as more bullets slammed into it.

The now-dead driver had driven them into the middle of a warehouse, pitch-black in the late Vegas evening and a lack of lights.

"At least one sniper; won't be just one," he said quickly.

"Full court?" Kate asked and David hesitated. They were allowed to use the full suite of their supernatural abilities in self-defense, but it was discouraged unless necessary.

Then he felt magic flare in the dark and it was *not* Kate.

"*Move!*" He grabbed her and ran, dragging the Mage with him as more bullets smashed into the ground around them—and a bright blue fireball incinerated the taxi and where they'd been hiding.

"Right," Kate gasped as he dropped her next to a wall. "Mage. Guessing vampires. Full court."

"Cover me," David told her as he pulled out his phone and hit a very specific four-digit sequence without unlocking it. Dropping it to the ground, he stretched into the future…and then dropped to the ground as a heavy silver bullet ripped through three full crates of potato chips to cut through where his head had been.

"Help is on the way," he said softly. "We just have to stay alive!"

———

"I can't stop silver bullets for very long," Kate warned him. "And I bet you anything you care to name they're already moving more shooters around."

"Agreed."

There was no telling how long it would take the closest ONSET team to respond to his emergency signal. Assuming they were at the Nevada base and not tied up in another call, it could be as little as twenty minutes…but if the team was at one of the other state bases or was already in action, it could be a lot longer.

Another heavy bullet slammed into the crates they were hiding behind, losing enough of its velocity that Kate's shield stopped it cold, silver or not.

"They're trying to keep us pinned down," David noted. "Let's…see about that."

The Omicron Silver held twelve rounds, but as a caseless automatic, it was capable of firing a three-round burst—a mode most of its users couldn't use. David, on the other hand, was *far* stronger than most of the Silver's users and had the bulk to use that strength to absorb the recoil.

When the next shot echoed through the warehouse, he spun out from behind the crates in a perfect two-handed shooting stance and opened fire. Two three-round bursts slammed into the catwalk the sniper was firing from, and someone shouted in pain as a rifle fell and clattered to the ground.

The response was roughly as David expected: four shooters that had been trying to sneak up on them returned fire, assault-rifle fire echoing in the open space—and allowing Kate Mason to localize them. A blue inferno tore across the floor of the warehouse, and the assault rifles were silent.

Rejoining Kate behind their somewhat worthless cover, David met her gaze silently as he switched the Silver back to single-fire. He wasn't carrying any spare clips. The six rounds left in his gun were all he had and he wasn't carrying a blade of any kind.

"We need to get out of here," he told her.

"Taxi came in that way," she pointed. "I'm not betting on us being able to make it, though. Probably closed."

"That won't stop me," David replied. "But bullets might."

"I know. We have to do something."

He nodded.

"Cover me?"

"Always."

Fire flared from her hands, a ball of white light rising up to light up the whole room. She couldn't duplicate the power of the sun that would endanger the vampires, but she could certainly light up the room so no one could hide.

Hoping they were blinded by the flash, David set off for the door. No mortal human could match his speed...but vampires weren't mortal humans.

Four of them emerged from the darkness with blurring speed, intercepting him in the middle of the warehouse floor. Two of them charged him with long knives while two others opened fire with submachine guns—and others began to pepper Kate's cover with assault-rifle fire to keep her from taking out the ones charging David.

He shot the first vampire to come at him with a knife, the heavy fifty-caliber silver slug ripping out most of the creature's chest and sending it flying back. The second managed to close to knife distance, forcing him into a delicate high-speed dance of bullets and blades as his friends opened fire into the melee and David tried to take him down.

In a knife fight, even his prescience cut down to fractions of a second, enough to live but not enough to necessarily *win*—but unfortunately for the vampire, David had been trained by the inhuman Sages ONSET used as combat instructors.

It cost him three of his remaining five bullets, but the vampire went down—and the last two bullets shattered the skulls of the vampires shooting at him.

Several of the rifle-armed shooters on the roof were down, Kate flinging efficiently deadly bolts of fire at her attackers, and David left her to it—she certainly didn't need *his* protection. Dropping his pistol, he charged for the door again...only to find his path cut off by a wall of blue fire.

"No, Commander, you don't get to run today," a calm male voice said behind him.

His prescience spiked and he dodged to the side as a bolt of blue flame cut through where he'd been standing. The Mage approaching from behind was floating an inch or so off the floor, a Victorian-style burgundy cape flaring out over a black modern designer suit.

The man held a silver-topped walking stick in his right hand, which he pointed directly at David.

"No sword, no gun, what's left, Commander White, but the man? And however strong, a man is no match for a Mage."

The vampire wasn't wrong, though David was hardly going to simply give up just because he happened to be unarmed. He sidestepped the vampire's first burst of flame, charging the Mage with his fists clenched.

"David, catch!" Kate suddenly shouted, and he flung his right hand out, unseeing, to grab whatever she'd thrown him.

The bolt of fire seared into his skin for a moment, and then adjusted to a gentle warmth—while a blade of icy blue fire flashed up from his grip and lit up his face as he grinned coldly at the vampire.

"That's when it's nice to have friends," he told the Mage—and charged.

The vampire might have been surprised, but there was nothing wrong with his reflexes. David knew how fast he was, but the Mage brought his walking stick up to parry the flaming sword Kate had conjured. White light flared around the stick and David bounced away, thrown by the vampire's magic.

More bolts of fire lit up the floor, but he was already moving, the blue sword arcing around at waist height—only for the vampire to leap above the sword and smash downward. Even with his prescience, David only barely dodged the heavy silver top of the cane.

"You die tonight, White," the vampire told him, casually hovering in the air four feet up. "My Lord wills it, and so it shall be done."

David leapt into the air, slashing coldly as the vampire dodged back, losing his balance and falling off whatever spell levitated him. The Mage crashed to the floor on his back and David landed and charged at him again.

The vampire crab-walked backward, a motion that even David couldn't replicate, and then leapt back to his feet. The cane flashed out in the light Kate had summoned, and his cape billowed, power flaring around him as he channeled magic.

Unfortunately for him, David was faster. Blue flame slashed through the gorgeous burgundy cape, barely missing the vampire as he abandoned his spell, dodging David's strike…but that much power couldn't be easily grounded.

Especially not when someone *else* was around to use it.

The aura of power that David had Seen the vampire gather stayed with him as he dodged…but he was no longer in control of it and it took him a moment to realize what had happened as the magic locked onto him, freezing him in place for several precious moments.

"Friends are *very* important," Kate Mason said sweetly—and then fired her revolver into the trapped vampire's head just as he shattered the spell.

The warehouse was suddenly silent and David realized that while he'd been fighting the vampire Elder, Kate had been methodically eliminating the rest of the ambush.

"Thank you," he said softly.

"Thank *you*," she replied. "I couldn't have dealt with his guards *and* him at once."

David glanced around, shaking his head.

"I guess I didn't need to call for backup," he noted.

"I wouldn't count on that," Kate said grimly. "Do you want to bet there wasn't a second string to their bow?"

He sighed.

"One Elder versus both of us? No, there's something else in play." He grabbed his phone.

"This is Commander White, emergency status is still active," he said into it. "We've been ambushed and cut off; we are expecting incoming vampires or other hostile supernaturals in short order. What's the status on our backup?"

"This is Commander Wu," a voice with a faint Chinese accent replied. "ONSET Sixteen is inbound. We are at least five minutes out—but we have surveillance-satellite tasking approved. We'll have overhead in fifteen seconds, linking in Leitz to keep you updated."

"Cynthia, good to hear from you," David greeted his control. "How much trouble am I in?"

"I don't know yet; how bad was it?" she answered.

"One Elder, fifteen-to-twenty troops. Could have been worse; I'm just worried about the *rest* of it."

"That's fair," she replied, her voice suddenly distracted. "Commanders, I have a *major* aetheric event triggering outside the warehouse. I don't know what's going on, but you need to get out there and stop it.

"Now."

THE VAMPIRES HAD CLOSED the front door that the taxi driver had entered the warehouse through, but the corrugated metal tore and lifted easily when faced with David's superhuman strength. What he saw on the other side, though, made him realize the vampires had bitten off far more than they could have chewed.

Six pots marked the corners of a hexagon, each of them spewing smoke that he could smell contained blood and sulfur and other, less identifiable things—and power.

Magic arced from pot to pot, smoke weaving together with energy, and the familiar scent of ichor began to waft from the ritual circle. David's Sight warned him as reality *tore*, black slime dripping through onto the concrete and beginning to take humanoid shape.

Kate squeezed his hand, restoring the flaming blade as she stepped aside to open her line of fire.

"Wu, Leitz, the bastards opened a rift through the Seal," David reported into his phone. "Get here. I don't have *Memoria*; I can't seal this."

"Three minutes," Wu replied. "Hold the line."

David tossed the phone aside and advanced on the forming demons with the flaming sword.

"Easy enough for him to say," he muttered. Four minor shadow demons had managed to come through already, and the ichor continued to drip onto the ground from the other side.

They sensed his approach and turned to the attack. Black claws appeared out of nothingness, slashing out as they charged at him. The flaming sword cut the first one in half, then David ducked under the second while Kate vaporized the third.

He caught the fourth with a backhand blow from the conjured blade, but the second was coming back around as four *more* spawned into reality.

Black claws stabbed into his flesh as even his prescience wasn't enough to dodge every attack. The last of the first wave came apart, the flaming blade slicing it in two even as its claws tore into him, cold seeping through his body as the ichor tried to poison him.

His regeneration repelled it almost instantly, the wound closing as fast as it had formed as he charged into the growing swarm of demons.

Kate conjured a wave of blue fire that wrapped around him, blasting half a dozen of the little horrors into chunks...but more remained and he could *feel* something larger coming through.

The flame sword sliced through the smaller demons, clearing a space around David even as their numbers grew. The portal was expanding, with more and more of the minor demons coming through, and a sinking feeling took hold in David's stomach.

A rift was a nightmare when he had a sword that could seal it and an entire team backing him. With just him and Kate, this could get very, *very* bad.

"Break the smoke pots!" Kate shouted. "It won't break the rift, but it should stop it growing!"

David took a deep breath and charged into the swarm. Claws slashed at him and shadowy hands tried to grab him as he twisted and turned through the demons to reach the rift itself. The flaming sword lashed out, collapsing one of the smoke pots as he kicked another over.

Then the rift spat out the next level of demon, a man-sized abomination of ichor and black flame. A whip of black fire slashed through the sword Kate had conjured, shattering the spell and leaving David unarmed, surrounded by lesser demons, and face to face with a low-court demon warrior.

Then the demon exploded as a chain gun walked its fire up the creature's torso and several air-to-surface missiles exploded across the field. Ichor scattered across the warehouses surrounding him as the missiles blasted the smaller demons to pieces, and then the chain gun walked across the remaining smoke pots.

"Mason," Wu's voice bellowed over the Pendragon's loud speaker. "Close it!"

Power flared in the Nevada evening as Kate Mason channeled magic and slammed it past David into the rift. For a moment, the tear in reality glowed a bright blue, and then it finally collapsed.

David stood in the middle of a scattered puddle of slime, the gentle warmth of his regeneration rippling through his skin and dealing with the scratches of being even near to a missile strike as he breathed heavily, looking up at the circling helicopter and giving Wu a calm, even salute.

[17]

"Most people go to Vegas looking for a party, Commander White, not a knife fight with vampires and demons in a warehouse."

Standing in the Major's office on the Campus, there wasn't much David could say in response to Major Warner's caustic commentary, so he simply shrugged and waited for her to get it out of her system while he studied the Rocky Mountains through her windows.

"I can't even ask what you were thinking," she continued, "because it's not like you did anything wrong, so far as I can tell. What the hell happened?"

"I'm not certain," he admitted. "But I would guess that there was a call out to taxi drivers known to do such things that they'd get paid for delivering us to that warehouse."

"Given that the footage from ONSET Sixteen's helicopter includes what might be the half-melted wreckage of a taxicab, I'm guessing that didn't end well for the driver," Warner replied.

"No. They shot him."

"And then tried to open a rift in Las Vegas." ONSET's second-in-command shook her head. "Are you all right?"

"I'm fine," David told her. "Commander Mason is in the Campus hospital, but even she just picked up scratches and a few burns. I was a bit worse off, but..." He shrugged.

He needed to be careful to not think of Commander Mason as Kate here. For now, that part of what happened in Vegas was going to have to stay in Vegas.

"But you healed," Warner finished for him. "The vampires seem to have put you high on their list of most wanted, Commander. That will probably help with one of the big concerns being placed in front of the board."

"Ma'am?"

"You've now met and spoken to two senior vampires without fighting them," she reminded him. "The circumstances made sense both times, frankly, but that's still twice more than the vast majority of our agents. The suggestion that you have been compromised has been floated with a certain degree of seriousness."

"I see," David replied, swallowing his initial response of a string of curses. "And do you believe so, ma'am?"

"Hardly," she chuckled. "There's too much of an iron stick up your ass, David White, for you to be compromised."

That was a vivid mental image.

"That the vampires clearly think you're someone they want dead, at almost any cost, is still reassuring. I'm not sure how they knew you were in Vegas, though. I would have expected you to be keeping a low profile."

He sighed.

"We tried, but something came up," he admitted. "We...kept it low-key, but we certainly weren't invisible."

Warner leveled her gaze on him, and he had the sudden impression of a gun turret bearing down.

"What did you do, Commander?" she asked.

"We won ten point five million dollars in one of the high-roller lounges," he confessed.

The Major's office was very quiet for several seconds, then Warner sighed.

"If you were anyone else, Commander, I'd assume you'd decided to break the rules to get rich, hoping we'd let you keep some," she said dryly. "But given the *iron stick up your ass* I mentioned earlier, I assume you had a reason."

"We had an opportunity to purchase intelligence on the Arbiter," he told her. "Ten million dollars, but we had to move quickly."

"So you did," Warner sighed. "And did you manage to close said deal before the Familias tried to summon *demons* into Las Vegas?"

He pulled the metal USB stick from his somewhat-scorched jacket and dropped it on the table.

"Such a small thing," he said softly. "For ten million dollars."

"I'm guessing there's still half a million dollars or so of casino chips in your room?" Warner asked, looking at the USB stick like it was a venomous snake.

"Yes, ma'am."

"I'll make sure the people we're sending to grab your gear know to cash it in for you," she told him. "You're not leaving the Campus for a while, David."

"Understood, ma'am. But…you need to know what we found."

"Take the stick to Charles," she told him. "I take it there's a key takeaway, though?"

"The Arbiter runs the facility where the Familias keep *all* of their fledglings until they regain control," David said softly. "It's the ultimate leverage on the vampires—if we ever want to force them to talk terms, it's the weapon for it.

"And if we keep going as we're going, taking their next generation out of the equation would make genocide easier, wouldn't it?"

Warner winced.

"For a man who hates to read, you sometimes use words like a knife, Commander," she pointed out. "I'll pass on at least the high level to Ardent. You talk to Charles, but…"

"Ma'am?"

"Your board convenes in two days," she told him. "We were about to recall you anyway."

INSTEAD OF HEADING STRAIGHT to Charles's underground lair, David instead went to the Campus hospital to check in on Mason. The guards and nurses let him through quickly. Despite his current technical suspension, no one on Campus seemed to be acting like he wasn't still fully on duty.

It was probably a good sign.

Mason was sitting up on her bed, reading on her phone. She laid it aside and smiled as he came in. It was a professional smile, exactly the same as she would have given him before…but her eyes said everything that they weren't allowed to say there.

"You don't look particularly beat-up for a young lady they rushed to the hospital, Commander," he told her.

"Scratches, cuts and burns are serious for most people, Commander," Mason replied. "Not *very* serious, but enough to need someone to clean them out and bandage them." She shrugged. "They're mostly keeping me in overnight for observation in case I got vampire blood or demon ichor in the injuries."

"You're vaccinated against the vampire virus, right?" David asked.

"Of course, and they gave me a booster," she confirmed. "But… observation anyway, with the antivenom on hand. The ichor's the bigger concern, but we have treatments for that, too."

David shook his head. There were many advantages to being a high-class regenerator, not least a high likelihood of near-immortality, but the ability to completely ignore most minor injuries and the potential for infection was definitely handy.

"We're turning the data from the Oracle over to Charles," he told her. "I don't even know how much data on the Arbiter's life they shoved on that stick, but I suspect we'll find some interesting tidbits."

"More interesting than the location of the Mountain?"

"More interesting?" he shook his head. "Potentially. Probably not more *useful*, but potentially more interesting."

"That man lived through practically every major historical event we know of," Mason said. "Probably wasn't there for them all, but just *think* of what his memories would mean to any historian worth their salt."

"Hopefully, we won't have to kill him, and we can lock him in a room with one," David replied. "An interview with *that* vampire would be worth an unimaginable amount, and not just in money."

"From what you said, it sounds like he wants peace somehow."

David shook his head.

"He might," he agreed, "but the rest of the Familias doesn't, which leaves us with very few options."

CHARLES WAS WAITING for David when he finally entered the dragon's lair, the big lizard pacing back and forth impatiently like a child waiting for a new toy.

"Ye have something for me, Ai'm told?" he asked gruffly. "Something that Warner made sound fascinating."

David produced the USB stick, only for it to be snatched out of fingers by massive, if surprisingly delicate, claws, and slotted into a machine.

Menus and file structures popped up on the massive array of screens Charles used as a monitor, and the dragon hummed to himself as he studied the data, then coughed hard.

"Who gave this to ye?" he demanded.

"An intelligence broker, basically," David said slowly. "Why?"

"It was encrypted. Hard. But Ai didn't even *notice* because it decrypted as soon as it recognized my computer," the dragon told him. "Not just an Omicron computer, David. *Mine*. Specifically."

"Shit."

"So, who gave this to you?"

"The Tahoe Oracle," David explained. "Loring put us in touch; we paid ten million dollars for that stick."

"The name is known to me," Charles admitted. "Not quite an urban legend; their Internet presence is quiet but known in our community. I thought they were much as ye described: an information broker. But this"—he waved at the data stick—"this is something else."

"Given the price and the reputation, I was guessing dragon," the ONSET Commander admitted. "But then…every time we interacted with them, it was via constructs. But these were like no constructs I'd ever seen. They were recurring, had memories, personalities...everything linked back to the Oracle so far as I could tell, but they were still more...complete than I'm used to constructs being."

"Aye. That's not dragon magic," Charles confirmed. "Yer not wrong that Ai have powers Ai've not shown ONSET, but that's not among them."

The dragon sounded thoughtful.

"What the hell did I meet with, Charles?" David asked.

"Something Ai did nae think was left in the world," the dragon told him, his tone awestruck. "Unless Ai miss my guess, ye met Lake Tahoe."

"I don't follow," David admitted.

"'Dragon' isn't a bad comparison," Charles explained. "But in the Chinese sense—a great elemental spirit, one of the Pure. There aren't supposed to be any left on this side of the Seal, and a being like you describe trapped by the Seal would have been destroyed or corrupted by the Masters Beyond."

The only Pure David knew of were...

"A demon?"

"Nae," Charles shook his head. "Though Ai know why ye went there. Yer body, David, is flesh and blood. Magic weaves through ye, but it does not sustain ye. Ye are Mantled.

"Mae body is stone and metal, *made* flesh by the magic within me. Ai am what ye termed Awakened.

"The Pure...have no bodies as ye understand them. They *are* magic, spirit. Before the Seal, there were many types, some who forged bodies of ichor like the demons you know, who others claimed godhood.

"Some were not so much as bound to places, a mountain, a water system as they *were* places. The greatest of these were mighty creatures indeed, but their essence could not be trapped by the Seal like the other Pure," Charles finished sadly. "The *genius loci*, the spirits of stone and water, torn from their homes, simply died—or were perverted into demons serving the Masters Beyond."

"And you're saying what I met was one of those?" David asked.

"It fits," the dragon told him. "Such beings would act through intermediaries that were alive in a sense but were only ever extensions of the Pure itself. The Oracle could have concealed itself in its lake, somehow, and slept through the ages of the Seal."

He shivered.

"If a sleeping Pure has awoken, the Seal is weaker than I feared," he confessed. "But its power would allow it to see the past and present with great fidelity, and it could use projections like those you met to enter that information into computers rapidly."

"Why would a being like that need money?" David asked.

"If the stone and water that sustain it are damaged or poisoned, it hurts it," Charles said quietly. "It will use that money to buy properties and buildings, construct water purifiers, shut down mines... Its priorities are not ours, but this one, at least, seems to value lives other than its own."

The dragon shivered.

"Be glad it seeks money and a peaceful solution, David White, for if that spirit were to turn its power against the humans on the stone it lives in, there would be no victory for mortal men, regardless of their power."

[18]

"THIS BOARD OF INQUIRY IS CONVENED UNDER THE ARTICLES OF Supernatural Law Enforcement Code of Conduct on May 15, 2017, to discuss the actions of Commander David White in Operation Golden Twilight," Commander Alexis Stall reeled off.

The tall brunette were-puma who commanded ONSET Four looked almost bored. Flanking her were three men, none of whom David knew well.

Commander Albert Frost led ONSET One. One of the oldest Mages in Omicron's service, his hair had gone white early to match his name, but he still sat upright and radiated both physical and magical energy.

Commander Orel Sokol, the leader of ONSET Six, was almost the complete opposite of Frost. Where the Mage was tall, Sokol was short. Where the Mage was graceful, Sokol was built with all of the grace and delicacy of a raging bull. Empowered like David, Sokol was almost completely invulnerable to harm and incredibly strong even by superhuman standards. If the man could fly, he'd have belonged in a superhero costume.

The last member of the four-person panel was Commander Loris Falco of ONSET Seventeen. David knew nothing about the hawk-nosed, dark-eyed man with the florid cheeks and the ready smile, not even what type of supernatural the man was.

"During the raid on the Golden Twilight Casino in Reno," Stall continued, "it was discovered that the Familias Romanov had sent four heavy transport trucks away the prior night under heavy guard. The decision was made by Commander White and Commander Mason that the trucks needed to be pursued to see what the Romanovs felt was worth that protection.

"Upon tracking down the trucks, Commander White engaged and destroyed the defenders, including several stolen Nevada National Guard antiaircraft units," she noted. "He secured the trucks with the competence and courage we would expect from an officer of Commander White's record.

"He then discovered that the trucks contained a number of vampire fledglings, restrained for transport. Major Warner confirmed that the situation called for the fulfillment of Standing Order Twenty-one and ordered the euthanization of the vampires in question for the protection of the surrounding area."

The small board room on the fifth floor of Building One was silent. There was no one in the room except David and the four members of the board. No prosecutor. No defender. The board had access to all of the records of that night, including the video footage of his entire conversation with the Arbiter.

"Before carrying out said orders, however," Stall continued, "Commander White was met by an Elder Vampire that wished to negotiate for the fledglings' release, offering—as I understand—that he would somehow guarantee that they would never harm anyone."

Stall's tone wasn't promising.

"Despite having no authority to negotiate with vampires under Standing Order Twenty-one, and facing active, specific orders to euthanize the vampires in question, Commander White chose to allow this Arbiter to leave the area with the four trucks that so much effort had been spent to acquire.

"While Commander White did suggest an attempt to track the vehicles, they were switched out with other truck cabs, and we have no idea where the forty vampires that we had the capacity to eliminate have gone."

David met Commander Stall's gaze levelly.

"There will be an opportunity for you to explain your thoughts later, Commander, but does that fundamentally sum up the events as you remember them?" she asked.

"Yes," he confirmed calmly. "That does accurately represent the sequence of events."

"Very well," Stall noted. "The purpose of this board, gentlemen, is to establish whether, in the opinion of his peers, Commander White's actions were, firstly, inside the limits of the authority granted to an ONSET Commander; and, secondly, were justified regardless of his authority to take them.

"There are specific particulars of charges that we are all familiar with, but fundamentally, they boil down to those two points.

"I suggest we begin by reviewing the camera footage of Commander White's conversation with this vampire."

It was strange watching the conversation as recorded by his own helmet camera. David remembered the whole scene vividly, but the slightly different angle of the camera mounted on the AR wargear was disconcertingly different.

The whole scene only lasted a few minutes, despite David's feeling like he'd spoken with the Arbiter for ages. The recording continued as the white-robed Keepers got into the trucks, including the one Mage levitating a truck into a driveable position.

Then Stall shut down the recording, turning her gaze back to David.

"So, Commander White. You took it upon yourself to release forty vampires to this individual based on nothing more than his promise. Why did you think this was justified?"

"Commander Stall, I am a Seer," David reminded her. "That is part of my record and my file. I can, as it has been poetically phrased to me, 'see into men's souls.' The Arbiter may change his mind, may be forced into a different action, but at the moment he made that offer to me, he meant every word of it."

Stall turned to Frost.

"Commander Frost, correct me if I'm wrong, but is it not possible for a Mage to conceal their emotions and truthfulness from another aura reader?" she asked him.

"It is," Frost confirmed. "However, if one has encountered that before, it is relatively obvious when we are shielding our emotions. At this moment, for example, Commander White is shielding his emotions from my own Sight and I am doing the same in turn. Can you tell, Commander?"

"No," David admitted. "Though in this case, that is because the table you are all sitting behind is enchanted to shield all of your auras from my own Sight. I *can* tell under normal circumstances, and the Arbiter was not doing so."

"Is it not possible that the Arbiter, who so far as we can tell may well be the oldest vampire alive, would be capable of shielding his emotions so you could not tell?" Stall demanded.

"It is entirely possible," David told her. "But if we assume that the Arbiter possesses powers we are not aware of the existence of, then fighting him would have been even more unwise than I thought it was at the time."

Stall looked taken aback as Frost smirked and nodded.

"Commander White is correct," the old team leader said. "Part of the consideration of his actions has to be that the Arbiter is a complete unknown. We have not, to our knowledge, encountered any vampire more than five centuries old. Nor has any other supernatural agency we exchange data with. The Arbiter represented a level of threat that could not be easily judged—and he certainly seemed quite confident in his ability to defeat ONSET Thirteen."

"Should we allow our decisions as Commanders to be shaped by fear of our enemies?" Stall snapped.

"May I interject?" David asked.

"Certainly," Frost told him before Stall could refuse.

"The Arbiter at that moment in time did not appear to wish to *be* our enemy," he told them. "He had an objective: the retrieval of the fledglings. His objective did not require him to fight us, and he sought a peaceful solution first.

"You ask if we, as Commanders, should shape our decisions by fear of our enemies. I say we should not...but we should consider the power of *potential* enemies before making them such."

That seemed to strike a nerve and he pressed forward.

"I would also request that, to understand the sequence of events more fully, that the video of the interior of the truck be played," he said.

"I don't see how that's relevant," Stall replied.

"I do," Frost objected. "Sokol, Falco?"

The other two men nodded.

"Let's play it, Alexis. We've all seen it," the old Commander told her. "I know what Commander White wants us to see."

Stall fiddled with the projector for several moments, and then the video played.

David physically winced at the sight. He'd remembered it, but his own memories were overlaid with his Sight. In many ways, that had been worse, seeing the hunger and desperation of the fledglings, but it had also helped obscure some of the visual horror of their situation.

Each of them was chained to the side of the side of the truck, clad in the ragged and torn remnants of whatever clothes they'd been wearing when they'd been turned. They'd probably been somewhat clean when they'd been loaded into the truck, but at that point, they'd been in it for over twenty-four hours. The walls and floor were smeared with filth, despite the clear evidence that someone had *tried* to clean the truck up around the vampires. Smears of dried blood marked the lips of the fledglings, left over from a feeding that David was relatively certain now had been animal blood.

They were pathetic. Even as they struggled against their chains to try to reach and eat him, they were pathetic. Helpless. Vulnerable. Lost.

"Let's not hide behind euphemisms and self-deception," David told the other four Commanders. "'Euthanizing' these fledglings would have required me to walk into that trailer again and shoot each of them in the head.

"We are police officers, first and foremost. What kind of police are we if we can find it in ourselves to murder chained-up people who had no choice in what they had become?

"What kind of police are we if we hide behind 'standing orders' to commit cold-blooded murder?"

ONCE AGAIN, the boardroom was silent. Then Stall leaned forward, studying David…no, studying David's *neck*.

"Your record shows you were bitten by a vampire," she noted. "A fledgling, in fact. I'm surprised by your sympathy for them."

"One of a group of semi-delinquent teens in my town Mantled as a vampire," David explained slowly, realizing at least part of Stall's objection in this whole affair. She, too, had been bitten. Even among Omicron's personnel, it wasn't a particularly common thing. "That teen bit and fed on his friends, killing half and turning the other half into vampires like himself.

"The girl who bit me was one of the half that turned. She had no idea what she was doing. All a fledgling can truly process is hunger—and they do not *choose* to become vampires. Especially not in the case of a random Mantling like that and its victims."

He shook his head.

"Many fledglings are at best innocent and at worst criminally insane," he concluded. "In the absence of Standing Order Twenty-one, there would be no grounds for finding them criminally liable for their actions."

"Fledglings are actively *dangerous* to those around them," Stall objected. "A newly Turned fledgling will feed and kill until stopped. They are hardly innocent!"

"They have no concept of their actions, no control over their mental state," David pointed out. "The definition, roughly, of *criminally insane*.

"It has often been necessary for ONSET and Omicron officers to shoot and kill vampire fledglings in self-defense or the defense of others. There is certainly no argument that we are functionally at war with the Vampire Familias, and the deaths in combat of Familias foot soldiers are hardly to be regretted, but…"

He shook his head.

"Standing Order Twenty-one makes a virtue of an unfortunate necessity," he told them. "The vampires may prove an insoluble problem, and the fledglings a hideous wrinkle to that problem, but if we embrace genocide as the only solution, just what have we become?

"And if we were to *commit* the genocide we have made an explicit goal, would any of us be able to look at ourselves in the mirror?"

The answering silence was split after a moment by gentle applause, and everyone in the room looked to Commander Falco, who was softly clapping.

"I think you've made your point, Commander White," he told David in an Italian accent. "And you can stop twisting the knife. I suggest we send the good Commander out while we debate. We have enough for our decision, don't you think, Commanders?"

DAVID WAITED in the attached room for just over an hour, deprived of any updates or contact with the outside world. It wasn't a comfortable wait, the time passing slowly as he waited to find out if his words were going to have any impact or if his actions were going to see him demoted or relieved.

Finally, the door swung open and Frost stuck his head in.

"We're ready for you, Commander White. Please, join us."

The other Commanders waited behind the table as Frost guided David back into the room and into his seat facing them. The old Mage was shielding his emotions still, and the table continued to shield the auras of the Commanders behind it, but some of the tension seemed to be lacking now.

Stall leaned forward, clearly still the elected spokeswoman of the group.

"Firstly, Commander White, I must make clear that any judgment on the constitutionality or ethicality of Standing Order Twenty-one is entirely outside the purview of this board," she told him. "We find ourselves in agreement with you that these events highlight issues with the Standing Order that will need to be considered, but this board of inquiry is not the place for them.

"Do you understand, Commander White?"

"Yes, Commander Stall."

"Good." She leaned back in her chair, a small smile playing across her lips.

"It is the unanimous judgment of this board of inquiry that, considering the existence of and weight given to Standing Order Twenty-one, that your actions were outside your normal authority as an ONSET team commander."

David swallowed. That wasn't an auspicious start.

"However, this board also concludes that the circumstances were unusual and a rapid decision was required," Stall continued. "Under those conditions, we feel a broad latitude must be given to the officer on the scene."

There was probably some degree of conflict of interest in ONSET Commanders deciding how much latitude ONSET Commanders deserved to get, but David wasn't complaining today. Not yet, anyway.

"On consideration of those circumstances, the unknown threat level of the Arbiter himself, the fact that it appears his compromise was legitimate and the lack of threat represented by the fledglings in question, this board rules that your actions, while somewhat questionable, were justified and acceptable.

"We recommend no censure or discipline, but we will require that a copy of this judgment and a record of this board of inquiry be included in your permanent file, Commander White. While your actions appear justified today, it is possible that future events may change the light in which these events are viewed, and the decision of this board of inquiry does not disqualify these actions or evidence from being included in future charges, boards or other prosecutions.

"Do you understand this board of inquiry's ruling, Commander White?"

"Yes," David said crisply. "Thank you."

"Thank *you*, Commander," Stall told him. "You've given us all a great deal to think about, and I think it is to be benefit of us all—and of Omicron itself—that this board was held and these questions asked.

"For today, we are done, and you are free to go. This board of inquiry is over."

[19]

Somehow, David wasn't surprised to find all three members of his team waiting for him when he returned to ONSET Thirteen's residence. Stone, Hellet and McCreery were sprawled around the couches of the little apartment building's central lounge.

"Aren't you three supposed to be on vacation somewhere?" he told them.

"We got recalled to hear the results of your board, boss," Stone replied. "So, are you still the boss, boss?"

"Still the boss," David said. "The board might not have necessarily agreed with what I did or why, but they understood enough to sign off on it. If nothing else, it's a stretch to ask four ONSET team commanders to undermine the authority of the ONSET Commander on the ground!"

"It was the right call, too," Hellet said. "I don't think we'd have survived fighting him. It was going to be an ugly scene either way."

"It was already an ugly scene," David pointed out. "A lot of dead vampires and some serious questions as to what was going to happen next.

"Now, that mess is over, and we have a job to do. I don't know what our next tasking is going to be, but I can tell you this: if they're not sending us into the field by tomorrow, *I'm* sending us right back to the training gyms. We have work to do."

"What, no celebration at all of getting to keep your job?" Stone asked.

"Plus, I heard something about a big casino win?" McCreery added. "Rumor travels fast around this place."

"That part's complicated," David explained. "I'm not allowed to gamble, remember? There was a reason, but I still don't know if I get to keep the leftovers."

Hellet chuckled.

"Good luck with that, sir," she told him. "Don't mind me if I'm unsympathetic."

"I live in government-provided housing. What use do I have for money?" David replied.

"You, boss, are a fundamentally odd man," Stone said. "I'll take it if you don't want it!"

"I'm not going that far. Like I said, people, we're going to have to work to do. Command has had us grounded for over a week—we might get tomorrow, but I wouldn't bet on it. Make sure your gear is clean and prepped."

"Yes, sir!"

1#

RETURNING TO HIS QUARTERS, David opened the safe and withdrew his own combat webbing, including *Memoria*'s scabbard. He'd checked on the sword when he'd returned to the Campus, but there was no purpose to carrying it around there. If something made it through the defenses surrounding him right then, even the demon-forged blade wasn't going to make much of a difference.

If he was going out into the field, however, that was a different matter entirely. He carefully drew the red-tinged blade from its extradimensional scabbard, laying blade and sheath next to each other on his table as he went through the rest of his gear.

By the time he'd made it through the contents of his safe, he had a collection of dismantled parts that made up his M4-Omicron carbine, his Omicron Silver caseless automatic, and the full set of his augmented-reality wargear.

With practiced hands, he began rapidly cleaning and reassembling the gear. The pistol came together first, electrical ignition and solid-state parts having created a weapon with surprisingly few moving parts.

Then the combat webbing. Slabs of computer circuitry went into custom-made pockets, followed by plates of enchanted ceramic armor. Physical leads ran through channels intended for them and connected the pieces of technology to each other, and then he hung the armor back up.

The carbine followed as he carefully cleaned and assembled each part. Between the sword and his own speed, any firearm was secondary—but he still didn't want them to fail on him.

Finally, he turned to the sword itself. He carefully cleaned the hilt and blade—the soul-forged steel didn't required sharpening—and checked the spell on the extra-dimensional scabbard. He couldn't refresh or replace the spell, but he could tell if it had any problems.

He wasn't surprised that it didn't, and slowly sheathed *Memoria*, clipping the scabbard and its protruding hilt onto the hanging combat webbing before dropping onto his bed and studying the array of gear.

When every encounter with a vampire had involved them coming to kill him, Standing Order Twenty-one and its blanket instruction to terminate all vampires on sight had made perfect sense. Now, however, he'd met two senior vampires and spoken with them—and had a chance to see the new-turned fledglings the way he suspected the Arbiter did: as helpless, dangerous, children.

Caleb Dresden had been calm, charming, charismatic…and arguably evil. Even the intelligence he had provided, intelligence that had allowed David to ferret out treason in the ranks of the Elfin, had only helped him.

The Arbiter had been…something else. The sole concern of that ancient vampire had been that the fledglings not be caught up in the war the Familias fought. The protection of people who, at least by his standards, were innocents.

That was a concern that David understood, a cause he couldn't begrudge anyone.

Not even a vampire.

———

DAVID WAS SITTING at his kitchen table, drinking one of the beers from his fridge and watching the sun set over the Rocky Mountains, when the knock came on his door. There were only a handful of people likely to show up at his door in the evening.

"It's unlocked," he declared.

The door swung open and two of the short list of people likely to be outside his door wandered in. Kate Mason came first, in uniform for once, accompanied by the immense bulk of Michael O'Brien, the commander of ONSET Nine and the man who'd once commanded both David and Mason.

"Have a seat," David told them. "Want a beer?"

"Sure," O'Brien rumbled. "I can get them myself. Want one, Kate?"

"Sure."

Mason pulled up a chair and waited for the big werewolf to return to the table, popping the tops off the bottle and passing one over to the Mage.

"How are you doing, David?" O'Brien asked. "Boards are never fun."

"Came out about as well as I could hope," David replied. "I was honestly expecting *some* sort of censure, though I'll admit I was figuring it would be token."

"It was your call to make," the werewolf said gruffly. "Can't say most of our Commanders would have made it, but it was your call to make."

"Would you have?" David asked his old commander.

"I don't know," O'Brien admitted. "It's easy to fall into the kind of trap that gave us Order Twenty-one. I haven't met many vampires who wanted to sit down and have a chat—but that could just as easily be because I've left enough dead vampires behind me to fill a couple of graveyards."

"We all have," Mason added. "Even OSPI has always gone for a *shoot first, don't really bother to ask questions* attitude on the vampires."

"And that's why we don't truly understand the Familias," David told them. "An entire, massive aspect of their culture—where their next generation comes from! —slipped completely under our radar. We didn't even know there was such a thing as the Keepers."

"And without knowing about them, we may have dramatically misunderstood our enemy," O'Brien agreed. "I already gave Warner my recommendation as to what to do with them."

"Do I want to know?" David asked.

The werewolf laughed.

"Given that my recommendation was 'Give David a giant stick and tell him to go negotiate', I suspect you were going to hear about it either way," he said. "We have to go to this Mountain, now we have the data we have to act on it.

"But we don't have to go in boots first and shooting," he continued. "We need to bring a big stick, enough to make the vampires stop, but I'm willing to admit that if there's *anywhere* we should stop and talk to the fanged fuckers, it's there."

"If the Keepers truly avoid human blood, have they even done anything worth taking them out for?" Mason asked. "Technically, they aren't even guilty of a crime."

"Except Standing Order Twenty-one," David told her. "And, well, we are at war with the Familias, and the Mountain represents leverage we can't give up. But I think Michael's right. We *have* to talk to the Keepers and the Arbiter—but we have to do it from a position of strength."

"There's no 'we' here, Commander White," O'Brien said, his voice suddenly level. "It has to be you. You killed Marcus Dresden—but you spoke to Caleb Dresden peacefully. The Romanov Sisters died by your hand—but you let forty Romanov fledglings live.

"Even more than any of the rest of us, you have dealt death to their leaders while offering life and mercy to those who cooperated. Even more important, you have spoken to this Arbiter.

"No, David White, it'll be another multi-team strike—and it *has* to be under your command."

O'Brien shrugged and saluted with his beer.

"That, at least, is what I told Warner. She seemed convinced, but I don't know if the Colonel will agree."

"Is he really going to argue with the man who could have his job in, what, three phone calls?" David asked.

The old werewolf chuckled and shook his head. Once, Brigadier Michael O'Brien had commanded the OSPI High Threat Response teams. Commander of just one ONSET team, the HTR team's successors, was his "quiet retirement."

"I don't want Ardent's job and he knows it. He's far better qualified to talk to politicians than I am."

"If we talk to the vampires," David pointed out, "we're going to have to take the results back to the Committee. Only they can lift Standing Order Twenty-one, after all, let alone do anything else!"

"And that, Commander White, is part of why I volunteered you for the command!"

The werewolf chugged his beer and glanced at the two younger Commanders at the table, a wicked grin spreading across his face.

"Now, however, that I have oh-so-accidentally provided an excuse for Kate to be in your apartment, I'm going to sneak out," he told them. "I suggest Kate avoids being seen leaving too, but it'll be easier once it's actually dark."

Both of them gaped at O'Brien and his grin widened.

"I remind both of you that I am a lot older than anyone else here—and I didn't get that way by being blind!

"Have a good night, Commanders."

[20]

THE NUMBER OF SILVER OAK LEAF LAPEL PINS LURKING OUTSIDE THE briefing room the next morning was a surprise to David. Despite the alliance between Omicron and the Elfin—officially, the deputization of their Elfin Warrior paramilitaries as US law enforcement agents—few members of the Tolkien-obsessed supernatural social club were ever allowed on the Campus.

"David! Get over here," a familiar voice barked, and the pieces fell into place.

Elfin Lord Jamie Riley, the Lord General of the Elfin Warriors and arguably one of the two or three most powerful people in the somewhat disorganized Elfin leadership, was a slim older man with short-cropped black hair.

He also had standing authorization to be on the Campus.

"What's going on, Lord Riley?" David asked as he approached the Elfin Lord, nodding to several of the Elfin he knew, including Klein, who stood just behind his commander.

"David, by now you can call me Jamie," Riley told him crossly. "If nothing else, I'm the reason you still have a damn arm, aren't I?"

"Fair enough...Jamie," the ONSET Commander allowed, carefully ignoring the visible wince from Riley's bodyguard. "My question still stands."

"Ardent called me in," the Elfin answered. "He wanted us to validate what we could of what appears to be the intelligence windfall of the century—a windfall I understand we have you to thank for."

"And Majestic," David demurred. "She put us in contact with the Tahoe Oracle, which was a...different experience."

Riley shivered.

"I've met its projections once," he said quietly. "The price is always worth it, but damn if talking to a construct with a personality all its own doesn't throw me off. *Mordo onna, mal saira.*"

David shook his head.

"I don't speak Quenya," he reminded the Elfin Lord.

"The Oracle is strange but wise," Riley translated. "There's much in that data dump I can't confirm, David. Ancient history, far beyond the reach of my network. But..."

"But?"

"The Mountain exists," he said flatly. "We *know* that. We know it has a guardian of immense power, which matches the Arbiter's description. I think we've validated enough of the Oracle's information, and the Oracle is a reliable-enough source in my experience, for you to launch an operation."

"It'll be Ardent's call," David replied. "But even if we aren't certain, we can't pass up even the chance that it's accurate."

"I'll make what arguments I can," Riley promised. "But this is your territory, David, not mine. I can't push Ardent at all."

"I know," David conceded. What influence the Elfin Lord had needed to be preserved for keeping ONSET from abusing his people. Such abuse wasn't *likely*, but...there was something about Colonel Kyle Ardent that made anyone with the Sight uncomfortable.

"Seems easy enough, though," Klein pointed out, interjecting himself into the conversation. "We go to this Mountain, blow in the doors, kill all the vampires. What's the difficulty?"

David smiled grimly.

"The difficulty, Klein, is that we're cops. And, so far as I can tell, the vampires in that facility aren't actually guilty of anything."

DAVID WASN'T sure he'd ever actually been in this particular briefing room before. Most ONSET briefings he'd attended had been either individual Commanders briefing their teams, or at most two or three team Commanders being briefed simultaneously.

Today, they'd needed a room for almost thirty people. A dozen Elfin Warriors surrounded Riley on the other side, while Major Warner and Colonel Ardent had both brought matching sets of young, black-suited bodyguards.

David, O'Brien, Mason, and every member of David's board of inquiry filled the rest of the room. Seven ONSET Team Commanders was more than he'd ever seen gathered in one place in the entire time he'd been in ONSET.

"Ladies, gentlemen, thank you all for coming," Ardent told them from the podium at the front of the room. He was a gaunt man, almost skeletal, with brown hair and a ready smile that never touched his eyes or his aura.

His aura, in fact, rarely changed. It wasn't shielded or otherwise blocked from David's Sight; it just…didn't change. Where most people's auras were a constantly shifting pattern of colors showing personality, emotion and supernatural powers, Ardent's was simply…flat.

It was disconcerting.

"Most of you are here, well, because you were on Campus," Ardent admitted. "Lord Riley was requested to attend to validate some information that Commander White brought into our hands. While it isn't possible for us to deploy all seven ONSET teams currently here on the intended operation, I wanted to make certain everyone is in the loop, as the risk factors mean you may be required to rapidly redeploy as backup.

"To begin, I want to ask one of our intelligence chiefs, Charles, to give us a summary of what we have discovered about the vampire known as the Arbiter and the secret Familias facility called the Mountain. Charles?"

The big projector lit up with the image of the Arbiter from David's encounter. The dark red Catholic robes accentuated the vampire's pale skin, shaven head and glittering black eyes. He was creepier in the image than he had been in person.

"This, ladies and gentlemen," Charles's brogue said over the speakers, "is the vampire who identified himself to Commander White as the Arbiter. We have most of his life story now, but little of it is relevant to us prior to his entry into the United States in 1790 as Adam Waters.

"What is important to know about him is that he was Anaxis of Athens during the reign of Philip of Macedon," the dragon continued. "He is approximately twenty-four hundred years old, which makes him the oldest vampire Omicron is aware of.

"Those priestly robes are his by right. He was a Bishop in France prior to the French Revolution, and fled the country about two steps ahead of the guillotine.

"He was at that time already a Keeper, part of an order of vampires Omicron was not aware of until we acquired this intelligence," Charles noted. "They apparently give up human blood as a necessary component of their task of raising the fledgling vampires to be useful adults again."

"Vegetarian vampires?" Klein asked. "That seems hard to believe."

Ardent's glare silenced the Elfin, but Charles caught the question.

"They're hardly *vegetarian*," the dragon pointed out. "Details are hazy, but they appear to subsist on animal blood. Cow and pig, by preference."

"That doesn't fit with what we know of vampire feeding," Riley objected thoughtfully. "They consume the life force as well as the blood. It's part of why their victims usually die instead of turn."

"I believe that they have to drink from the live animal for just that reason," Charles replied. "Or did, at least. Some of the intelligence we have acquired suggests they have established a solution for that in recent years, but it wasn't relevant to the question, so our source didn't provide us details.

"What is relevant is that the Arbiter is the single most powerful vampire in North America...and always has been," he concluded. "That said, he has also always stood apart from Familias politics. He is the most powerful nursemaid in the world.

"The Familias send all of their fledglings to him, and he returns them as adult vampires a year or so later, restored to their senses and taught what it means to be a vampire and how to survive in this world."

"You can understand, everyone," Ardent cut in, "what this means as a potential weak point. The Arbiter's facility is their future. Without it, they will have a far harder time expanding their numbers and replacing their losses."

"It also represents an opportunity," Commander Frost noted, the old man's voice thoughtful. "If we were to co-opt that facility, *we* would control what those fledglings were taught about 'what it means to be a vampire.'

"That is not a possibility we can ignore."

"This is true," Ardent allowed, "but it's also not a possibility that we can allow to blind ourselves to necessity. The Arbiter and his Keepers represent an unknown but extremely high level of threat. He himself appears to be an extraordinarily powerful Mage, and his Keepers include several more Mages of unknown power levels.

"But the most important thing is that we now know the location of the Mountain, *if* this intelligence is correct. Lord Riley?"

Riley rose to his feet.

"Colonel Ardent provided me with a copy of the information around these Keepers," the Elfin Lord told the group. "Apparently unlike Omicron, we were aware of the existence of the Keepers."

Riley managed to not sound *too* surprised, but it was clear the possibility that Omicron *didn't* know about the Keepers hadn't occurred to the Elfin.

"We have, in fact, had several peaceful interactions with the Order in the past," he noted. "This was a surprise to us because we, like Omicron, have basically been in a low-grade war with the Familias for years. This brings me to a major point: the Keepers are *not* part of the Familias. They stand entirely separate."

"They are a support network for the Familias," Ardent objected. "They are hardly separate from our perspective, even if they keep apart from the vampires' point of view. The intelligence, Lord Riley?"

"We, obviously, cannot confirm the details of the Arbiter's past,"

Riley replied. "Our encounters with the Keepers have been at a much lower level and, well, transactional. We were aware that there was a central facility for teaching the fledglings, run by the Keepers, but our attempts to locate it have been fruitless.

"We have, however, heard it referred to as the Mountain," he noted. "And have localized it to the Rocky Mountains in Nevada. That's a vast expanse to search, so we didn't try—but it lines up with the location you have acquired."

"Given the verification that Lord Riley has been able to provide," Ardent told the briefing, "I have made the decision to move forward with an assault on the Mountain."

"Sir," David interrupted, "on what grounds? So far as we know, these Keepers are guilty of no crimes."

"This is true," the Colonel admitted, his tone unwilling. "However, their support of the Familias renders them an active, immediate threat to the security of the United States of America, and Standing Order Twenty-one gives us the authority to do whatever we have to to neutralize that threat.

"Do you understand, Commander?"

"Yes, sir," David accepted.

"Good. I must confess that I have never seen nearly as unanimous a recommendation from my subordinates as I have for this operation," Ardent replied. "Everyone, from Major Warner to Commander O'Brien to members of the Committee of Thirteen itself, appears to agree, Commander White, that *you* are the only suitable officer to command this operation.

"Given your...misgivings, are you prepared to take on this task?"

"I am," David agreed instantly. Certainly, he wasn't going to leave it to anyone *else*. "I must say, however, that given the circumstances, it may be wisest to summon the Keepers to surrender before we kick in the door."

Ardent glanced around the room, clearly take the temperature of the Commanders and Elfin in the room before responding.

He must not have seen what he hoped to see, because he sighed and nodded.

"That is reasonable, Commander White," he allowed. "I doubt

these vampires will so blithely stand down as that, but that will be within your authority." Ardent paused. "It has also been made clear to me by the Committee that *if* the fledglings are, in your opinion, safely contained, they are to be *kept* so until we have a chance to study the facility and its occupants."

"There will be no massacre under my command, Colonel," David replied softly, only for Ardent to bark a laugh.

"I don't think anyone in this room or on the Committee expected a massacre under your command, White," he replied. "We just want to be clear on what's actually expected.

"You'll command a three-team strike force: your own ONSET Thirteen, Commander Mason's ONSET Fifteen, and Commander Sokol's ONSET Six, plus two platoons of Elfin Warriors under Deputies Klein and Santiago," Ardent reeled off.

"We have arranged for you to have air and artillery support if needed," he continued. "There will be two squadrons of F-22s on standby at Mountain Home Air Force Base. The squadron COs are in the know, but the pilots will be only briefed in the air if you call them in.

"There is an artillery battery on the road from Sacramento as we speak," he noted. "They will be in position with eight M109A7s by sixteen hundred hours, marking the beginning of your operations window.

"Officially, it's a mobility training exercise, but, again, the battery CO has been fully briefed."

"That's a lot of firepower, sir," David pointed out.

"It is," Ardent confirmed, "but there's a reason for it. Charles, can you brief everyone on just what the Mountain *is*?"

"Certainly," Charles agreed. The image on the big screen switched from the image of the Arbiter to an overhead satellite image of a chunk of the Rockies.

"This is the Crater Lake National Park," the dragon told them all. "On the east side of the lake, on the lower slopes of Mount Scott, facing towards Russia, there is an old Strategic Air Command ICBM base. Four Minuteman II silos and a central command bunker.

"The siloes were decommissioned, imploded, and the sites and intact upper levels sold to civilian developers in the nineties," he continued. "The command bunker was sealed and abandoned. It was not officially sold, but the land it sits on was.

"Between the four silos and the surrounding land, no less than six developers were involved in the purchases of the land, which, unlike most portions of the Park, is cleared for development.

"They've spent twenty years arguing over how to develop the site, with multiple conflicting plans issued with local authorities."

"And in truth, they are all owned by the Keepers?" Riley asked.

"Exactly," Charles confirmed. "While the paperwork showed the rights and work tied up in years and years of problems, the Keepers simply moved in and set up. While only the top few floors of the silos are intact, that still provides quite a bit of real estate, especially as it appears that they accessed the command bunker and reactivated the generators.

"They also appear to have quietly moved in a large quantity of boring equipment and have dug out multiple floors inside the old silos as well as linking tunnels and…well, they've built quite the underground warren, though they appear to be using the old command bunker as their central home.

"That bunker is built into the mountain. Its most vulnerable sections are under twenty feet of concrete, and much of it is buried under several hundred to several thousand feet of mountain. It was rated to survive a direct nuclear hit on the silos themselves."

David whistled softly as he studied the overhead.

"Entrances?" he asked.

"At least five, one for each of the SAC facilities," Charles told him, highlighting them on the screen. "All of them were powered, foot-thick steel doors. Those were removed or destroyed at the decommissioning…but the intelligence and overhead suggests they were replaced with functional equivalents.

"The Oracle's intelligence suggests there are approximately sixty Keepers and four hundred fledglings in the facility," he noted. "Armament available to the Keepers is unknown; they may be relying on the ability to lock down the base to defend themselves, but the original facility had remote-controlled weapons and concealed firing positions to protect the entrances, at least."

Several people in the room inhaled sharply as Charles gave the numbers, but David had been expecting something similar from the moment he learned just what the Arbiter was doing. There'd been forty fledglings in the convoy they'd intercepted. Even assuming that was an unusually large number, he'd presumed there had to be hundreds of vampires in the "school".

Four hundred new vampires a year didn't seem like much, but it was likely the largest expansion of the supernatural population going on, too.

"I leave the details of the operation to Commander White and his people," Ardent told them all. "But this appears to be one of the most important missions of our time. Success, however it ends up occurring, could change the entire nature of the war with the Vampire Familias.

"All of you need to be aware that this is going down," he continued. "Do not hesitate, Commander White, to call for aid. The Arbiter and his Keepers must surrender or be destroyed.

"Nothing less will secure the safety of our country."

[21]

"All right, people, now that Charles has filled you in on the background, we're going to talk specifics," Commander David White told the crowd of people he'd assembled in the same briefing room Ardent had given him *his* briefing in.

Three ONSET Commanders. Nine ONSET Agents. Eight mundane Pendragon pilots. Forty Elfin Warriors. Elfin Lord Jamie Riley and his Second, Brianna Young, sat with the Elfin. Those last two weren't supposed to be in the operation per David's briefing, but no one was going to tell Riley he *couldn't* be here.

And the Elfin Lord's presence was welcome. The Arbiter was terrifying; any extra magical firepower was going to be worth its weight in gold.

"This was Strategic Air Command Base Crater Lake," David continued, the screen behind him zooming in on the facility. "We have confirmed five entrances, but it looks like this one, to the old command bunker, is the main access."

It flashed on the screen.

"We have detailed maps of the interior of the structures as they were after decommissioning," he told the crowd. "We have some intelligence on the modifications made since, as well as the portions of the complex the Keepers have dug out since. The accuracy of that new information should be good, but relying on that is a good way to get people killed.

"We have designated each of the entrances Targets One through Five," David noted. "ONSET Thirteen is going to go door-knock at Target One and demand the Keepers' surrender. If we get it, we can all feel relieved and glad we brought a massive amount of overkill."

He smiled grimly.

"I put the odds at maybe twenty percent," he admitted. "According to my one meeting with the Arbiter, he and his Keepers are sworn to nonviolence—*except* in the defense of their fledgling charges.

"I think we can safely assume that if we attack their crèche facility, fighting us won't count as a violation of their oaths. We can expect heavy resistance, headlined by a supernatural who may well be the equal of Ekhmez or another high-court demon."

That shut up most of the mutters. Ekhmez had taken over OSPI headquarters by a mix of mind control and outright slaughter, and the only reason David had managed to kill the creature was that it had underestimated the will of the seven people it had forged into *Memoria* —the sword had betrayed him, and that surprise had allowed David to triumph.

If the Arbiter was of a similar power level, which David suspected might be *under*estimating him, it could easily take all three Commanders, Riley and Young to take him down. Five Class One Supernaturals, all of them of phenomenal power, and it might well not be enough.

"ONSET Six and ONSET Fifteen will move in Targets Two and Four," he continued. "Klein, your people will go with Mason. Santiago, you're with Sokol."

"What about the other two entrances?" Sokol asked.

"When I give the go signal, our Pendragons will bombard those entrances with heavy anti-armor missiles and collapse them. We know the exact specifications of the access tunnels, and given the skillset of Agent McCreery and the other pilots"—he nodded toward the ONSET Thirteen pilot—"I am fully confident in our ability to bring the entrances down.

"Once that is done, Six and Fifteen will move in through their entrances, supported by the Elfin. ONSET Thirteen, having knocked on the main door, will hold position to prevent any escapes."

"Which means the Arbiter is likely to try to go through you," Riley pointed out. "If you will permit, Commander White, I would like to attach myself and Second Young to ONSET Thirteen for this strike."

"The addition of two Mages of your and Brianna's strength would be more than welcome, Lord Riley," David told him. "We have very little idea of what a two-thousand-year-old Mage is capable of, but I suspect he can overpower any of us.

"The Pendragons will provide overwatch for breakouts. Sunlight alone should help contain our targets, but escape by Thrall-driven vehicles is possible. Any vehicle that attempts to leave is to be taken out," he ordered grimly. "Preferably by the Pendragons, but you will be linked into our artillery and air support.

"Use whatever means are necessary," he concluded. "Even once we move in, people, we want even the Keepers alive if possible. I don't want anyone taking unnecessary risks, but we *will* be accepting surrenders, Standing Order Twenty-one be damned.

"Do you understand me, people?"

THE GUEST QUARTERS on the Campus looked much like the rooms in a nice hotel. For that matter, the *building* the guest rooms were housed in looked like a nice hotel, though missing the pool and restaurants of the hotel.

Lord Riley had been given one of the nicer rooms, one with a balcony overlooking the entire compound and a gorgeous view of the Rocky Mountains around them. He and David stood on that balcony as Young poured all three of them wine.

Riley took his glass and studied the mountains.

"Brianna," he addressed the Mage who served as both his bodyguard and his apprentice. "Leave us, please. There are certain topics you…need to be at least officially unaware of, my dear."

The young woman with the dyed pixie cut bowed slightly, then took her glass of wine and withdrew in silence, leaving David and Riley alone.

"Your organization provided me with such nice chairs, it's a shame to waste them," Riley said, taking a seat in one of the four patio chairs as Young closed the door behind her. He glanced back at the door she'd left them through with a fond gaze.

"I don't deserve her, you know," he said aloud. "She carries an elf-blade of my forging by her own choice, not necessity." He chuckled. "I figure it's been at least a year since she had enough knowledge to forge her own."

David shifted uncomfortably, suddenly reminded of the tightness and occasional pain in his shoulder from the wound that had never fully healed—the wound from an elf-blade. Every Elfin Lord and their Second carried one, but it was *forging* one that made someone an Elfin Lord.

"I think she thinks I need nursemaiding more than I do," Riley concluded. "She could easily be a Lord if she wanted. She tells *me* she doesn't want the attention, but…" He shrugged. "I wonder."

"I don't know her well enough to say," David replied cautiously, taking a seat and sipping the wine himself. "But I'm guessing that wasn't what you wanted to speak to me about."

"It wasn't," the Elfin Lord confirmed. "You should know, though we haven't told Omicron, that the Conclave was approached by a delegation of Keepers two days after your encounter with the Arbiter."

David sat bolt upright, studying the older man.

"What did they want?" he asked carefully.

"They wanted the Conclave to act as an intermediary between the Keepers and Omicron in the pursuit of peace negotiations between the Familias and Omicron," Riley said quietly. "I wanted to hear them out, but I was outvoted. The Conclave declined their petition—not least because the Keepers do not speak for the Familias."

"Who does, these days?" David asked.

"Romanov and Dresden, both," the Elfin Lord told him. "Same as it's been since you killed Marcus Dresden. The Romanovs are weakened, badly, but their allies are terrified of Petrov's wrath if they betray him at this point—and of Caleb Dresden's punishment for siding against him.

"But..." Riley trailed off, raising a finger. "The vampire civil war is almost over. You and Dresden have broken Petrov Romanov's resources and family. Only Petrov's personal power holds together his faction now...once he is dead, the war is over."

"And I'm guessing he's high on everyone's hit list," David noted.

"The very top. That is part of why we didn't want to get involved," the Elfin told him. "The Keepers could make a deal, but if Caleb Dresden doesn't agree to it, it's a waste of everyone's time.

"And the Conclave is divided over if peace is a good idea."

"As opposed to what?" David asked.

"Genocide."

The word hung in the night and David nodded with a sigh.

"Standing Order Twenty-one," he replied. "It's a prettier name for the same damn thing, but we *know* it won't work. We could kill every vampire in North America, and we'd still have poor random bastards cursed by Fate to be Mantled as vampires."

"But without the Familias and the Keepers, a handful of fledglings popping up here and there can be handled," Riley pointed out. "It's the vampiric *nation* that is a threat. The elder vampires that can personally challenge the Elfin Lords."

He shook his head.

"Of course, it wouldn't fall to us to actually carry out the act," he admitted. "And it's far easier to contemplate that when the blood will be on Omicron's hands, not ours."

"They are man-eating monsters," David said. "It's not like Standing Order Twenty-one exists without reason."

"Agreed. On the other hand...the Keepers exist," Riley said. "An entire section of their society that never touches human blood. A sign, perhaps, of what they *could* be."

"We'll find out, I suppose," David told him. "One way or another, the Mountain holds the answers."

"May they be ones we like," Riley replied, toasting him with his wineglass.

[22]

THERE WAS A FAMILIAR FEELING TO WATCHING PENDRAGONS SWEEP IN AND land on a mountain field, high above the cities below. This field had less snow than the Montana field where the disaster that had been Operation Sun Net had kicked off, but it was rapidly turning into the same kind of semi-military staging ground that that night had seen.

There were no questions of warrants or authorities tonight, though. Much as David was starting to grow uncomfortable with Standing Order Twenty-one, its existence meant he had full sanction to do whatever he felt was necessary.

"Should we be pitching tents or prepping to go in?" Mason asked, approaching from behind him. "We're still waiting on the gear for Santiago's people, but everyone is here. We just don't have AR wargear for half the Elfin Warriors."

David looked to the west, studying the slowly setting sun.

"I don't want to go in without everyone on the tacnet," he told her. "And it's late; sundown's in two hours at most. There's tents in the gear for a reason; we'll set up and hold until dawn."

"Makes sense."

She was silent for a moment, then stepped up next to him, looking over the expanse of Oregon stretching out beneath them.

"In a staging area in the mountains again," she murmured.

"Last time we did this, I kind of died," David replied. "I'm hoping for a better outcome this time."

"I'm looking at everything the Colonel set up for you to command, and I just wish I could think it was overkill," she admitted. "If the Arbiter fights, is this…is this enough?"

He shook his head.

"If he decides to fight, it will be me, Riley and Young against him," he told her. "And all I expect us to be able to do is hold him in until you and Sokol can reinforce us. With the five of us together, I have more faith, but…we have no idea what he's capable of."

"Do you think he'll talk?"

"No," David said. "I know Michael figured showing up with a big stick would get him to listen, but I'm afraid it's going to have the opposite effect. If we threaten his charges, he has to fight."

"You could…you know, leave everyone behind and go in yourself," Mason said slowly.

"If I tried a stunt like that, you and Sokol would have to relieve me —and you'd be right," he told her. "No, Ardent's right. We can't permit the Mountain to continue as it is. One way or another, the current state of affairs has to end."

They were both silent for a while.

"I won't forgive you if you get yourself killed," Mason told him. "Not now, when we're just starting to figure this out."

He chuckled.

"I'm not sure life and duty are going to leave us much to figure out," he said. "But no, Kate, I have no intention of getting myself killed. You damn well better stick around for me."

Unspoken was that he was a lot harder to kill than she was. She was more dangerous in a lot of ways, but also far more fragile than a Class One Regenerator.

He wasn't willing to lose her. There just was nothing he could do that wouldn't be stopping one or both of them from doing their duty.

"We move in at dawn," he finally concluded, letting business push aside personal. "I'll pass that message on to our backup if you can make sure everyone here knows."

"I can do that, Commander White," she said formally.

"Thank you, Commander Mason," he told her, then smiled. "We'll make it work, Kate," he said more softly. "Both this mission and... everything else. We'll make it work.

"It's what we do."

Rejoining the main body of personnel milling about in a semi-orderly fashion, David made his way up to his Pendragon and grabbed his "work phone": a satellite communications system linked into the military networks.

A precoded channel linked him into a conference call and pinged the COs of his backup units. A different code would have done the same thing while sending an urgent alert. A third, completely different code would have them getting their units in motion and *then* calling in.

This was the lowest-priority channel he had with them, and he waited patiently for the two Air Force and one Army officer to get on the conference call.

"Major Wilbur here," the artillery battery commander linked in first. "This is...Commander White, correct?"

He sounded unsure of the rank.

"It is, Major Wilbur," David confirmed. "We're waiting on your Air Force counterparts."

"Always waiting on the Air Force," Wilbur said gruffly. "Wouldn't want to get their uniforms dirty."

"Of course not, Major," a new voice interjected politely. "Why, if we got mud on the uniforms, people might think we were infantry!"

Wilbur chuckled. "Would take more than that."

"It might," the voice agreed. "This is Colonel Dallas, USAF. I also have Major Lange on the line."

"Thank you for linking in, gentlemen," David told them. "Right off the bat, I'll let you know you can stand your units down overnight. We had a logistics issue and one of my teams isn't ready to deploy yet.

"Plus, sunlight is our best ally here. We're going to hold off until at least an hour after dawn."

"Sunlight," Wilbur repeated. The headshake was silent but still managed to come through. "This is seriously a vampire nest?"

"You *were* briefed, right?" David asked. He'd been told Wilbur was in the know, but it sounded like a lot of this had come at him cold.

"Yeah...right before we left on what was supposed to be a mobility exercise, I got pulled into an office by a three-star General and two suits and given the rundown on 'supernatural affairs in the USA'," the Army Major told him. "I was *briefed*.

"Doesn't mean it really sank in. It all seems rather...fantastical, no offense."

"More like a horror movie," David told him. "I didn't realize you were quite so freshly briefed, Major. Do you have any immediate concerns I can help with?"

Silence for several seconds.

"I take it you're...not exactly normal yourself, Commander?"

That question brought back horrifying memories of David's more-than-somewhat-xenophobic father, but he forced them down with a pained smile.

"I am Empowered," he said shortly. "Give or take...think Greek hero. I am faster and stronger than a regular human and see approximately a quarter-second into the future in combat situations."

"Shee-it," Wilbur breathed. "I...I'm sorry, Commander that's a lot to take in."

"That's fair, Major. Imagine what it felt like for *me*," David replied.

That got a chuckle from the Major.

"Fair enough. So. Vampires. Do we need to be staking them or some such? Holy water?"

"Staking them through the heart will kill them, yes, but it's damned ineffective," David pointed out. "Holy water has no effect, but they are *severely* allergic to sunlight. They can survive it, if they're careful, but it has a high likelihood of killing them.

"Most importantly for your battery, blowing them to itty-bitty pieces is quite effective at ending them," he concluded. "You put those hundred-and-fifty-five-millimeter shells where we call for them, and that's all we need."

"I've got a briefing paper for my men, but..."

"It'll fall to you to make them understand the orders are legitimate," David said gently. "There's very little I will be able to do at that point."

"I know it's all legit," Wilbur conceded. "Just...yeah. I'll sell my men," he said flatly. "Just having a hard time selling *myself*."

"I'll trade you, Major," Colonel Dallas told him. "My pilots are realizing we've strapped GBU-28s to half of the wing and are wondering what the *hell* is going on."

"The target is an old SAC missile facility that's been co-opted," David replied. "Those bunker-busters might be necessary."

And he was grateful they'd managed to dig up the squadrons of F-22s to carry them. The five-thousand-pound bombs normally required bombers.

"The thought of dropping one of these things, let alone the twenty we're carrying between the two squadrons, on American soil makes my teeth itch, Commander," Major Lange pointed out. "There isn't much bigger these birds can haul."

"I expect we'll need your Hellfires more than the GBUs," David told them, "but if everything goes to hell, it will fall to your squadrons to destroy the facility from the air—and it was hardened against nukes."

"We'll need direct hits if it's that hardened," Dallas said grimly. "I've got the specs, but briefing my people in the air is going to suck."

"It's better than the alternative," the ONSET Commander pointed out. "The last time I went on a mission with this high a threat index, my backup was a B-2 bomber with nuclear cruise missiles."

"Just...just *what* did my battery get drafted for?" Wilbur said, sounding vaguely sick.

"From some of the shit the Commander's people have pulled me into over the last few years, literally the war against Hell, Major," Colonel Dallas told the junior Army man gently. "And the front line is wherever we find them."

"We're hoping it won't get that bad this time," David told them. "These are vampires, not demons, and however fucked-up the vampires are, they're still fundamentally human."

The channel was silent.

"I take it there are things you fight that aren't?" Wilbur said levelly.

"Unfortunately."

"I'm glad that's *your* job, Commander," the Army man replied. "But my guns and I have your back. All the way."

"We'll be in touch again in the morning," David promised. "Have your units back on standby by nine hundred thirty hours.

"The plan is go in at ten hundred."

[23]

THE SIGHT OF ELEVEN PENDRAGON JET HELICOPTERS LIFTING OFF IN SYNC was both awe-inspiring and somewhat eerie. Even sitting aboard the last helicopter, David couldn't hear a thing: all eleven helicopters were in full stealth mode, which activated limited-duration spell effects that completely smothered the noise.

"We're in the air, ETA ten minutes," McCreery reported. "Staying just subsonic; the spells can't do much with sonic booms."

The Pendragon had started life as a prototype jet-equipped version of the Blackhawk helicopter with a limited supersonic capability. Omicron had quietly mass-produced them and enchanted the pieces prior to assembly.

The Black Dragon helicopter had been deemed an impractical waste of money. Layering in magic, however, created an extraordinarily fast and stealthy aircraft capable of delivering a team of six and a pile of heavy weaponry wherever Omicron needed them.

The lead eight helicopters carried the Elfin Warriors, a five-supernatural fireteam and an Omicron pilot in each helicopter. The last three carried the three ONSET teams, twelve supernaturals and two mundane pilots.

McCreery would stay aboard the helicopter and coordinate their close-in air support. Air support was far more valuable than one more sniper today.

"Leitz, anything new on overhead?" David asked his control.

"We've got satellite coverage locked in for the next forty-eight hours," she replied. "It's pretty obvious looking at it that the place isn't as abandoned as it's supposed to be. Someone's been maintaining the fences and roads, and I see traces of recent vehicle movement."

"Nice to know we're not dropping in an on abandoned ruin," he said. "That would be embarrassing."

"I'm not seeing much motion, but it is daylight," she told him. "We didn't see much overnight, either. It's quiet."

"Too quiet. Anything else useful?"

"Heat signatures are picking out the vents for the generators scattered around the mountainside. Lots of little ones, we'd have missed them if we weren't looking for them," she noted. "I'd say they've rebuilt the diesel plant at the bottom of the command bunker and probably have generators elsewhere as well. They've done a good job of hiding it, but we knew where SAC had *their* vents, so…

"There isn't a lot of power being generated, but enough to keep the lights on and a computer system running," Leitz concluded. "Somebody's home."

"A lot of somebodies," David agreed. "Get yourself linked in with Wilbur, Lange and Dallas," he ordered. "I'll be on the ground; I won't have the high level. It'll be up to you and McCreery where the strikes need to go once the call is in, understand?"

"Yes, Commander. I'll have a conference channel set up before you land."

"I hope we won't need it," he said quietly, "but worst-case scenario, Control…Lange and Dallas have enough bunker-busters loaded to collapse the whole damn complex in on itself.

"If we're forced to fall back and I'm down, I want them to bring the whole damn Mountain down. Understood?"

"Yes, sir."

Leitz paused.

"Good luck, Commander."

As they came around Mount Scott, David caught himself holding his breath and studying the threat detector system over McCreery's shoulder. Given what Familias Romanov had pulled together to defend their convoy of fledglings, it was entirely possible that the Mountain had significant concealed anti-air defenses—defenses that could very easily ruin his people's day.

"I am negative on ground radar, I repeat, we are negative on ground radar," the lead helicopter reported. "We are in clean."

"At least as far as tech goes, anyway," McCreery muttered to David. "As I recall, the Arbiter knew exactly where we were even with Hellet veiling us."

"He did," he confirmed. "I doubt we're truly going to sneak up on him. I just want him focused right on the front door."

"How are we doing that?" the pilot asked.

"The most obvious way possible. Drop our stealth, Agent McCreery, and then land us right outside the bunker doors. Let's…see what happens."

The flotilla of helicopters split apart, five headed to each of the target silos while the last helicopter, ONSET Thirteen, suddenly became *much* more visible and charged right down the center.

This was the moment where one asshole with a Stinger missile could destroy whatever chance of a peaceful resolution there was, and David stopped himself from holding his breath again.

Nothing happened, and McCreery dropped the Pendragon into a carefully maintained but empty parking lot directly in front of the bunker access tunnel.

"It's on you now, sir," she told him. "I'm linked in with Leitz and the fire support. Go get 'em!"

Grabbing his carbine, David stepped back into the main passenger compartment, where Stone and Hellet were waiting for him, exchanging a nod with Lord Riley as he entered.

"Are we good?"

Stone slammed one of his custom-made hundred-round drum

magazines into his M60 with an audible *thunk* and a grin visible even through his tinted faceplate.

"Oh, hells yes, sir," he replied, his voice even higher than usual with excitement.

"Young and I are ready," Riley replied cheerfully.

"I'm ready," Hellet said more sedately. "This place...feels very strange, sir."

David had been focused on the flight and the plan, but now that Hellet pointed it out, he Saw it. There was a strange aura seeping up into the helicopter from the ground. It was nothing like the aura of death and decay he was used to associating with vampires.

It was...calming, soothing. And he could also tell he was only catching the very fringes of the spell that was being woven somewhere under his feet.

"Well, now we know at least part of how they keep the fledglings under control," he told her. "You've got the explosives?"

Hellet patted a satchel at her side, presumably filled with the multiple kilograms of magically enhanced C4 that would act as their doorknocker if the Keepers declined to cooperate.

"Let's move."

―――

David led the way out of the helicopter and across the concrete outside, studying the area around him with both his mundane gaze and his Sight.

The soothing aura had sunk into the stones and concrete around them, an aftereffect of a long-sustained magic. He could hear birds in the distance, and a gentle breeze swept across the compound, rustling the branches of the trees surrounding it.

It didn't feel at all like what he'd been expecting, and he shook himself, jerking his head for his two Agents to follow him as he set off toward the big security doors.

There'd been no attempt to pretend the bunker hadn't been reopened, he noted. That was probably reasonable, as it wouldn't be obvious to an overhead flight and the bunker was at the heart of the old SAC compound, surrounded by forests, mountains, and park for twenty kilometers in every direction.

The vampires would have known someone was coming long before they reached this door. The massive steel doors looked like the bunker had never been decommissioned, an impressive feat, given that the original doors had been stripped out and the entrance blocked with concrete.

"They don't seem to be expecting guests," Stone pointed out. "They blocked up the old security gatehouse." He pointed at a chunk of the concrete wall that had once held a window and door, a side access for people on foot.

"Cameras on the top," David replied, gesturing toward them. "They know we're here. Let's go say hi."

He paused, considering.

"Lord Riley, Second Young." He turned to the Elfin. "I'd like you to hang back and keep an eye on things. If there's any surprises…well, feel free to come save our asses, but a second string to our bow sounds healthy."

He wasn't quite sure what to expect as they approached the big steel doors. The cameras were clearly active, moving slowly in the midmorning light. Whoever was watching through them would have seen the helicopter landing and the approach of the three Agents in black body armor.

The soothing air to the whole place struggled against David's sure knowledge that violence was going to tear this place apart shortly.

"Ready the explosives," he told Hellet as they approached the door. "Looks like we're going to need to knock."

"Wait, look!" she replied, waving to the door.

It had begun to open, the two big doors slowing swinging outward. They moved enough to open a space that would fit one person, then stopped.

There was no light inside, just pitch blackness. A man-sized gap leading into the abyss.

David swallowed.

"Well, it seems a shame to waste the invitation, doesn't it? Riley, keep an ear to the radio; we'll call for help if things go south.

"Stone, Hellet…let's go."

Stepping between the massive, foot-thick steel doors into the darkness inside the bunker gave David pause. With his every action being recorded by cameras in both his helmet and his subordinates, however, he forced down the atavistic caveman afraid of the dark and pushed through.

"I've got no lights," he murmured into his microphone. His own vision could pick out some details, but even he had problems seeing when there was no light at all. "Nothing at all. Even the vampires can't see much in this shit."

He glanced around, comparing what he could see to the map running on his HUD.

"Looks like they dug out the concrete plug but otherwise left the structure the same," he concluded. "Stone, Hellet, switch to thermal and follow me."

"Should I give us light?" the Mage asked.

"Not yet," David told her. "Let them play their games…but as I give the word, light this place like up like the Fourth of July."

"Wilco."

The entrance tunnel was wide enough for two eighteen-wheelers to pass abreast with comfortable room to spare and a good two hundred feet long. The three ONSET Agents made their way down it in silence that grew more uncomfortable with each step.

"Somebody opened the door," Stone finally said, breaking it. "They know we're here. I feel like I'm trapped in a fucking kill box."

"Hellet?" David asked.

"Shielding us," she confirmed. "Unless they drop the entire mountain on us, I think we're good from at least the first surprise."

"Don't tempt fate," he advised. "Keep moving."

As they reached the other end of the tunnel, they ran into a matching set of massive steel doors. It wasn't clear from their intelligence if the inner doors had been removed, but the Keepers seemed to have replaced them either way.

David was about to order Hellet to break out the explosives, then decided to wait and see what happened.

Somehow, he wasn't surprised when the doors began to swing open, a dim light—bright enough to eyes adjusted to pitch blackness but still soft and gentle—spilling out to frame a small woman with long blond hair wearing a plain white robe.

As she stepped out into the tunnel, orbs of the same gentle, warm light came with her, hovering around the vampiric Mage as she faced David and his people from barely ten feet away.

David left his weapons at the ready, knowing that Stone would have the Keeper covered.

"We are here—"

"We know why you're here," she told him. "You are Commander David White of the Office of the National Supernatural Enforcement Teams and you are here under the authority of Standing Order Twenty-one of the United States Supernatural Law Enforcement Offices."

David said nothing, leaving the silence to grow.

"Since you haven't tried to shoot me yet, I suppose you are at least willing to talk," she finally continued. "Come with me, Commander White. The Arbiter is waiting for you."

"Is he?"

"Yes. We've been waiting for someone like you for quite some time now."

That was going to sound great on the recordings later.

"Like me?" he asked carefully.

"Someone willing to listen," the Mage, who was almost certainly older than the late teens she looked. "Someone willing to give a peace a chance."

[24]

The white-robed vampire led David and his people deeper into the Mountain. Just past the second set of big doors was an underground loading dock, with space for ten eighteen-wheelers. A single big truck sat at one end of the space, clearly visible to David despite the dim lighting.

Their guide kept a trio of floating balls of light drifting around them, making it easier to see where they were going. The dim lighting was fine for David—and he suspected it was fine for the vampires—but it might have been a problem for Stone or Hellet.

That the lighting was clearly targeted for vampire senses was telling, in its own way. This wasn't a place that they expected to have mundane humans or Thralls or guests. This was purely a place for the vampires themselves.

There were half a dozen other white-robed vampires in the loading area, making no attempt to conceal themselves but also not visibly armed. They didn't *look* like a defensive contingent, but David saw no other reason for anyone to be in the dock.

Once they exited the docks, his entire image of the Mountain took a shattering body blow. Their guide led them through a set of double doors decorated with a mural of an old cathedral and into the main spaces of the underground complex.

He'd been half-expecting it to look like the ONSET bunkers he'd been in: utilitarian blank concrete and steel. He had not been expecting dim lighting, quiet music and soft carpet. The concrete walls had been carefully painted, the flooring installed with delicate competence, and speakers added to pipe through relaxing music.

David lost half a step in sheer surprise—and the wry smile the woman leading them gave him the impression she'd anticipated his reaction.

"This is not a place mortal eyes were meant to see," she warned him. "Your presence risks the calm we work to achieve to help the *teknon* find themselves once more. For them, the smell of human blood is a...trigger. They easily lose what little control they have."

"I see no reason for us to approach the...*teknon*, you called them?" David said.

"There is none," she admitted. "But we are extremely careful about even who enters this facility. No human has set foot in the Mountain since we first brought the *teknon* here. It should be fine, but I worry."

She acted more like a nurse than the bloodthirsty monster he was used to vampires being.

"Come," she instructed. "I am to bring you to the Arbiter as swiftly as possible, before your friends above us decide you have been missing for too long."

David checked his radio connection. So far, so good, but he wasn't sure if he'd lose it as he went deeper—at which point, the Keeper's concern would be very real. If he went dark for long enough, Mason and Sokol *would* come in looking for him.

"Let's not let it get to that, shall we?" he agreed.

She nodded and continued down the hallway, taking several turns that he carefully made sure his augmented-reality systems were recording. So far, everything they'd seen had the same bones as the old SAC bunker; the vampires had just redecorated.

"Here," she told them, stopping at a door that didn't look particularly different from any others. "He is waiting for you."

"Thank you," David replied. "I didn't catch your name."

"I didn't give it, Commander White," she replied calmly, then opened the door for him to enter.

He nodded his understanding of her deflection and then led his people into the lair of the Arbiter.

THE ARBITER WAS NO LESS creepy on repeated exposure. He sat behind a massive oak desk, leaning forward with his hands clasped together on the table as David and his team entered. Three chairs were in front of the desk, on an absolutely gorgeous geometric rug the ONSET Commander hesitated to guess either the age or value of.

Except for the rug, the desk and the chairs, the room was empty. Its size, given that at this point they were under several hundred feet of mountain, was grandeur enough—and the Arbiter clearly knew that.

"Anaxis," David greeted the vampire with a bow of his head.

The creature chuckled and gestured the ONSET people to the chairs.

"I am impressed that you know that name," he admitted, "but it has been over two *thousand* years since Anaxis of Athens died and almost as long since I used that name. I'm more impressed you found this place, though I must admit I suspected it was inevitable."

"What should I call you, then?" David asked. "Bishop Adrian François? Adam Waters?"

The Arbiter chuckled again.

"Please, Commander, call me the Arbiter. It is the only name I have used in almost two hundred years. Besides"—he smiled—"if it wasn't for the Revolution, it would have been *Cardinal* François. We were having inevitable problems arranging my trip to Rome, and then, well, my country exploded."

He made a throwaway gesture with one hand, then clasped them back together.

"I suspected it was coming, but my attempts to ingratiate myself with the elements that fomented revolution were undermined by the rest of the Church. Such were the times, Commander. Times such as those—and times such as today—are chaotic tides. You cannot guide them, only choose if you will sail upon them or be swept away."

"You know why I'm here," David told him. "I am ordered to intern this facility and take all members of the so-called Keepers prisoner."

"I have told you my oaths," the Arbiter replied. "You know I will fight you if the *teknon* are threatened...and I will not if you will guarantee their safety. These are my fetters, the oaths I chose long ago.

"I do not regret them, Commander White, only that the collision of our duties may require me to destroy you."

In David's experience in reading auras, no one ever told the entire truth with entire sincerity all of the time. Except...in both of his conversations with the Arbiter, that was what the man had done.

Two thousand years of self-examination, he supposed, allowed you to know yourself far better than most people's four score and ten.

"My orders with regards to the fledglings from the Committee are quite specific," David told the old vampire. "If, in my judgment, they are safely contained, they are to be left as is. I think the incident with the trucks struck a chord in my superiors."

The Arbiter was silent and David *saw* the relief flood through the ancient being's aura...followed by trepidation?

"Then, I have one single additional condition on the surrender of the Mountain and all of its inhabitants," he said. "If you take control of this place, you *must* defend it. If you will refrain from harming the *teknon* and I know the Familias will not harm the *teknon*, then my Keepers can have no part in the battle to come."

"The battle to come?" David asked carefully.

"Every Familias has agents in my ranks," the Arbiter said calmly. "By now, they all know you are here. Come nightfall, they will move. They will hold back *nothing*, Commander, for this facility represents their future, and they are aware of its lack of defenses.

"So long as Omicron holds this facility, I offer a truce: if Standing Order Twenty-one is lifted, every vampire that leaves this place will be Truce-bound, sworn to harm no human and observe the laws of the United States.

"That is the Truce I propose, that I will bind all future vampires on this continent to," he concluded.

"And yet they must feed," David said carefully. "We would be forced to destroy any of them that broke the truce."

"There is no human blood in the Mountain, Commander," the vampire pointed out. "I own and operate a number of cattle ranches and pig farms across the United States and Canada, as well as several slaughterhouses.

"It took me fifty years to find a way to transport animal blood to provide all that we need, but I have done it," he concluded. "At one point, we had to throw live animals in with the *teknon*. It worked, but it delayed the maturation process. Now, we can feed them aetherically stabilized blood, containing added vitamins and minerals and the magically captured life force of the original beast."

That was something new. Something David hadn't even realized was possible.

"The logistics infrastructure is mostly in place to provide that same animal blood to every vampire in North America and large chunks of South America," the Arbiter told him. "If the Committee will grant my *teknon* the rights of their citizenship, then I shall do all within my power to have them honor the responsibilities of it."

David inhaled sharply.

"I can't guarantee that," he warned. "That falls to the Committee."

"I know. What falls to you, Commander White, is to guarantee the safety of my charges, and the security of this facility against the storm my brethren will shortly unleash upon it."

David sighed and nodded.

"That, Arbiter, I can do," he admitted. "If you are prepared to accept the warrant and surrender."

"The safety of the *teknon* is everything."

"What does that word even mean?" David asked.

"Children, Commander White. Their adulthood, their *selves* have been stolen from them by the transformation. We teach them how to be people again."

"My orders are that they are to be unharmed. Securing this facility is a requirement," David noted. "We cannot allow the Familias to retake it."

"Then my oaths leave me no choice," the Arbiter said calmly. "Neither I nor my people will fight you. We surrender the Mountain."

"What aid can you give me to defend it?" David asked. "You would after all, be protecting the *teknon*."

The Arbiter shook his head.

"We…cannot so broadly interpret our oaths," he pointed out. "More so than most of parahumanity, we are predators and must struggle with our oaths. We must err on the side of pacifism, Commander, especially when we know that the Familias will do all in their power to avoid harming our charges."

David stared at the vampire for a few seconds. That was nuts—even with both sides trying not to hurt the fledglings, collateral damage was a distinct possibility.

"Accidents happen," he finally pointed out.

"Yes," the Arbiter agreed. "But we are bound by our oaths, Commander, as are you. What aid we can give—materiel, intelligence, assistance with the Mountain's systems—we will give. But we will no more fight for you than we will fight you."

[25]

STILL FEELING SOMEWHAT OFF-BALANCE, DAVID STRODE BACK INTO THE main loading dock. He glanced around the dozen Keepers still standing there.

"Where are the controls for the doors?" he demanded.

"Over here," the same blonde Keeper who'd been his guide earlier told him, materializing out of the shadows like a ghost. "I've been assigned to keep you informed and enable your operations," she continued. "What do you need us to do?"

"For now, open both main doors and turn on the lights," David ordered. "Then I want all of you to go to your living quarters and stay there, except as needed to take care of the fledglings."

"I am to assist you, but otherwise, those were the Arbiter's instructions as well," she told him calmly. "Come with me and we'll open the doors."

The woman turned to the rest of the Keepers.

"You heard the Commander," she told them. David hadn't spoken loudly, but given that everyone there was a vampire… "The Mountain has fallen; we now answer to Omicron.

"This is necessary for the salvation of our race," she continued. "We are oathbound, and the Arbiter's Truce binds us as well. The same oaths that bind us to yield if the *teknon* are safe mean we will not fight *with* Omicron, either—our kin will not harm our charges.

"We know the Familias will come. We will not fight them. We will not help them," she said flatly. "This is the Arbiter's command.

"Go back to your rooms. Fulfill your duties. The next few days will decide the fate of our race…and our oaths demand that we do nothing."

More Keepers had appeared in the big open space as she spoke. Whoever the blonde was, her voice clearly carried weight. When she finished, the vampires began to disperse, disappearing back into corridors and tunnels leading deeper into the mountain.

"This way," she said, turning back to David. "I'm trained on the control systems for the bunker."

"Everyone seems to be listening to you," he replied. "Just who *are* you?"

"The Elder Sister," she explained with a grin. "You met the Younger Sister when you met the Arbiter the first time. We are his bodyguards, aides, and"—she shrugged—"occasional lovers. We speak for him, help him with computers and the other modern technology he occasionally has trouble with."

"Do you have a *name*?" David asked.

"You can call me Jenna," she replied with a giggle. "My sister is Gabriel. Come, Commander."

"I'm surprised you're so willing to be helpful," he said as he followed her into the control room and she began to tap keys on the computers.

"The Arbiter thinks that a formal Truce, re-binding us to human law in exchange for the right to exist, is necessary for our survival," Jenna told him. "Without such a deal, Omicron will eventually exterminate us, and *that*, Commander, my oaths do not permit."

David heard motors whir to life and the doors begin to open.

"I cannot follow you outside, of course," she noted. "But I would hope that you can talk down your strike forces and fire support *before* they blow up my charges. I and the Arbiter would be…upset if this went wrong now."

Jenna handed David the keys to a Jeep and sent him back outside. He could have reached his people by radio inside the Mountain, but he suspected that being visible while telling people to stand down was a good idea.

"All right, people," he said into the radio, stopping the vehicle in the parking lot where Jamie Riley and his Second were waiting beside McCreery's helicopter. "The good news is that so long as we aren't planning on massacring the fledglings, the Keepers have surrendered.

"We have achieved our initial objectives without bloodshed, but that always means there's another shoe coming," David continued. "I want everyone on the ground in the main lot by McCreery ASAP. This isn't a briefing I want to give over the radio."

Plus, he needed to check in with Warner before things went further.

"Lord Riley." He inclined his head to the Elfin. "I'm going to call home. Can you get everyone organized and ready?"

"And here I forgot my orange jacket and flares," Riley told him, but nodded. "We'll make it happen. Good luck."

"Thanks."

David stepped into McCreery's Pendragon to take advantage of the aircraft's sound-dampening. With ten helicopters headed his way, even magically stealthed ones, any tool to make the conversation easier was useful.

"Major Warner, this is White," he pinged the base commander. "Reporting in."

A few seconds passed while she got on the channel.

"What's your status, Commander?"

"You'll probably want to have Charles or Leitz pull the footage from my camera of the conversation I just had with the Arbiter," David told her. "The summary: if we'll commit to protect the facility and not harm the fledglings, the Keepers have surrendered."

"The Committee made a good call," she replied. "That's fantastic, Commander, the best possible outcome."

"The Arbiter also has a suggestion for a long-term truce," David continued. "At the minimum, he has the ability, on his own, to bind any new vampires who leave the Mountain to honor our laws and not harm humans. Assuming, of course, that we're willing to accept these 'Truce-bound' vampires as exempt from Order Twenty-one."

Warner was silent for a few seconds, then exhaled heavily.

"Damn. That's…"

"Hope for the future, ma'am," David said. "For us and them. And if we can convince some of the Familias to sign on, too…"

"Then suddenly, we have vampire Elders and commandos to throw at the demons," Warner finished for him. "I'm not sure the Committee would sign off on that, David. You're talking beings with rap sheets a mile long and piles of dead bodies to their name."

"I know. The Arbiter didn't even suggest it, but I think it's something we need to realize has to be on the table."

"I don't know if we can sell the Committee on a blanket pardon," Warner told him, putting into words what they both knew would have to be the Familias's requirement for signing off on the Arbiter's Truce. "But…to end the violence, to bring the vampires back into the fold as productive citizens?"

"I'll make the case before the Committee myself if we need it, ma'am. I'm pretty sure the Arbiter will come with me to do it—and any of them that break the Truce are fair game for us."

"That might be enough, Commander White. But I get the feeling there's a catch you're not telling me."

"The Arbiter admits the Familias have agents among his Keepers. Their oaths forbid them from violence, not sending text messages."

"Oh. *Fuck.*"

"I figure we're probably safe enough tonight, but tomorrow night, we're going to see the massed firepower of the North American Vampire Familias thrown at this base," David stated. "How long can I keep those planes and artillery?"

"I'll make damned fucking sure you have them that long," the Major told him flatly. "I don't know if I can scrape up Omicron or Elfin reinforcements, though; you already have everything we can spare."

"I know." He paused. "Ma'am, this is going to cost us if we hold. It's the right thing to do, but I'm not certain I have the authority to make this call."

"Fuck that," Warner said. "You made the call already. We'll back you. Hold the line, Commander White."

She chuckled softly.

"The survival of the vampire species may depend on it."

Exiting the Pendragon, David found himself facing a field of confused and questioning faces. It was intriguing, to him at least, that he could almost tell who had worked with him before and who hadn't by how calm they looked.

Mason and Klein both looked curious but unbothered. Riley and Young were even calmer. Most of Klein's usual squad and Mason's ONSET Fifteen looked concerned but confident.

Sokol, ONSET Six, and the thirty or so Elfin Warriors who hadn't worked with David before looked like they were half-expecting the ground they were standing on to explode.

"All right, people," he addressed them. "We just had a major change of mission profile. The good news: the Arbiter and the Keepers have surrendered. *We* now control this facility.

"The bad news is that Familias knows this," David warned them, "and they cannot, if they wish to survive as they currently are, permit us to maintain that control. We have seen the resources even a single one of the Vampire Families can bring to bear: when we hit the Golden Twilight casino, we met mobile artillery, modified antiaircraft units, and heavy military weapons.

"When *all* of them bring their worst to the table, we can expect that we are facing a conflict that we have not seen in some time. It appears to fall to us to fight a war on our own soil, against an enemy we have battled for years now."

"Why?" Sokol asked. "Let's just blow this place and go home."

"We promised the fledglings would be unharmed," David pointed out to the other ONSET Commander. "If we are to *end* the war with the vampires, once and for all, we need to hold the Mountain. So long as the future of the vampire species is in our hands, we can dictate peace.

"But to do so, we must hold the Mountain."

"So, what's the plan?" Mason asked, stepping forward. "Everything we'd briefed on, everything we prepared, was for an all-out assault on this place, not a defense."

"So, we know how *we* were going to hit it," he replied. "So, we set up countermeasures to those. The Pendragons will need to act as close air cover, but I've been told we will continue to have both artillery and air support.

"We're going to want to pre-sight artillery target zones and airstrike corridors," he continued. "The facility itself has no weapons, no defenses beyond being a giant concrete bunker. My preference would be to fight the bastards *outside* the Mountain, so we will prepare positions on the surface here.

"The vampires can only move so much in terms of personnel and gear during the day, so we will likely only face light attacks tonight. Tomorrow, though, we can expect to face everything the Familias can throw at us."

David smiled grimly at them all.

"If we hold, ladies and gentlemen, we end a two-hundred-year-long war and allow our government to lift a standing order that is arguably the worst violation of the Constitution Omicron has been forced to embrace.

"Let's make it happen."

[26]

DAVID LEFT HIS PEOPLE PULLING SUPPLIES OUT OF THE HELICOPTERS IN THE main parking lot and returned to the shadowy underground of the Mountain. Jenna was waiting for him, accompanied this time by the raven-haired woman in the black armored bodysuit who had driven the Arbiter to their first meeting.

"We are limited in what our oaths allow us to provide," the bodyguard—Gabriel, Jenna had said her name was, the Younger Sister—told him. "But there are supplies and resources you can access. Sandbags and so forth would be useful, I believe?"

"They would," David allowed, gesturing for Stone to join him. "Stone, pull a work team together from the Elfin and follow Miss Gabriel here. Any addition we can make to the surface defenses will be of value."

"Any guns?" Stone asked bluntly.

"We keep very little in terms of weaponry in the facility," Gabriel replied. "Some sidearms, a few assault rifles. Nothing that would qualify as heavy weaponry."

"After what the Romanovs protected the convoy heading this way with, I'm surprised," the Agent grunted.

"That convoy was Petrov Romanov's last chance to expand his

Familias and make up for the losses you inflicted," Jenna pointed out as her sister led Stone away. "They pulled out everything they had to make sure they reached us safely…and you stopped them."

"They made it here," David replied.

"Because the Arbiter promised they would be oathbound," she noted. "Such would be of no use to Romanov." The blonde vampire smiled. It was a…toothy, predatory thing. "He *hates* you. I don't think you even begin to comprehend how deep Romanov's hatred of you runs.

"You have destroyed his dream of ruling the Familias, but his own power means he can only lose by dying." The predatory grin widened. "He knows he is doomed, and whoever kills him in the end, it is *your* hand that set into motion his downfall."

"Or his own," David suggested. "Omicron never sought war with the Familias, only to protect people."

"And enough of our kind truly were bloodthirsty monsters to set into motion events that could not be stopped," Jenna told him. "I wish I could say differently, but the conflict was inevitable. And now it must end. We cannot conquer humanity, we never could, and as the world moves forward, we can no longer hide."

"You speak like you were there," he said.

"I was," she admitted. "My parents brought me to the signing of the Declaration of Independence, Commander White—a ten-year-old blonde thing struggling to see over the shoulders of others. I have seen the growth of our nation from the beginning, but for much of it, I have been hidden in the shadows, avoiding a war my own kind started."

She shook her head.

"Gabriel is five years younger than me. We were in our twenties when we turned. We owe everything to the Arbiter, more so than many here. We will die for him."

"How does being a Keeper reconcile with Gabriel being his bodyguard?" David asked.

"Gabriel isn't a Keeper," she replied calmly. "She swore never to touch human blood, but she refused the rest of the oaths to allow her to defend us. Come," she continued. "The Arbiter wishes to speak with you with less…time pressure, shall we say."

David gestured for her to lead the way, wondering suddenly how many of the white-robed vampires around him were *actually* sworn to nonviolence...and how many could turn on the people he'd committed to defend them if things went wrong.

JENNA LED him into what appeared to be the main control center for the Mountain. Dozens of screens showed the view from cameras mounted around the exterior, and David suspected that the computers there could also open and close the various doors into the complex.

It had chairs and stations for easily a dozen people, though from the look of them, only four or so were currently in use—and the room's only occupant was the red-robed Arbiter. The vampire stood alone in the middle of the room, his head shifting minutely every few seconds to study another set of screens.

"Welcome, Commander White. Thank you, Jenna."

With a wordless bow, the blonde vampire withdrew, leaving David alone with the master of this facility for the first time.

"You realize, I presume, that you cannot trust my Keepers not to open the way for the Familias," the old vampire said without preamble. "They will honor their oaths, they will not fight you, but that does not mean they necessarily *agree* with me.

"And even if they do, the bonds of loyalty and blood run strongly in our kind. If Reginald or Romanov or Sakura order a Keeper of their blood to open the door to one of the silos, it will happen."

"I suspected as much," David agreed. "I intend to meet them outside the Mountain. We will need maps of the interior, though."

"Gabriel should be providing them to your Agent Johnson as we speak," the Arbiter told, still facing the screens instead of his guest.

"Jenna said Gabriel was not a Keeper," David noted. "Are there others like her here?"

"You worry about knives at your back," the old vampire replied. It wasn't a question. "No. Gabriel is not unique, but she is alone here. I once swore the oaths she is now bound by. I failed, Commander. If you know the names you called me by earlier, you know what happened."

"The Paris Crèche."

"I was its Guardian, as Gabriel is the Guardian here. I did not believe the Revolution was a danger to the Crèche, only to me. I…was not wrong, but I misjudged the movements in the shadows."

"My information was only that the Crèche was destroyed," David admitted. "We weren't told how."

"I'm surprised you even learned as much as you did," the old, old man in the room with him replied. "If you can tell me…how? I know of only three entities in this world—and perhaps a dozen beyond it! — who would know who Anaxis of Athens was."

"It's not like you can threaten them," the ONSET Commander replied with a chuckle. "We bought the information from a creature calling itself the Tahoe Oracle. I have no idea what it is."

"Ah," the Arbiter said with a long exhalation. "I was aware of the creature you refer to. It was not on my list, but yes, its powers would suffice to learn that which I thought forgotten."

He shook his head.

"I would not expect your sympathy for the destruction of the Crèche at Paris," he concluded. "I am…gratified that you are as willing to consider peace as you are, Commander. My kind have done you no favors."

"In my experience, only monsters judge an individual by their race or their badge."

"Even us, Commander White?" the Arbiter whispered. Age and exhaustion seemed to radiate from his frame, overwhelming even the soothing aura that filled the entire Mountain. "My race *are* monsters; don't let Hollywood or the trends of romance fiction fool you otherwise. I believe I can teach them a different course, but monstrosity has been our path for millennia."

"I am a Seer," David reminded the vampire. "Feral as those fledglings were, they were still…innocent. Helpless. I am a police officer. It is my duty to *protect* the helpless…even from themselves, sometimes."

"You should have met Aléxandros," the vampire told him. "That was where he started, you know. Protecting the Hellenic cities from themselves." He laughed bitterly. "History shows where that ended."

The whole conversation had gone somewhat off-course, but David let the Arbiter get whatever was in his system out.

"But Paris, yes. Understand me, Commander, I do not blame the men who burned out my Crèche," the Arbiter told him. "The Knights Hospitaller knew what they'd found. There was no better way then. No hope of a peaceful compromise.

"The Keepers I had left behind fought, but the Keepers are nurses and doctors, not soldiers. They died. The Knights set the whole place ablaze, burning the *teknon* to ash so they could not flee."

David remained silent. He could understand exactly what those eighteenth-century Knights had been thinking—and also exactly how the Arbiter felt about it.

"I failed to defend a Crèche and could no longer claim I was a Guardian," the Arbiter said simply. "I swore the full oaths of a Keeper and set into motion the sequence of events that led to where I stand today, able to finally offer a compromise and a new path for my people."

"If we help you," David noted.

"If you help me. If you defend this facility." The old vampire sighed. "I have no resources to give you, Commander. Only my word that I will make this worth it."

"I know."

The Arbiter gestured.

"Your artillery battery arrives." He pointed at one of the cameras, showing the green-painted shapes of Major Wilbur's M109A7 Paladins and their support vehicles driving up the road towards the compound. "The road is better maintained than it looks; it can support them."

"There won't be any more help coming," David said. "We can't commit mundane troops to this beyond those already briefed."

"I do not know what the Familias will bring," the vampire admitted. "But what I am hearing is…dangerous."

"How so?"

"Romanov has invited Dresden's faction to work with him to retake the Mountain," the Arbiter explained. "A brilliant move on his part, one that places him at the forefront of protecting the race. If he succeeds, he will snatch victory in his civil war from the jaws of defeat."

"What will Dresden do?" David asked. He'd been counting on the civil war to disorganize his enemies' response.

"I don't know, Commander White," the old vampire admitted. "I know what his father would have done—and it is for everyone's benefit, I think, that you killed him."

"Your politics make me nervous," the ONSET Commander replied.

"*Yours* created a standing order to exterminate my species."

DAVID MADE it back outside just in time to greet the assemblage of US Army vehicles as they came rolling in. Eight big tank-like vehicles with massive cannons led the way, accompanied by eight similar-looking tracked vehicles without the cannon.

The lead self-propelled gun came to a halt and the hatch popped open. A small sandy-haired man in US Army fatigues and a gold oak leaf Major's insignia jumped down, a massively impressive mustache flapping around his face as he moved.

The man took a moment to calm his mustache and glanced around, his gaze settled rapidly on David.

"Damn, that is some Space Age shit your people are carrying," he noted loudly. "You White?"

"Commander David White, ONSET Thirteen," David confirmed. "You're Wilbur?"

"Major Miles Wilbur, US Army," the smaller man said. "I take it we aren't shelling this place anymore?"

"That remains to be seen," the ONSET agent admitted. "We have successfully taken control of the facility, but we expect…disagreement on that point from the main vampire forces."

Wilbur shook his head.

"I had to brief my boys on the way up here," he told David. "Now, *that*, Commander, was a weird-ass fucking conversation."

"I can only imagine, Major. We expect to come under attack by vampires and potentially Thrall or mercenary forces starting tonight,"

David told him. "I expect the major thrust to be about an hour after dark tomorrow, but they're going to probe tonight to see what we do."

"My men may be uncertain and confused, Commander, but I've still got eight hundred-fifty-five-mike-mike guns and more than a thousand high-explosive rounds to drop wherever you want them. How badly do you want us to fuck up these guys?"

"That's what I was hoping to hear, Major," the Commander replied. "For now, I think we'll want to move your guns higher up the mountain and out of the immediate threat zone. I'm assuming once you're in position, you can pre-plot target zones all the way up the roads?"

"We can do that," Wilbur agreed. "Both my guns and my ammo CATs have secondary weapons, though. You sure you want us that far back?"

"Unless your secondaries are loaded with silver, they aren't going to be much use," David told him. "Your big guns will blow whatever they hit to hell, and even vampires can't reconstitute themselves from scattered fragments, but regular bullets aren't going to do much. I'd rather have you on hand to rain fire from above."

"It's your call," the Major told him. "My orders are clear: you're in command, Commander White."

"I'm a glorified cop, Major," he pointed out. "What I know about properly deploying artillery can be written on a small pin. I want your people set up to back up mine with direct-fire mission, and I want them out of reach of the pissed-off fangs I expect to be swarming the mountain tomorrow night."

David shook his head.

"I'll want your boys ready to drop fire tonight, but I don't expect to call on you until tomorrow," he concluded. "Tomorrow…tomorrow I expect to need you to turn half of this mountain into hell."

"We can do that," Wilbur said grimly. "Though if you've got something all-terrain-capable, I'd rather run myself and the Battery Sergeant-Major up the mountain and find a decent spot to ground the guns. I don't really want to run thirty-five ton vehicles into a forest without an idea of where I'm taking them."

"We've got full topographical maps, and the Keepers have given us half a dozen Jeeps," David offered. "Or you can borrow a helicopter."

"Jeep's better. Need to the see the ground."

"Stone." David pinged his Agent through the coms. "Can you bring one of the fangs' Jeeps out? Our artillery CO wants to reconnoiter the slopes."

"Can do."

David returned his attention to Wilbur.

"Jeep is on its way. Any more questions?"

"Yeah, though probably not relevant," the Major said slowly, his gaze on David's weapons. "Is that a *sword*?"

NAPOLEON BONAPARTE HAD ONCE FAMOUSLY SAID, "ASK me for anything but time."

By the time late afternoon was rolling around, David was wishing his own superiors followed the same philosophy. Everyone accepted that the vampires were a threat, that they were probably going to try and retake the Mountain...but no one was willing to move unusual resources into play.

This was shaping up to be the kind of defensive battle where a battalion—even a company or two—of conventional troops could make all of the difference. Vampires were tough and hard to kill, but a solid-enough line of machine guns—preferably with silver bullets— would still make short work of them.

"We have no authority to commandeer conventional troops," Warner told him in response that request. "ONSET itself has nothing to spare; you know that. The supplies and heavy weapons that are on their way are all you're going to get, David; I'm sorry.

"To borrow Army troops or even National Guard troops, the Committee has to sign off, and I don't think they're prepared to accept that the Familias may be able to fight a real war on US soil."

"What *am* I getting?" David finally demanded.

"Two dozen heavy machine guns and about a million rounds of steel-jacketed, silver-tipped, ammo," she reeled off. "Same 7.62 millimeter rounds your M4s use, so you can load them into the carbines as well as the machine guns.

"We also apparently have a few crates of silver-loaded claymores someone put together and we never found a use for. Those are heading your way as well."

"It's something, at least," David admitted.

"You'll have two heavy-transport choppers on the ground by an hour before nightfall. It's not a lot of time, Commander, but our hands are surprisingly tied."

"That has implications I'm not sure I like, ma'am," he pointed out.

"I know," Warner admitted. "I've dropped some commentary in the appropriate ears at OSPI. If someone—or more than one someone—on the Committee is in bed with the Familias, we have a problem."

"If the Arbiter has his way, not for much longer," David replied.

"Oh, believe me, Commander White, even if the Committee accepts the Arbiter's Truce and we start reintegrating the vampires, I will bloody nail anyone who worked with the Familias to the wall for treason," the Major said flatly.

"The good news is you *are* getting heavy weapons and you have one of the largest concentrations of combat-trained supernaturals Omicron has ever fielded at your command."

"Apparently, it's going to have to be enough."

"I know. I'm sorry."

[27]

Twilight felt both eternal and far too short as David paced the surveillance center, his attention flickering from camera to camera on the screens around him.

Everyone else was out on the mountain except for Mason. The two of them represented the only reserve he had. There were too many approaches, too many entrances, for him to let the vampires anywhere near the bunker itself.

That meant his fifty supernaturals were scattered around the perimeter, waiting for the call from David to move to intercept the scouting parties they were expecting tonight.

"That's it," Mason murmured. "Sun is down." She shook her head. "Not exactly what I had in mind when I was thinking about watching the sunset together."

David shot her a shocked glance, checking to make sure their radios were muted.

They were, of course. His lover was significantly smarter than he was; he knew that. She wasn't going to be careless with a secret that could make both of their lives a thousand times more complicated.

"Be careful," he told her anyway, then turned his attention back to the cameras.

The Arbiter had installed the best of the best for the sensor systems that surrounded the Mountain. As darkness swept over them, the screens tinged green as they automatically switched over to infrared. In night vision mode, the overlay for the attached motion sensors was more visible as well.

David toggled his radio on.

"Leitz, are you seeing anything on overhead?" he asked the analyst.

"Nothing yet… Wait," she replied. A moment paused. *"Might* be coincidence. Might. But pattern recognition just IDed two dozen cars and SUVs headed your way with similar arrival estimates.

"We're watching for an earlier wave, but I'd say you're definitely going to have problems in an hour."

"Thank you," David told her. "We'll pass the word."

He nodded to Mason and switched his radio to the main channel.

"Control has flagged incoming vehicles with a shared ETA of approximately one hour," he told his people. "Now, the fangs *know* we can do that, so I'm expecting we'll see the actual first wave sometime in the next thirty minutes."

He paused, considering his words. There wasn't much to say.

"Keep your eyes peeled, and good luck."

Even as he watched the screens around him, the video from the cameras was being fed into the tactical network running inside David's AR wargear. His heads-up-display could show him any of the cameras, plus the locations and status of any of his people.

It could easily get confusing, and the system worked best with teams of six or less. Right now, the main thing he was using it for was to know which of his people were near each camera—so when the motion detector tripped, he could direct people to deal with the situation.

"Stone, Hellet," he said calmly over the radio. "Motion detector just tripped on camera D17, two hundred and fifty feet southeast of you." He studied the camera.

"I've got three…no, four, bodies at seventy degrees," he told them. "Flagging to your wargear."

"Moving," Stone replied crisply.

Their icons blipped on his HUD, and a moment's study allowed him to bring up the cameras to watch them moving into the area. The four vampires—nothing else looked like a human but had a seventy-degree-Fahrenheit body temperature—moved up and past camera D17, clearly unaware of the device.

Tapping commands, David brought up cameras C16 and C17, allowing him to pick up the continued advance of the vampires and the movement of his own team.

Hellet moved closer to C17 and stepped out into the open, clearly visible to the incoming vampires.

"I can see you," she said loudly, her voice carrying over the radio to David. "This facility is now secured by the Federal Government; surrender or we will use lethal force."

On the cameras, David saw the vampires freeze—and then go for their weapons. The lead vampire got off a single shot that ricocheted off Hellet's defensive shield.

Then both cameras lit up with flashes of bright light as Stone opened fire with the big machine gun. Silver-tipped bullets tore through the trees, shredding foliage and trunks alike.

The four highlighted figures on David's screens reeled backward and fell.

"Clean sweep," he told them. "Well done."

"Camera E12 has motion," Mason announced as he turned his gaze back to the screen. "Linking in with Klein."

David's followed her words, studying the video feed from E12. Another set of four vampires was moving through the bushes, but the Elfin Warrior was already on the radio with Mason and he left that sector to her, turning his attention to the rest of the Mountain.

Moments later, another flare of motion caught his attention.

"Camera D36," he said aloud, studying it. "Agent Dupond, I have motion in your sector, camera D36. One hundred seventy feet to your south-south-east."

"Moving," the massive Empowered grunted from Mason's team

grunted back. Two of ONSET Fifteen's Agents, Pierre Dupond and Hiro Tsimote, moved on David's screen, intercepting the vampires as they approached camera C38.

There was a blast of fire that was visible from half of the east-side cameras. When the heat and light faded, there was no sign of the group of vampires moving up the side of the hill.

"Neutralized," Tsimote noted flatly, and David sighed. The flame elementalist *hated* vampires—he'd had an even worse first encounter with them than David had, and they both carried the scars of vampire fangs. They were *supposed* to be summoning people to surrender, but...

"Understood," David replied shortly. It wasn't like he had any illusions about the intent of any vampires sneaking up on the Mountain tonight.

"Motion sensors are clear," he noted a moment later on the general channel. "Continue to watch for contacts; the vehicles are forty minutes out but we *know* they're going to try and be sneaky."

Two more teams tried to sneak their way in while David watched and waited for the vehicles to arrive. A total of twenty-five vampires all told had tried to make an approach. None had surrendered when called upon to do so. None had survived their first encounter with the defenders.

Either the Familias spearheading the attack had no idea just what surveillance net was woven around the Mountain, or they had presumed ONSET wouldn't have control of it. Either way, they tried stealth and failed miserably.

"We may need to up our estimate of just how many vampires are going to be coming our way," David quietly noted to Mason as he studied the fleet of vehicles converging through Crater Lake National Park.

Twenty-five vampires had already died on the slopes of Mount Scott. The vehicles heading his way almost certainly contained at least as many, and that was assuming there were Thralls in some of them.

"Quite possibly. What's the plan for these guys?" Mason asked, gesturing toward the screen. Fourteen SUVs and ten sedans had joined together and were now turning onto the main approach road.

"That depends," he noted. "Think they're going to try and drive all the way up, or dismount somewhere and approach on foot?"

"If they've been in touch with their friends, they've got to realize that stealth isn't going to work," the other Commander replied. "I figure they floor it and head straight for the bunker."

Ten seconds later, Mason was proven correct as the lead pair of SUVs, massive four-wheel-drive monstrosities, spun gravel off the rough road and charged up the hill.

"Lord Riley," David greeted the Elfin Lord General over the radio, "you have incoming. Looks like our friends in the cars are coming in hell for leather."

There was a pause on the radio.

"I see none of *them* went to Afghanistan," Riley said quietly, his voice almost sad. "We'll deal with it."

The vehicles came barreling up the road, turning the final curve from the gravel road onto the maintained section that led into the old SAC compound—and then the lead two vehicles basically disappeared as the roadside anti-vehicle mines went off.

Four crisscrossed cones of fire and shrapnel disintegrated the front vehicles, and the second pair of cars had barely begun to slam on their brakes before they skidded into the debris field.

Surviving the wreckage of their companions, they bounced onto the still-intact road…and triggered the second set of mines. Another quartet of fireballs lit up the night, and two more vehicles disappeared.

The following vehicles managed to come to a halt in the middle of the half-wrecked road, spilling out men and women in body armor with an assortment of weapons.

"McCreery."

David didn't need to say more. As the vampires began to spread out, the Pendragons swept in. Ground-bombardment missiles lit up the sky with their engines and machine guns opened fire, explosions sweeping the ground around the road.

The attackers scattered like bowling pins, explosions smashing them to the ground—but not fast enough to stop them from opening fire with Stingers. The missiles exploding on the ground were matched by explosions in the air for several seconds, and then the remaining Pendragons pulled away.

"McCreery, report," David snapped. They hadn't anticipated anti-aircraft missiles—and they *should* have.

There was no response for several moments and a sick feeling began to take over his stomach.

"Here," she finally replied, her voice twisted with clearly forced calm. "We lost three helicopters and are down half our missiles. Orders?"

"Pull back to the depot and rearm," David ordered. "Riley? You've still got incoming."

"I see them," the Elfin Lord replied. "It looks like they've stopped underestimating us."

The survivors of the air strike were still moving forward. With the fires, it was hard for the thermal scanners to get a count, but they were now moving like real soldiers. A squad would advance while the others held covering positions, clearly sweeping for the resistance they knew had to be there.

They made it halfway to the main bunker before Riley's people started shooting. The Lord had kept five of the Elfin Warriors with him, and now it proved he'd picked the best shots. Rifle shots rang out, silver bullets hammering into the lead squad and sending them scattering to what cover they could find.

Then Riley hit a button and that cover revealed itself to be a trap. Twenty claymore antipersonnel mines, placed with carefully vicious thought, detonated in a single instant. Over half of the remaining vampires simply *disappeared*.

Then the Elfin Lord charged down the hill with his Second. The cameras couldn't quite process what they were seeing correctly, but David knew what the blue auras flaring to life around the two Mages were. When the remaining vampires opened fire on the charging defenders, their bullets deflected from the shields.

There was at least one Mage among the survivors, however, and fire tore through the night as they conjured power to try and take down the two Elfin. Riley, however, simply made a dismissive gesture with his sword as he approached the vampires, scattering the attack as he halted twenty feet from them.

"I see one of you has some talent," the Lord said casually. "I challenge you, then. Fight me, with steel or fire or magic as you will. Defeat me, and your companions will be allowed to leave. Fall, and your companions will surrender."

He gestured widely with the sword—but the response to his challenge was a lance of *something* that the camera only picked up as pure black light and a hail of gunfire.

The elf-blade flashed in the night, reflecting the black light back at its origin, and then both Elfin began to glow, the blue light of the shield fading into the stark white spells of Andúril, the Flame of the West—the magical martial art practiced by the Elfin Warrior-Mages.

A blur of motion followed as Young and Riley closed the distance, the vampire Mage attempting to stop them, and then the infrared cameras proved incapable of tracking the action. When the lights began to fade, the Elfin Lord and his apprentice stood alone, surrounded by wreckage and bodies.

"Secure," Riley reported over the radio. "But this is only the beginning, White."

"I know, Lord Riley."

"Sir, you have a problem," Leitz reported as midnight turned over to one AM.

"I have several, potentially," David replied. "What exactly is this one?"

"Echelon just flagged a California Army National Guard communication as a potential cause for concern," she told him. Echelon was the artificially intelligent, magically enhanced, officially nonexistent-even-in-Omicron-documents, computer program that the Omicron branches swept all official communications in the United States with. It searched for certain keywords and flags, and occasionally its algorithms threw up something that didn't match any of those keywords or flags…but usually turned out to be supremely important.

"They had a detachment of mechanized infantry doing maneuver exercises near Redding in Bradleys. Regular training, so they weren't exactly checking in every minute or so."

"But?" the Commander asked, a sinking feeling warning him where this was going.

"No one has heard from them since about six PM," Leitz warned. "Echelon flagged it when CAL ARNG contacted them asking what had happened to their GPS transponders."

"Where were their transponders when they went dark?" David asked.

"Crossing over into Oregon, about a hundred miles north of their AO on the I-97. I'm collating local police reports as we speak, seeing if anyone called in an *armored column* moving up the interstate."

"If they were heading here, ETA?"

"Just after two AM," she told him. "These aren't race cars; they're light armored vehicles. 25mm chain guns and anti-tank missiles in the default loadout. I'm checking the TOE for the platoons in question to see if there's any unusual variants."

David met Mason's eyes and exhaled heavily.

"How many vehicles am I looking at, Leitz?"

"Three platoons," she said. "Twelve BFVs. I don't know how many ground troops, but…the company the APCs belong to had a hundred and twenty people."

A hundred and twenty people who were almost certainly now dead. David felt sick.

"Find them on the overhead," he ordered. "If I have an entire company of vampire mechanized infantry heading my way, I need to know that for certain."

He was also going to need to wake up Major Wilbur. It appeared they might need the artillery tonight after all.

[28]

Leitz found the APC column on overhead roughly fifteen minutes before they expected it to arrive. Twelve tracked vehicles trundling along the interstate at thirty-five miles per hour in a neat column, the sparse nighttime traffic swerving to pass them in surprise.

"Overhead can't give us decent thermal," she warned. "I have no idea how occupied they are."

"Do we have anyone checking in on the company they belonged to?" It was possible, though certainly a worst-case scenario in many ways, that the BFVs on their way to attack the Mountain were still manned by their original crews.

"A local OSPI Inspector is on their way," Leitz confirmed. "But we won't have any real information for several more hours."

"And in about ten minutes, these are going to come charging up the roads into the compound," David noted. "All right. Thank you. Keep me updated on any other potential flags, but this is now our problem."

He studied the targeting grid the artillery battery had given him, checking it against the map.

"Major Wilbur, I need you to dial in a strike," he told the Army officer, reeling off the grid coordinates. "We've got what appears to be the commandeered vehicles of a mechanized infantry company heading our way, and I don't care to discover how many vampires they've crammed into them."

"Understood," Wilbur replied. "What are we looking at, Commander?"

"Appears to be M2 Bradleys, according to the TOE we've pulled."

"Okay," the artillery commander sighed. "They're pretty well armored against our shells, Commander. They're not going to enjoy the barrage, but there's a decent chance at least some will make it through.

"We have specialized anti-tank ammunition with a decent chance of one-shot kills, but I only have twelve of them."

"Hold on to them for now," David told him. "I have the feeling we're going to need those later."

There was silence on the channel for several seconds.

"That's what I was afraid you were going to say, Commander White," Wilbur told him. "We're dialed in and I've brought the closest cameras on my screens. Any of them that reach your positions will do so through a wall of fire and steel, courtesy of the US Army."

"I DON'T SUPPOSE you have any more of those anti-vehicle mines?" Riley asked over the radio as the lead Bradleys showed up on the Mountain's camera systems. "I have one set left on the road and I'd love to put a few more in these guys' way."

"I was surprised we had a dozen of them," David told him. "You're going to have to settle for artillery support."

"That's going to be new and interesting," the Elfin Lord General replied. "I haven't been this close to an artillery barrage before."

The ONSET Commander paused, considering the Elfin words.

"So, the anti-vehicle mines *weren't* new and interesting?" he asked.

"...I take the Fifth," Riley replied after a long pause. "Deputizing or no deputizing, there's still some things I am not going to tell Omicron."

"Targets approaching the zone," Wilbur cut in. "Time-on-target barrage beginning…now."

The Paladins were high enough up Mount Scott that David couldn't hear or feel them firing. One of the surveillance network's cameras was close enough for him to see the billowing blasts of flame as the big guns fired.

Fifteen seconds later, the barrels adjusted and fired again. And again. And again. The guns fired four times in a minute, then returned to rest position to cool. David wasn't sure how long the howitzers could maintain the four rounds per minute, but he knew it wasn't long.

Different angles and firing charges meant all twenty-four shells arrived in a ten-second span, smashing down onto the forested road moments after the last Bradley left sight of the main highway. The cameras trained on the incoming vehicles showed the entire column disappearing in a cloud of superheated smoke and debris they couldn't penetrate.

"Do you see anything?" Riley demanded. "I need to know how many made it through."

"We're not getting anything useful from the cameras," David told him. "Hold position and prep those anti-tank rockets."

"Oh, believe me, they're already prepped," the Elfin replied. "I'd *love* for you to tell me the artillery took them all, though."

"No such luck," Mason told them. "Looks like we got most of them, but I have four BFVs still moving up. Ninety seconds to the last set of mines."

"Let's see how much attention they're paying," David murmured. The first eight mines had left a giant mess in the road. The tracked APCs could easily traverse it, but if they recognized just what they'd hit…

The BFVs slowed as they spotted the debris. They knew artillery was in play, which made that dangerous, but whoever was in command clearly recognized the aftereffect of anti-vehicle mines.

David wasn't entirely surprised. If the Familias didn't have any veterans of the war in Afghanistan on staff, he'd be shocked.

"They're going off-road," he warned Riley. "Moving around where they suspect the mines are."

"If you can hold them up, we can drop another salvo on their heads," Wilbur promised.

"Oh, I'm pretty sure we can do that," the Elfin replied grimly. He reeled off a set of grid coordinates. "As soon as we engage, drop fire on that zone."

"Can do."

"I see the trees coming down," Riley told them. "Let's see just what the vampires brought to the party—and how well they play."

David was realizing how much he hated being behind the lines, commanding via camera and radio as others took on the enemy and the risk. There was nothing he could do to help Riley and his half-dozen Warriors from there except watch.

The Bradleys emerged from the forest at high speed, smashing aside trees with their frontal armor as if speed was the only thing that could keep them alive. One of the lead vehicles took a pair of LAAWs from Riley's men and went up in a massive fireball, but the other managed to swerve and throw off the targeting.

More explosions marked the ground, but the troops inside the APCs were dismounting at speed, jumping out of the back of the moving vehicles as the machine guns opened fire on the sandbagged position holding Riley's people.

That action at least confirmed that the troops probably weren't the National Guardsmen the vehicles had originally belonged to. Thralls, empowered by vampire blood, *might* be able to pull off that stunt...but it looked like this wave were vampires.

Then the shells started falling...only to detonate *above* the vampires as they ran into a defensive shield. In the center of the vampire charge was a tall, white-haired man with familiar-looking Slavic features and his hands held above his head.

"That's...Romanov himself," Mason murmured. "Holy shit."

The curse was for the vampire's power—as he contained the explosive force of half a dozen massive artillery shells and *flung* it at the Elfin position. David had fought the man's daughters, powerful vampire Elders commanding dark magic.

Petrov Romanov showed where they'd learned it from.

The sandbags and concrete barriers the Elfin had assembled disintegrated and David cringed. Some of the Warriors were powerful enough to survive that—but not all of them. Pillars of black fire appeared around Romanov, sweeping toward the sniper positions with terrifying speed.

The 25mm chain guns on the Bradleys opened as well, walking their fire across the front of the bunker, clearly trying to drive the surviving Elfin into Romanov's fire strike.

Then another LAAW fired, a glittering blue corona shielding it as it slashed through the shield and hammered into the closest APC. The explosion staggered the vampire Patriarch, and his shield flickered for a moment—a moment in which the Elfin marksmen took down the closest of the closing vampires.

Then the chain guns chattered to life again—only for their shells to impact on a glowing blue shield that rose to match Romanov's flickering black one as Jamie Riley, Lord General of the Elfin Conclave, strode out of the wreckage of the defensive position.

White light flickered around the Elfin Lord, lighting up the whole parking lot in front of the SAC bunker with a stark, unnatural glow. Two vampires charged at him, only to disappear in flashes of blue light as Riley gestured at them.

"Petrov Romanov," the Elfin Lord spoke, his own headset carrying his words back to the command net. "Turn back."

"Stand aside, child," Romanov snapped as their shields clashed, the two spheres pushing against each other even as they blocked the gunfire flashing across the field. "My quarrel is not with you!"

"You cannot pass," Riley said calmly, magic projecting his voice across the concrete field. "I am a servant of the Secret Fire, wielder of the flame of Anor. You cannot pass."

"*Burn!*" the vampire screamed, new pillars of black flame conjuring into existence and charging at the Elfin Lord.

Riley continued his calm advance, his shield smashing the black flame aside.

"The dark fire will not avail you, flame of Udûn," he continued, and even David recognized the quote now. "Go back to the Shadow. You cannot pass!"

Romanov screamed, a wordless expression of rage, and charged the

Elfin Lord. Wings of black fire swept him from the ground as a whip of pure darkness slashed out, smashing through Riley's shield like tissue paper.

Riley met the whip with his sword, the elf-blade appearing in his hand without his seeming to draw it. The darkness met the blue glow of the weapon, wrapping around its blade and trying to pull it away or break it.

Then the whip shattered and the Elfin Lord took to the air to meet his enemy. No wings or visible magic surrounded him; he simply rose and met Romanov in the air. Their shields continued to press against each other, each trying to overwhelm the other and allow their allies to strike, and the two Mages met in the middle.

The cameras were barely able to track what followed. Only David's own superhuman senses allowed him to make any sense of the distorted, skipping-frames mess the screens showed—and what he saw was terrifying.

Romanov's wings and whip struck again and again at Riley, new ones flickering into existence as the Lord parried, balls of black fire appearing from nowhere to try and take the Elfin down.

Riley's sword seemed to be everywhere, the azure glow of the enchanted blade intercepting whips and wings and fireballs alike. Some made it past, only to disintegrate against the growing pure white glow around the Elfin Mage.

For a few seconds, it looked like Romanov was no match for Riley, then a whip, two wings, and three fireballs slammed home at once. The white aura flickered…and failed, the Elfin Lord falling from the sky like a homesick stone.

The light flared back into existence, halting Riley mere feet from the ground—and he'd somehow sustained his shield the entire time—but now the vampire was swooping down on him with terrifying speed.

Even David almost missed what happened next. A single shot, fired from outside the shields, charged with the azure blue aura of powerful magic, smashed through everything and collided with Petrov Romanov, sending the vampire Patriarch reeling backward at the impact of the heavy silver bullet.

Brianna Young might be Lord Riley's apprentice, but she was also his *bodyguard*. And no one had said this was going to be a one-on-one duel.

The vampire stabilized himself in the air, only for a second charged bullet to smash into him. The injuries, likely enough to kill even most high-class regenerators, were barely slowing him down—but they were enough to allow Riley to recover and rise back into the air as more shots punched through Romanov's shield.

A wordless howl cut through the air, loud enough that David could hear it *inside* the bunker—and the vampire charged Riley again, flame and darkness surrounding him as he threw all of his power into the strike.

His power focused on the attack, the Patriarch's shield collapsed, with the remaining Elfin firing rocket launchers before the vampires even realized they were defenseless. The last three Bradleys detonated simultaneously and the marksmen set to their lethal work as their Lord met the vampire Patriarch in the air once more.

White and black fire lit up the sky as a corona of pure power surrounded each Mage, both of them wounded and giving up subtlety for hammering magic into each other as hard as they could. Riley was maintaining the shield over his people and Romanov continued to slowly, inexorably push towards the Elfin Lord.

And then Riley calmly and perfectly dropped his shield. Unresisted, Romanov shot forward with mind-boggling speed—and met the Lord's elf-blade coming the other way.

The corona of black fire vanished as Petrov Romanov, Patriarch of the once-most powerful vampire Familias in the United States, hit the ground.

In pieces.

[29]

THE REMAINING HOURS BEFORE DAWN PASSED IN SURPRISING CALM, leaving the sun to rise over a mountainside that had been reduced to a war zone.

Three Pendragon attack helicopters were debris scattered along the main road along with their pilots. Four of Riley's Elfin Warriors were gone, their shattered remains covered by white sheets in a cold room the Keepers had offered them to use as a morgue.

Seven of the defenders were dead, but David's best estimate was that over two hundred vampires had already died assaulting the Mountain. He'd expected probing raids but ended up facing an all-out mechanized infantry assault.

He, Mason and Riley sat in what had been the base cafeteria and served a similar function for the Keepers. Vats of "stabilized blood," as the odd vampires called it, were stacked along one wall, keeping the animal blood at a constant temperature to feed the occupants of the Mountain.

There was also regular food. Vampires didn't *need* to eat, but it made it easier for them to go extended periods without drinking blood. The Keepers appeared to have adopted a mix of the magically stabilized animal blood and ordinary food as their main diet.

They freely shared the normal food with the Omicron and Elfin, though most of the Keepers refused to spend any actual time in the same room as their conquerors.

Exhausted after the night, David missed the Arbiter entering the room, the old vampire disturbingly soft on his feet as he approached and laid a tray with three steaming fresh coffee cups in front of David and his companions.

"You will need to sleep," the Arbiter told them in a calm, clinically assessing, tone, "but not yet. There remain preparation to be done and warnings to be given."

"Thank you," David told the vampire, drinking the coffee carefully. "I don't suppose killing Romanov changes anything?" he asked after a moment. "I thought he was leading the attack."

"He was, and now the Familias Romanov is no more," the Arbiter said sadly. "There will be a handful, at most, who didn't participate in last night's attack. You have destroyed one of America's eight vampire families, Commanders, my Lord."

"I'm surprised they had that much left," Mason admitted. "We've been smashing their operations across the continent for weeks."

"They were the most powerful single Familias when this civil war began," the old vampire pointed out. "In both numbers and resources, they were unmatched; that is why Petrov challenged Caleb Dresden for leadership. Those resources are now expended, those numbers only of the dead."

"What happens to the survivors?" Riley asked. "Not all of them would have been here; many of them are basically administrative staff with teeth."

"Tradition says they would become Keepers," the Arbiter told them. "The invitation will be extended when this is over, but we will see if they accept. Being a Keeper in North America is about to become a far different calling than before. More of a government job now."

David shook his head with a half-chuckle.

"But Romanov was leading this mess," he repeated. "So, what happens now?"

"Either Sakura or Reginald takes over," the old vampire explained. "Sakura has stood at Romanov's right hand the entire time, and many of *her* Familias now lie dead on these slopes. Reginald was Dresden's man but joined Romanov in this assault.

"Every family except Dresden's own did so," he continued. "If they fail to retake the Mountain, their betrayal will weigh heavy on them. They now must stand together, or Dresden will destroy them individually.

"So, they will keep coming, Commander, and you will see the true fury of the Familias still. Romanov's death bought you today—but tonight...tonight they will come with fire."

"Then we'll need to be ready," David told him. "How many attackers are we talking here? I wouldn't have thought Romanov could put two hundred soldiers into the field!"

"Half of those were Sakura's," the Arbiter replied. "But yes, it seems you continue to underestimate the numbers of the vampire Familias." He shrugged. "Not all are warriors. Not all will answer the call—self-preservation is a strong instinct for our race—but enough will."

"How many is enough?" David demanded.

"Perhaps a thousand, and as many again Thralls. Perhaps half the living vampires in North America."

"They wiped them out," Warner reported over the radio. "Every member of the National Guard company those Bradleys came from is dead, Commander White. It looks like a poison gas attack, which means it was probably magic."

"Damn. I was hoping he'd have just put them to sleep or something," David admitted.

"About the only good news is that it *does* look like poison gas, and they were sufficiently out of the way that we can call it an accident," she told him. "I hate lying to the families, but the truth isn't going to help anyone here."

"Ma'am, if the Familias repeats that assault on a broader scale, we could be in serious trouble," he pointed out.

"I know," Warner said. "The Committee has outright refused

deploying any additional conventional troops to your support. You've got your artillery and your standby air support, but that's all they're willing to sign off on."

"It might not be enough."

"I know," the Major repeated. "We've managed to get our hands on a few containers of gear courtesy of friends in the Army, but they're purely conventional. No silver ammo, no special payloads. Just rockets and claymores."

"We'll take everything we can get," he told her. "What about reinforcements from our own people?"

"As usual, it never rains but it pours," she admitted. "We've had a new flare-up of minor dimensional portals, and we're playing firefighter. I've got nothing to spare, Commander White; it's going to be up to you."

"Two thousand vampires and Thralls," he said quietly. "That's not a few rifles and Mages, Major. That's a goddamn army. You're asking for a miracle."

Warner was silent for several long seconds.

"The problem, David, is that the Committee doesn't see any value in saving the Mountain," she told him. "I've been authorized—*ordered*—to provide you with a fifteen-kiloton nuke that you are to embed in the facility. If you no longer feel you can hold, you are to withdraw your people, lure as many vampires into the bunker as possible, and then detonate the nuke."

David was shocked to silence.

"We have a chance for peace here, ma'am. For a solution to the vampire problem."

"I know you think so," Warner said calmly. "And I'm willing to throw resources at the chance, but I've been overruled. Standing Order Twenty-one remains in effect, David. You have a specific exemption for the Keepers and their charges, but the Colonel and the Committee would rather see them destroyed than lose your teams.

"Do you understand me, Commander?"

"Yes, ma'am."

"I'm sorry."

"I understand, Major," David repeated. "But I suggest you don't bother sending the nuke. We both know damn well I won't use it."

THEY'D TAKEN over a block of guest quarters to catch up on their sleep, since David knew they were going to have to be awake all the next night as well, facing down the coming of hell and everything the vampires could bring with them

He knew *he* needed to sleep. With what was coming, he wasn't going to be coordinating from the surveillance room this time. Leitz would have to do that by remote, because he was going to need everyone outside, holding as long as they could, as hard as they could.

Despite his brave words to Warner, he knew that he'd need to be awake when the cargo containers arrived later that day. There was no way they weren't going to send the nuke, and much as he hated the very idea of it, he had to conceal it from the Arbiter's people.

He didn't have to arm it, but he wouldn't be doing anyone any favors if he proved to the Keepers that the Committee was perfectly willing to blow them all to hell if it was remotely convenient.

Instead, however, he found himself sitting on the bed, staring at the wall. There was an army coming his way, and instead of helping, his superior's orders were to abandon the Keepers and blow the whole facility.

The Arbiter was giving them a chance, an opportunity to make peace even at the cost of hundreds of his fellow vampires—and they wanted to respond to the old vampire's olive branch by burning it up with nuclear fire.

There was a knock on the door. He stared blankly at it for a moment, until the knock repeated.

"Come in," he ordered.

He wasn't surprised to see Kate Mason open the door and step through. She was still wearing most of her Omicron wargear, the black bodysuit with its computer-containing webbing.

"Your radio was turned off," she told him quietly. "Riley said you were going to sleep, but...I doubted that."

"Been a rough night," he replied carefully, but Kate closed the door behind her and dropped her own helmet on the ground.

"Yeah," she agreed. "My own radio is off too. Riley's holding down the fort. He knows where I'm supposed to be."

"And?"

"And where I actually am," Kate admitted. "He suggested I check on you, though I don't think he knows anything."

"Ah."

The next thing David knew, Kate had her arms wrapped around him, holding his head against her.

"I'm not as skilled at aura reading as you are," she murmured, "but I can See and you aren't shielding. What happened?"

"We're not getting reinforcements," he told her. "Instead, they're sending us a nuke. For 'if we no longer feel we can hold.'"

"Fuck. And the Keepers?"

"We're to blow them to hell with the facility," David confirmed. "I won't do it. I *can't*."

"You know I hate vampires," his lover said quietly.

"More than I do, and I was bitten by one," he agreed.

"Yeah. Well, I hate vampires," Kate repeated. "But the Arbiter, the Keepers…they understand that what has been cannot continue. They realize things have to change and have accepted the sacrifices that have to be made to get there."

She rested her head on his.

"I have to respect that," she told him. "I have to honor that. They showed this much courage; how can we betray them?"

"I won't."

"No," Kate agreed, then kissed him. "Because you've got an iron stick up your ass." She shook her head, then kissed him again.

"That isn't a particularly *nice* descriptor," he pointed out.

"No, David, it isn't," Kate confirmed. "But it's an accurate one for your sense of justice. And this time, I'm with you. Whatever it takes."

"Whatever it takes," he echoed. "We hold."

"We do," she agreed, and he realized she'd taken hold of his hands and guided them somewhere specific. She smiled down at him as he realized what she'd done.

"First, however, we both need to sleep—and I have a *brilliant* idea how to make that happen."

[30]

The heavy transport helicopters came in from the northwest, skirting Mount Scott as they carried their cargos around to drop them onto the concrete parking lot outside the central bunker. Four containers, each the same size as anyone would see on a truck or a freighter, were carefully lowered onto the concrete, and then the four helicopters took off again.

"It almost feels like they didn't want to say hello," Riley quipped as they approached the containers.

"Those are Army helicopters," David pointed out. "I'm not entirely sure they were even supposed to be here."

"Politics." The Elfin Lord shook his head, wincing slightly as he pulled the bruises from his clash with Romanov. "I live them these days, but that doesn't mean I like them."

"Yeah, well." David glanced around. "There's a reason we're opening these first. I'm looking for a specific crate, should be labelled W-80 with no further descriptors."

Riley stopped, his hand on the lever to open the closest cargo container.

"That's a nuke, Commander. Why the fuck is there a nuke in these containers?"

"Because my orders are to blow the crèche if we can't hold it," David told him. "Orders I have no intention of fulfilling, which means I need to make sure no one *else* realizes it ever arrived."

"Why are you telling *me* this?" the Elfin Lord asked.

"Because most of the people I trust in this place right now are too damned junior to carry that weight, and I needed Mason to go over the perimeter positions," David replied, then pointed at one of the containers. "Come on, I'm Seeing something in that container I've never seen before, so I'm going to guess that's the nuke."

Opening the container revealed neatly stacked sets of boxes with various labels. Stepping in, David gestured to the ones right next to the door. The crates were labelled *M19 (4)*.

"There's your anti-vehicle mines," he told Riley. "Looks like you got quite a few."

"I'm happier about those than I am about the nuke."

"Here." David stopped at a tall box that glowed in a strange purplish-green he'd never seen with his Sight before. He checked the label. Four stenciled characters, that was it.

They could have at least labelled the damn thing as radioactive.

He pulled the crate out from the wall, his Empowered strength easily handling the three-hundred-pound weight of the box as he lifted it and carried it out of the container.

"So, what do we do with this thing?" Riley asked.

"Hide it," David told him. "Somewhere away from the compound. I'll take care of it."

The Elfin hesitated.

"I hate to say it, David," he began, "but if they're not going to reinforce us, that thing might not be a bad idea if it all goes to hell. I'd *rather* get a damn truce, but given a choice between dying and changing nothing, and blowing the compound to hell and destroying the vampires' ability to produce reinforcements…"

"I'm not prepared to nuke innocents, Jamie," David replied. "And I think at this point, we're all agreed that while the fledglings are *dangerous*, they are also innocent."

"Criminally insane, but it passes," the Elfin Lord agreed with a sigh. "Look, all I'm saying is that damn thing is a hell of an ace in the hole. Remote-detonated, I assume?"

"That's what Warner implied," he said reluctantly.

"Then I find myself compelled to point out that this complex was built to withstand a nuclear strike," Riley told him. "That bomb will only take out the crèche if you detonate it *inside* the Mountain."

David looked at him with realization.

"You're insane, you know that?" he finally told the Elfin Lord.

"I spent last night quoting Tolkien while fighting a vampiric Mage Lord," Riley replied with a chuckle. "Why is this news?"

MOST OF THE contents of the containers were mines of one sort or another, though there were replacement shells for the ones Wilbur's artillery had shot off the night before. There were also more sandbags, stockpiles of grenades—something ONSET didn't issue in quantity—and crates of 7.62 ammunition for when they ran out.

The fact that David was even considering issuing his people non-silver-tipped ammunition was a sign of how desperate the situation might become that night. Silver disrupted magical spells and impeded regeneration. Strong-enough shields—like those Romanov and Riley had being wielding the prior night—could withstand a lot of silver, but they'd stop an almost infinite amount of regular ammo.

Sandbags reinforced the positions out on the slopes, but more went into building a fallback position in the main parking lot. They'd have to fight the vampires on the slopes, bleed them and delay them, but David expected he'd need to pull his people back.

He didn't know how they were going to stop two thousand attackers with fifty people.

The sandbagged positions in the forest would be the first line. Then his people would fall back to defensive positions around the bunker and silo entrances, hopefully luring the attackers into a killing zone for artillery and air strikes.

After that…

David sighed.

He needed to talk to the Arbiter.

He found Jenna in the surveillance center, the white-robed Keeper watching the many screens for activity.

"Your people are busy," she told him. "Those mines…they terrify me."

"They terrify *me*," David agreed. "There's a reason most places in the world have banned them. We have ways to get rid of them afterwards, but we're expecting to be outnumbered forty to one."

"I apologize for this," Jenna said. "I wish there was a more peaceful way to make this happen. It…doesn't seem right that there should be so much violence when all we want is to make peace."

"People aren't willing to let go of what they have, vampire or human," he told her. "Many of them don't even realize what this is about. They've been told Omicron has seized the Crèche and they have to retake it for the future."

He shook his head.

"And the Thralls don't even have *that* much choice. They simply…obey."

The blonde vampire shivered.

"I've met some of them," she noted. "They are disturbing. Intelligent, sensible beings, and yet fundamentally broken by my people's power." She smiled sadly. "I was always a Keeper, Commander White. In a quarter-millennium, I have never been involved in violence. I am…not representative of my race, I am afraid."

"The point of this whole affair is to *make* you representative," David told her. "If all of this is to mean anything, your people will have to change. And that's a scary thought to everyone."

"Not just my people, I take it," Jenna replied. "I doubt it's an accident you have no reinforcements, Commander."

"No," he admitted. "I need to speak to the Arbiter."

"He is resting," the Elder Sister told him. "But…" She sighed.

"I will take you to him. He would want to speak with you."

SHE LED David down corridors and tunnels that went even deeper into the Mountain than he'd expected. They were definitely out of the original SAC bunker construction now, into sections that had been carved later and with somewhat more care. Decorative patterns were woven into the concrete, and the aura of the calming charm that filled the entire facility was even stronger here.

Finally, they came to a halt at a gorgeously ornate wooden door that looked like it might have come from the Arbiter's pre-Revolution French residence. Gabriel stood outside the door in her armored bodysuit, a sword and a rifle strapped across her back.

"This is closer to the *teknon* than he should be brought, Sister," the bodyguard snapped. "The smell of human blood will agitate them."

"We both know he doesn't smell human," Jenna snapped back, the first David had heard of such a thing.

It wasn't a reassuring thought.

"He needs to speak with the Arbiter," she continued. "He asked to be awakened in such a case."

"He did," Gabriel admitted. "Give me a moment."

The younger vampire opened the door and stepped through, closing it behind her.

"He doesn't wake easily," Jenna told David gently. "He is very old and his memories are not gentle to him."

That was an eerily poetic description of the PTSD that someone could accumulate over two thousand years of life and conflict.

David heard *something* through the thick wooden door, but even his enhanced hearing couldn't decipher it.

Finally, Gabriel opened the door again. She looked far more tired than she had a few minutes before, but she nodded to them.

"Come in," she told David. "Coffee, Commander? I am brewing some for him."

"I'll take some," he replied.

"Sister, please take him to the reading room," the vampire asked Jenna. "I'll bring coffees for us all."

Jenna led David through the door into a room that looked like it had been stolen from Louis XV's France. Rich tapestries and plushly upholstered furniture filled the spaces that she led him through, until they stopped in a seating area with six chairs that looked like they'd eaten a couch's stuffing each.

He waited patiently, though he couldn't help checking the time, for the vampire to enter.

He was somewhat surprised when the Arbiter finally did join them. It was the first time he'd seen the old vampire in anything except his pseudo-priestly robes, but he joined them in slacks and a polo shirt that would have looked perfectly normal on a Wall Street CEO.

Of course, the Arbiter's black eyes and shaven head somewhat ruined the normalcy of the clothing, but he took a seat in silence as Gabriel entered the room with four large steaming mugs of coffee—and a temperature-controlled thermos of something else.

"Excuse me, Commander," the Arbiter said politely, "but I must eat before we continue."

David tried not to watch, but there was a degree of morbid fascination as the old vampire picked up the thermos of stabilized blood and chugged it down the way an athlete might drink a protein shake.

Jenna was waiting with a cloth napkin when the Arbiter finished, wiping away the leftover blood almost before David saw it. The whole process was disturbingly normal, almost mundane for a two-thousand-year-old creature drinking blood.

"I apologize; I would have preferred not to eat in front of you, but I got the impression your request was urgent," the old vampire told him. "I do not require much sleep, but I am not easily awoken from it."

He shook himself like a tired dog.

"How can I assist you, Commander White?"

"We're not going to be able to hold on the surface," David told the Arbiter. "We're going to need to fall back into the bunker, and I don't want to put your people in danger."

"Ah." He gestured and Gabriel handed him the coffee. The vampire took a long drink before he responded.

"I had hoped for more assistance from your superiors, but I suppose I can see where they stand," he admitted. "What would you have me do, Commander? They will no more threaten the *teknon* than you; I cannot oppose them unless they actively attack my charges.

"I serve the race, not any particular cause or family."

"I don't need you to fight them," David replied. "I need you to help us seal the entrances at the silos, and then pull your people as deep into the bunkers and tunnels as you can.

"I don't want your people in the fight"—he didn't exactly *trust* them, after all—"and this is all for nothing if they get killed. We'll need to fight the Familias in the tunnels, but I want your people safe."

"Of course," the Arbiter replied with a nod. "We will assist as we can, within the limits of our oaths. Your assistance is my best hope of preserving the race."

"Even if we kill half of the vampires alive in the States?" David asked bluntly. "You're setting up a lot of death here, Arbiter."

"They will not all fight to the death. Many will surrender once the battle clearly turns against them. I will take what opportunities I can to speak to them as well," he promised. "I am not without influence with my people."

"I hope it's enough," David admitted. "If this all goes wrong, I don't know if the Familias will ever trust you again."

"Peace will be harder if you fail," the Arbiter agreed. "I request that you do not."

[31]

"Well, Commander, are the planes going to get some exercise tonight, or should I be sending my boys and girls to bed?" Colonel Dallas asked David over the radio as the sun edged down towards the horizon.

"Colonel, I'm expecting a multi-battalion-scale attack sometime after the sun goes down," David replied. "Believe me, I have *every* intention of using your people." He considered for a moment. "Are you equipped for air interception at all?"

"That depends on what you need," Dallas replied. "Our missile loadout is all air-to-ground, but we still have our cannon and could pull an intercept on, say, transport planes."

"You read my mind, Colonel," David told him. "We're expecting to see heavy transport in the air in the near future, but identifying it is going to be a pain in the ass. If we can confirm them, we'll pass the information on."

"How heavy are we talking, Commander?"

"Heavy enough for tanks and APCs, Colonel. I'm expecting to see a good chunk of several National Guards' budgets and armories go missing and show up here in the wrong hands," the ONSET

Commander admitted. "I'm not *expecting* airplanes, but it wouldn't be out of scale with some of the crap they have managed to get their hands on."

"Shit, Commander, that's a hell of a worst-case scenario," Dallas pointed out. "Who *are* these people?"

"That's not even my worst-case scenario," David admitted. "They're vampires, Colonel. They've had their fingers and minions in every branch of our military and country for as long as the USA has existed. Layer in blackmail, threats of violence and outright mind control…"

"I'm going to be glad when this is over," the Air Force Colonel told him. "And I'm going to have nightmares about it for the rest of my life."

"Welcome to my world, Colonel. When this is over, I'll buy you a damn drink."

"Be ready to buy the damn bar, Commander. I'm going to need it."

David could almost hear Dallas shaking his head.

"We're ready, Commander," he finally concluded. "You'll have your intercept if you can get us targets; you'll have your airstrikes either way. We'll get you through this."

"I hope so, Colonel, because my intelligence is starting to make me wish I'd updated my will."

"Don't bother," Dallas said with a chuckle. "The Air Force will save the day, we promise."

Letting the channel drop, David turned back to the sunset. He sat on top of the big concrete entrance to the main bunker, looking out over the parking lot and down the slopes of Mount Scott.

The parking lot looked like something from World War One now, with machine guns and sandbags forming a solid semicircle around the bunker entrance. There was no one in those defenses yet, with even Riley having moved to the outer layer of positions.

Mines and defenses would hopefully funnel the vampire attack up the main road, where Dallas and his F-22s would turn the already-battered section of forest into a preview of hell. Artillery and machine guns could do a lot, but it was the Air Force's missiles he was counting on to truly even the odds.

No matter how this turned out, the Vampire Familias of North America were going to have a bad night.

Unfortunately, David was relatively certain he and his own people weren't going to have any better of one.

"Sir, I've got good news and bad news on the enemy," Leitz told him as night finally set in.

"Lay it out," David ordered. There was no point trying to soften the blow at this point.

"The good news is we've located their assembly point," she noted. "There's an old private airfield on the side of the Park. It hasn't been active in twenty years, but the runway is apparently intact."

"And?" he asked quietly.

"There's at least a dozen heavy transport planes, C-130s and even bigger ones, already on the ground," the analyst replied. "Several are taking off, too, likely going for more personnel. They've got a temporary hangar set up that would allow them to off-load vampires if they're careful."

She sighed.

"That's…at least a thousand troops, plus vehicles. They're all under cover, so we can't be entirely certain, but…"

"But it's telling," David agreed. "Track the planes leaving; see if you can identify any planes heading there. Relay everything to Dallas and Lange. If we can hit that assembly point, it might buy us one hell of a chance."

"Understood, sir. But that's not all."

Something in her tone warned him that this was going to be even worse.

"What happened?"

"An Oregon national guard base went off the air just before sundown," Leitz said quietly. "It's an armor base, sir. At least thirty-two M1 Abrams tanks ready for deployment."

"Dear god," David breathed. "They can't possible have the trained crew to man them, can they?"

The fate of the likely *thousands* of people at the base was terrifying. The Familias truly was pulling out all of the stops tonight and apparently didn't care how many died along the way. It was hard not to feel responsible for the deaths, too. He was the one who'd initiated this whole mess, even if he was now on the defensive.

"I don't know," the analyst admitted. "We don't have overhead and no one is on the line, but the GPS trackers on the tanks are going down as we speak. They may not have them all, but they're less than two hours' drive away."

"Thanks," David replied. "We'll deal with it. One way or another."

"I'm sorry, sir."

"Not your fault," he told the analyst. "Keep me informed and get Dallas the coordinates for that assembly point."

He switched over to the channel for Major Wilbur.

"Major, how are your people feeling tonight?" he asked with a cheer he knew the other man would see right through.

"Still trying to sort out what the hell is going on, I think," Wilbur replied. "What do you need?"

"You said you had anti-tank rounds," David noted. "How many?"

"We had three Copperheads on each of the ammunition transports," the Army Major said slowly. "Picked up another half dozen in the drop-off, so...eighteen. Just what hell is coming our way, Commander?"

"We're pretty sure the vamps just commandeered an Oregon National Guard armor squadron, Major," David told him. "We're not sure how many of the tanks they can actually *use*, but there were at least thirty M1s at the base."

"My god."

"Can your Copperheads take out an Abrams?"

He heard Wilbur swallow hard.

"Yes," he said steadily. "We'll need your people to provide laser target designation, but the shells *should* be able to take them out. But I don't have enough to stop an entire *regiment*."

"I know. But I need you to stop what you can," David told him. "The rest will be up to us."

"How are you going to stop *tanks*?" Wilbur demanded.

"With mines, with rocket launchers, and with Mages. And if all that fails, with a goddamn magic sword."

With so many different irons in the fire, David found himself flicking back and forth between radio channels almost at random, trying to keep track of what was going on as his people prepared to defend themselves against the oncoming storm.

When Dallas reported his squadrons were ready for takeoff, he locked onto that channel. Leitz had a direct line to him that would get through regardless, and he had the command network still up as well. Between the analyst, Mason, Sokol and Riley, he knew he'd be informed if something came up to need his immediate attention.

The air strike, however, could short-circuit half of their problems in one swift stroke.

"All right, people, we are going black," Dallas told the two squadrons' worth of pilots as the last of them reached cruising altitude. "All external coms are to be relayed through my plane; this entire operation just went Top Secret.

"As you can guess, this is *not* a training flight. We are operating under special authority for combat operations on US soil," the Colonel continued grimly. "We are intercepting a number of hijacked military transport aircraft and then carrying out an air strike on a hostile assembly point.

"Major Lange and I have been fully briefed, but many of the details involved here are classified above Top Secret," he told them. "We have an active hostile domestic force that we are tasked to neutralize."

"Sir...that's a lot to swallow," one of the pilots responded. "We can't just...shoot down our own planes because you say it's okay!"

"If you double-check your orders, you'll find a sealed packet with orders signed by the Vice Chief of Staff of the Air Force. People, this is a real and present threat to the United States, the entire reason we have been on standby at Mountain Home for the last seventy-two hours.

"NSA is relaying coordinates for the aircraft as we speak. They are believed to carry multiple stolen armored vehicles and militia troops. We will attempt to force them to land at Mountain Home AFB, but if they do not turn back, we *will* shoot them down.

"Do you understand me, gentlemen?"

David missed the responses as he brought up the map of the area on his HUD, checking for the coordinates. Leitz had identified an entire second wave of aircraft, another dozen heavy transport planes, heading towards the vampires' stolen landing site.

Twenty-four F-22s would be able to easily take down the transports and then level the assembly site. The tanks would still be a huge problem, but locating the assembly site and tracking the planes had just changed the entire shape of the battle to come.

"Unidentified aircraft, this is the US Air Force," Colonel Dallas's voice rumbled in David's headset. "We have reason to believe you are illegally transporting stolen munitions and vehicles. You will divert ninety degrees south and prepare to be escorted to Mountain Home AFB for internment and search.

"If you do not divert, we will be forced to shoot you down."

David watched the icons continue to move on his HUD. The closing USAF fighters were tiny green arrowheads, closing with the red icons of the transport planes. Red icons that did not appear to be changing course.

"Transport fleet," Dallas hailed them again. "You will divert ninety degrees south and prepare for escort or I will open fire."

Seconds ticked away, the jet fighters rapidly closing toward the limited but deadly range of their internal cannons.

"This is Alpha-One," Dallas declared to his squadron. "Going live. Guns. Guns. Guns."

Something happened…but not what David had been expecting. One moment, twenty-four green icons were closing on the transport planes and Dallas was about to open fire.

The next, green icons were disappearing off his screen with terrifying suddenness and finality. David suddenly had no connection, his radio link to Dallas cut off as the icons flashed out of existence.

"Leitz!" he snapped. "What's going on?"

"I don't know!" she exclaimed. "We lost contact with Colonel Dallas, overhead says..." She stopped, her words disintegrating into a shocked, choking sob.

"Overhead says that his own people opened fire on him," Leitz whispered. "I'm reading missile fire, cannon fire... most of the planes are just *gone*."

"Get me Lange," David ordered harshly, his hope of an easy victory turning to ashes in his mouth. "Get me *anyone!*"

"This is Lange."

The Air Force Major sounded broken. Exhausted. If David hadn't known he was talking to the same man, he would have thought Leitz had connected the wrong person.

"What happened?" he asked.

"We...failed," Lange said slowly. "The transports continue on their way. We...no longer have the ability to carry out ground strikes. I have...four fighters left. All are damaged. My pilots are in shock. We... we can't do it, Commander. I'm sorry."

"What *happened?*" David repeated.

"That's..." Lange inhaled loudly. "That's going to be for JAG and the MPs to sort out now, I'm afraid. If we ever work it out.

"Four of our jets opened fire when Dallas went in to shoot down the transports. They took out the Colonel before any of us even realized what was happening and just kept shooting." The Major sighed. "They had to know the only way they'd survive was if they shot down everyone else, so that's what they tried to do.

"We took them out. But...I'd known some of the pilots who *turned on us* for ten years. Some of the men they killed for twenty. My God. I don't...I don't understand."

Thralls. Either the squadron selection had been as unlucky as it was possible to be, or the vampires had explicitly infiltrated the squadrons with in-the-know COs—a grouping they shouldn't have been able to identify.

A Thrall wouldn't have been able to question *why* they needed to shoot down their friends. They would have been running a side communication channel, one Dallas wasn't aware of, and once they'd reported in what was happening...

Their vampire masters had told them to kill the rest of their squadron, and they hadn't even hesitated, even knowing that they almost certainly wouldn't survive the attempt.

"Major, you *have* to complete the air strike," David told the Air Force man. "You can't change the course of this anymore, but I need every edge I can get. I need you to hit that assembly point with whatever you have left.

"I know what you're feeling," he admitted, "I've lost people under my command to these bastards as well. But I *need* you to drop those bombs."

Seconds ticked by in silence, and then he heard Lange take a long, gasping breath through his oxygen mask.

"I understand," he said. "One pass, high-level. I can't ask these men for more. Not after they had to shoot down their friends."

"I understand," David echoed back. "But even that one pass will save lives, Major, and may make all the difference tonight."

Whatever conversation Lange had with his remaining three pilots was on a different channel. They diverted back toward the target several seconds later, though, and the command channel linked back up.

"We are inbound on target, increasing altitude to avoid potential AA fire," Lange said, his voice mechanical now as his training took over.

"Range is five miles and closing. Weapons free, weapons free," he chanted.

David didn't have enough information on his HUD to confirm any details on the aircraft. All he had was their location, closing in on the vampire's assembly site at high speed.

"Target is padlocked, we are engaging. Rifle away, repeat Rifle away." Pause. "Bombing range, Pickles away, Pickles away."

A moment of silence.

"Look to the east, Commander, you're about to have a light show. We're done and bingo on ammo. Good luck."

David followed the instructions, watching the bright flashes lighting up the horizon as, despite everything, the last four fighters delivered their weapons on target.

Hopefully, it would be enough.

[32]

THE CLOCK WAS TICKING.

David stood outside the main entrance to the Mountain, waiting for the hammer to fall. They weren't sure how much of the force the Familias had concentrated at the airstrip had survived, but he *did* know when the tanks the enemy had stolen from the National Guard were going to arrive.

Part of him hoped that the vampires were foolish enough to send the tanks in on their own. Without any support, even the immensely powerful Abrams would be vulnerable to the anti-tank weapons and Mages at his command.

If they had the crews to drive the tanks, however, he assumed they had people who knew how to *use* them. Most of the vampires the Familias commanded were under a hundred years old; they almost certainly had men who were veterans of the tank campaigns of the Second World War, Vietnam or Iraq in their ranks.

That meant they'd meet up with the lighter vehicles and ground troops from the airstrip and move on his position in the kind of combined-arms mechanized assault that had never *officially* happened in North America.

With Dallas and Lange's squadrons shattered, there was no way he could get further air support. There were, he was certain, other Air Force officers in the know, but none were close enough to be able to get ground-attack-equipped aircraft to his position tonight.

"We have movement from the airstrip," Leitz reported over his radio. "Hard to say what was there originally, but I've got Strykers, Bradleys, and M113s moving out in columns. That's a lot of hardware, sir."

"How much is a lot?"

"Twenty Strykers. Twenty Bradleys. Forty APCs," she reeled off. "I don't know how the hell they got their hands on that much gear or concentrated it in less than a day without us noticing." She sighed. "We've confirmed thirty of the M1s on the move, too. They are ripping the *hell* out of the road, but they'll be in position in just over an hour."

"Assume they rendezvous with the APCs," David told her. "When will they be able to bring the hammer down?"

"Midnight, sir. Give or take thirty minutes, depending on how long they need to coordinate. We don't know who's in charge out there."

"With Romanov dead and Dresden letting his enemies beat themselves to death on us, I'm guessing a committee," he replied. "If we have an advantage here, it's that there are seven Familias leaders trying to decide how to run this operation, and I doubt any of them are willing to hand it over to anyone else."

"Sir, that's over a hundred armored vehicles and a thousand vampires and Thralls," the analyst said quietly. "A disunified command is a slim thread of hope."

"I know. I need you to talk to Warner," he said. "If there's any chance, at *all*, that we can get some kind of reinforcements…"

"I'll try, sir."

"I don't think you'll succeed," David admitted. He knew what the plan that had been dropped on Warner was, after all. "But I need you to try."

THE LAST TRACES of light were long gone as David walked the perimeter, checking in with his Agents and the Elfin Warriors. Despite only having two days to build their positions, they'd done solid work. Multiple sandbagged bastions covered the slopes, their crisscrossing lines of fire making certain that nothing was going to make its way up to the Mountain without having to take fire from at least three positions.

The downside, of course, was that each position only had two or three people in it. They were all supernaturals, but the powers ranged from Klein and Mason, fully trained battle Mages almost up to the weight of an Elfin Lord like Riley, to men and women like McCreery, with "merely" superhuman agility and three-dimensional sense.

He stopped at ONSET Thirteen's position, where Stone and Hellet were checking over the two machine guns they'd dug in with. McCreery remained in charge of the helicopter bridge, the missiles they'd fired the previous night replaced for the new battle to come.

"All quiet so far," Hellet told him. "How long?"

"They're converging as we speak," David admitted. "Outside of range of Wilbur's artillery, sadly. Smart buggers."

"Most of that armor can take anything short of a direct hit or close miss from even his guns," Stone pointed out. "We needed a bigger battery if we were going to face off against a cavalry regiment."

"We were supposed to be assaulting a fortified position, not holding one," David pointed out. "It's been a hell of a few days and it's not over yet."

"We'll still be here when it is," the big Empowered told his Commander. "Since when have vampires been an insurmountable threat to ONSET, after all?"

David shook his head silently. The only group who'd been responsible for more ONSET casualties in actions he'd been involved in was the Black Sun cult, and they'd had a demon infiltrate OSPI to set up a massive trap.

A thousand vampires and their mind-controlled servants were a problem.

"We needed an army," he told his people. "But I guess we'll have to do."

"You've seen what everyone here can do," Hellet pointed out.

"Would an army really be more useful than fifty combat-trained supernaturals?"

"I don't know," David admitted. "We're not exactly used to fighting tanks and armored vehicles."

"And the vampires aren't used to using them," she replied. "They know how to fight ONSET with commandos and Mages. But they've never fought us with tanks—they might have people who can use the tanks, but they won't have fought Mages in them!"

"We can hope," he agreed. "One thing I'm sure of: they are *not* going to know what hit them."

"No question," Stone agreed, patting the heavy machine gun next to him. "Though I suspect they might work out relatively quickly that at least some of it is bullets."

"COMMANDER."

Leitz's voice echoed in David's ears as he stepped away from the sandbagged position, heading into the dark toward the next one.

"Yes?" he replied.

"They've completed whatever discussions they're having on command," she told him. "They're moving into road formation, with the tanks at the back."

"Makes sense. None of those vehicles are leaving the road in great condition, but the tanks will wreck it," David noted.

"Yes, sir." She paused. "They'll reach the access road from the highway in twenty minutes. After that…"

"They'll spread out and come up the mountain," he concluded. "They're not going to play games or make probing raids or any of that. They've assembled the kind of armored fist that's supposed to be the monopoly of the US Army, and they are going to hammer it right at us."

"Can you stop them?" the analyst asked softly.

"I don't know. But I do know this: when this is over, the Familias will be *broken*."

[33]

DAVID FELT THE RUMBLE IN THE GROUND FIRST. HIS EMPOWERED HEARING picked up the engines and the crunching of tracks through dirt and gravel only moments later, but the vibration of a hundred-plus armored vehicles traveled through the ground with terrifying speed.

"I have them in sight," one of the Elfin Warriors reported. "Laser designator online, pinging the lead unit."

"We have Target One," Major Wilbur confirmed. "I need designators on six targets, people. We're only going to get full efficiency on the first barrage."

"Roger," another voice reported. "Taking to the treetops. Lining up."

There were six Elfin Warriors with the Army's laser designators out on the edge of the forest, all supernaturals with an affinity for stealth and the forest, sneaking through the shadowy darkness to align invisible beams of light on their targets.

"That's six," Wilbur reported a few seconds later. "Copperheads loaded, targets acquired. Standby for barrage in five. Four. Three. Two. One."

"Fire."

The M109A7 Paladins were over a mile farther up Mount Scott

from where David stood, but the crash of the guns washed over where he stood in the final defensive position like a wave of water. There was barely enough time for the first shock wave to pass over before the next arrived, the big guns firing in sequence to allow the lasers to bring the guided rounds in on target.

"Hold your beams until terminal impact," the Major ordered. "Copperheads going terminal. Impact...now."

The shells were sequenced, each one dropping on a tank several seconds after the previous one. Powerful as the tanks were, they were also *exactly* what the shell had been designed to take out.

"Confirm kills, all six," the lead scout reported. "Remaining targets are now maneuvering. They know we're here."

"We are reloading. Get me more targets," Wilbur ordered.

Forty seconds later, thunder shook the mountain again and another salvo of guided shells dropped on the advancing vampire force.

"Two targets still intact. We are redesignating." The scout paused. "They are starting to fire on the trees; we've got machine gun fire from all units and grenade fire from the Strykers. This'll be the last clean shot you get, Major; we need to fall back."

"Understood. Barrage in five."

The guns echoed again, but now David could also hear gunfire down the mountainside as the vampires began to shred the forest around them, hunting out the scouts they knew had to be there with machine gun fire.

"Coral is down; her designator is out," the scout snapped. "Brown is hit—Lyle, Morris, hold your targets, then drag him out. Holland, you're with me."

More shells slammed home, but no one was telling them how many tanks had died.

"Silas, what's your status?" the artillery Major demanded. "Get out of there!"

Another explosion lit up the night as the tanks opened fire with their main guns, canister shells spraying their payloads through the woods.

"Still here," the scout replied grimly. "Fuckers are aiming too low.

They got Holland." He was silent for a long moment. "You got six rounds left, right, Major?"

"Yes."

"I'll ping 'em as they come. Make them count."

"Wilco, Silas."

The first gun fired. David closed his eyes, listening to the sounds as the artillery worked their way down. It took several seconds for each shell to arrive. More time for the Elfin scout to move and bring his designator onto a new target.

There was nothing he could do but listen.

Three Copperheads dropped. Four. *Five.*

"That's it, sir," Silas finally said, a new strained sound to his voice. "I'm hit, lost the designator. I'm going to ground; they won't find me... but before I Shift, you gotta know: they're dismounting ground troops and moving up the hill."

"Thank you, Warrior," David told the werefox, hoping he caught Silas before the man changed shape. "Major?"

"I have the grid," the Army officer said flatly. "Dumping the last Copperhead; stand by for rolling barrage. Give me thirty seconds."

"Understood. Let's see what they do."

WHAT THEY DID WAS CHARGE.

The tanks came first, the massive seventy-ton weight of the main battle tanks smashing trees to kindling as they hammered their way up the hill. The APCs and infantry fighting vehicles weren't far behind them, tracked and wheeled vehicles alike turning the forest to debris as the vampires deployed around them.

The first troops on the ground were definitely vampires. They kept up with the vehicles plowing up the hill at thirty miles an hour with bounding leaps, their guns swinging as they hunted the scouts whose laser designators had taken such a toll on their advance.

And then the artillery barrage arrived.

Six shells at a time slammed into the ground, a steady metronome of one salvo every minute as the vampires made their way up the hill.

A hundred guns might have stopped the advance, forging a wall of fire and steel no living being could cross.

Six…just wasn't enough. Not against vehicles that could shrug off anything short of a direct hit. Not against *infantry* that could survive near misses and keep coming.

The vampires simply swung around the craters and kept coming. Machine guns and grenade launchers opened fire as they spotted the first positions, rocket launchers and more machine guns returning fire.

Then the sky lit up with fire as the Mages on both sides lashed out and the lead tanks ran into the antivehicle mines. Most of the chassis of an Abrams leapt into the air, high enough that David could see it spin before it crashed down again.

"They're not slowing!" Klein reported. "Multiple Mages. Son of a *bitch*."

David couldn't see much…but he could See everything. The Elfin Battle Mage was dueling with three vampire Mages. None of them were his equal, but combined, they were destroying the dugout he was hiding in around him.

"Triggering the claymore line!" Riley snapped—and a wall of fire cut the forest in half. Hundreds of claymores, only about a quarter of them loaded with silver, detonated in one shot.

"Fall back!" David ordered. "Trigger the second line as they clear it, Riley. Second-line positions, cover the retreat."

Machine guns chattered as the Elfin Warriors and ONSET Agents in the forward dugouts abandoned their positions.

"Can't make it," Klein gasped. "They've got me pinned down."

"We can cover you," David snapped. "McCreery!"

"No!" the Warrior snapped. "You'll need them for the next fallback. Sorry, Commander, but it looks like you're going to have a lot less humor in your life."

Blue light glittered in the heart of the forest, and David made out the silhouette of a single figure rising out of the shattered wreckage, lightning flickering from his hands as Klein charged the vampires. An Abrams tank lifted into the air, lightning crackling around its hull as the battle Mage picked it up and threw it into the forward section of Strykers.

There was an explosion. Then another. A tank cannon fired, the spray of canister hammering into the flying Mage. Bolts of black fire intersected on Klein's flickering shield…and then the ball turned into a glowing blue meteor that smashed into the ground with earth-shaking force.

The light slowly faded around a new crater, and everything was silent for several seconds as David stared in shock at the site of Klein's self-immolation.

Then the next salvo of artillery arrived, and the vampires began to move forward again.

———

Klein's sacrifice had bought enough time for the defenders to fall back to the second set of positions, and the artillery continued to hammer the vampires as they moved up the slope.

This time, however, the vampires knew the mines were there. Magic lashed out ahead of the handful of remaining tanks, whips of flame and force that smashed into the ground. Detonators were fooled into thinking tanks were nearby even as impossibly hot fire detonated the explosives themselves.

Spring-damp trees ignited with terrifying pops of steam and splinters as the vampires plowed the way forward with flame and black magic. Machine guns chattered back and forth, and David watched icons flicker out on his HUD as defenders went down.

Then tank cannons cracked again, this time firing explosive shells into the forward positions. The icons for ONSET 6 flashed red…*all of them.*

"Sokol, report!" David demanded.

The only response was an incoherent scream of rage—and the sight of the team commander leaping out of the wreckage of his sandbagged position with a heavy machine gun in his arms. He charged the tanks at a run, shooting down the vampires in his path and ignoring the bullets that hammered into him.

Even David wasn't as immune to harm as Sokol. The man didn't even flinch until one of the tanks managed to hit him dead-center with an explosive shell...and that simply threw him back until he got back up and charged.

This time around, the Commander reached the lead tank and grabbed the barrel of the cannon as it swung towards him. David could have bent it or damaged it, rendering the weapon nonfunctional.

Sokol ripped the gun out of the tank, taking most of the turret with it, and opened a gap that he leapt into the armored vehicle through. The tank ground to a halt in the middle of the fight after Sokol dropped inside, and David could only guess just what violence had taken place inside.

Rockets took out another Abrams and several of the Strykers, but the whole advance continued around the halted tank until Sokol erupted from it again, dropping onto one of the remaining tanks—only to be met with a black blur of motion that sent him flying.

When the blurs resolved, the nigh-invulnerable ONSET Commander was locked in a point-blank struggle with two vampire Elders, enchanted knives glittering in the light of the burning forest as they dueled.

Steel flashed red and one of the vampires spun backward, his entire throat removed by the Commander's Mage-blade. Gunfire echoed and the second vampire collapsed as Stone dumped a full burst from his own heavy machine gun into the man.

"Get back here!" Hellet shouted, the Mage tossing firebolts to cover Sokol's retreat.

For a moment, it looked like he was going to stay out in the line of fire, continuing to fight, but then Sokol finally responded to Hellet's shout, running toward the remaining positions.

He didn't make it. He was still fifteen feet short of the bastions when a whip of black fire cut through the night, wrapping around Sokol and yanking him back toward the tanks as a tall woman in an old-fashioned cloak strode out of the advancing army.

"You do not kill my children and run," her magically amplified voice echoed over the field. "Face me, Orel Sokol. We have old blood to settle."

"Who the fuck is that?" David demanded.

"Elsa Ambrose," Riley told him. "Matriarch of the Ambrose Familias."

"Oh, fuck."

VAMPIRE MATRIARCH and ONSET Commander smashed together in the middle of the battlefield, the light of the burning trees around them a stark and horrifying highlight to their combat.

David wanted to order his people to just shoot her...but the *vampires* had temporarily stopped shooting and advancing, and his people needed the breather. Clearly, none of the fangs were going to steal a Familias Matriarch's kill—but he was quite certain they wouldn't stand by while his people riddled her with bullets, either.

Sokol used the momentum of her yanking him toward her to deliver a solid two-footed kick to the cloaked vampire's chest, but it barely seemed to faze her. She smashed him to the ground with a single hand, black claws that might or might not have been formed of magic flashing out to slash across his skin.

If she drew blood, the wound healed before anyone saw it. Sokol's invulnerable skin resisted her strikes, and he slashed out at her with his enchanted Mage-blade. She flung him away before the knife could touch her, however, and continued to advance on him, fire lashing out.

David could *see* her tearing off the other Commander's armor, piece by piece, but Sokol simply ignored the blows, rising to his feet and charging her. There was a blur of knife and fists and claws, and then Ambrose went flying.

From the way she landed, the blow would have crushed a mortal woman's ribcage—but Elsa Ambrose was an Elder vampire with centuries of learning how to control her gifts. She simply looked *angry*.

More whips of fire slashed out. Sokol had already proven she couldn't hurt him, and charged into them. Instead of trying to bring him down, however, the tendrils of fire wrapped themselves around his limbs. The Commander was once more yanked from the ground, dragged through the air to hang suspended in front of Ambrose, struggling against her spell with all of his inhuman strength.

"My dear Commander," she said loudly, running those black claws along the side of Sokol's face. "Did you think, after all this time, that I had not researched you? Studied you? Learned *just* what your strengths and weaknesses were?"

Her claws yanked the back of his head up, pulling his mouth open before the ONSET Commander could stop her. Then her free hand stabbed *into* Sokol's mouth, the claws presumably tearing down the inside of his throat.

David could *hear* Sokol choking over the radio for several long seconds before he went finally, dreadfully silent.

[34]

AMBROSE DIDN'T SLOW AFTER KILLING THE COMMANDER. SHE TOSSED HIS body aside like a toy and then advanced on the Omicron positions, the rest of the vampire force resuming their drive forward behind him.

"Mason, Riley," David said calmly as he started moving. This wasn't the kind of fight he could leave to his subordinates. One Familias Patriarch was dead, but so was an ONSET Commander.

The honors were even so far, and he couldn't take the risk.

"McCreery, stand by for air strike," he continued as he leapt the unmanned barricades of their final surface position and drew *Memoria*. "Wilbur, what's your ammo level?"

"We've emptied the ammunition trucks and are down to twenty or so rounds," the Army Major replied. "We can keep this up for a while yet, but the guns themselves are going to start having problems shortly."

"When I call in the air strike, go to rapid fire on all your guns," David ordered. "I take it they won't hold that fire for long, but I just need a minute. Once you've dumped as much fire on the bastards as you can…move out."

"Move out?"

"Yeah. I'm not going to shell my own position, and after we fall back to the bunker, there's nothing else you can do," he told the Major. "Once you cover our retreat, get the hell out of Dodge as fast as you can. This place isn't going to be friendly to anybody before the night is out."

"Okay," Wilbur acknowledged with a sigh. "Wilco, Commander White. Good luck."

He'd almost reached the remaining positions, leveling with Stone as the big Empowered, currently resembling a somewhat mobile statue, laid down heavy fire with a machine gun. They were delaying the soldiers, but Ambrose was simply walking forward like the gunfire was a light rain.

Mason and Riley converged on him as he passed Stone, Young attached to Riley as usual.

"What's the plan?" Riley murmured.

"Kill Ambrose," David said shortly. "See if we can get any of the other Familias leaders to come out and play. Then cover our retreat with fire from on high."

"Nice. Simple." The Elfin Lord drew his sword. "Shall we?"

Fire flared up around the three Mages and David smiled grimly.

"Do try to keep up," he told them, then launched into a full sprint toward Ambrose.

The vampire cackled as she saw them coming, a booming, twisted laugh that echoed around the mountains.

"Finally. A challenge!"

She lifted her hand and lances of black light flashed out, aiming at David. He dodged several, parried two more with his sword, and leapt over the last handful, his Empowered strength carrying him in a high arc that he knew was going to attract gunfire.

A quarter-second of prescience was enough for him to twist through the air and dodge each bullet, slamming to a landing facing Ambrose from only a few feet away.

The vampire tossed back the hood of her cloak, revealing Elsa Ambrose to still be astonishingly beautiful. Her raven hair was tied back in a teenager's ponytail above delicately pale skin and warm blue eyes, eyes easily lit up by the massive grin on her face.

"I haven't had this much fun in years, Commander White," she told him as the claws on her hands extended farther, growing to match his sword in length. "Come to me; let us see the strength that slew the great Marcus Dresden!"

David grimaced and focused, moving toward her with a speed he knew would be a blur to watching eyes, and lashing out with *Memoria*.

The shadowy claws parried, knocking aside the demon-forged blade with almost casual ease. One hand defended her from his strike and the other dove for his face, two-foot-long claws slicing at him.

David twisted out of the way of the claws, recovering from the parry and yanking the sword back to him in time to block Ambrose's next strike. The sword smashed into her shadowy claws and shattered the entire collection.

Shards of broken shadow scattered away from the vampire's hand, and she leapt back several feet, clearing an open space between them as she eyed him with interest.

"Less than I had feared, Commander, but so much more than I'd expected," she told him brightly. "I see how our beloved leader fell." She threw out her hand, conjuring new claws with a gesture, and smiled. "And you brought friends!

"I just don't think that's fair, do you, Commander?"

With a gesture, the vampires behind her opened fire. Bullets and magic hammered into the defenses of the three Mages closing up behind David, but they advanced regardless to stand by his side.

"I don't think anyone here thought this was going to be fair," David pointed out, stepping forward as his companions spread out, forming a deadly semicircle around Ambrose.

"Well, then, let us play!"

Ambrose *moved*. One moment she was standing still, the next she'd half-disappeared into a swirling, terrifying dance that conjured bolts of black lightning that hammered Young's shields, specifically, as the vampire charged.

David met her before she reached the Elfin Second, *Memoria* connecting with a force only Empowered strength could deliver as he bodily collided with the vampire Matriarch. The blade scored along her flesh and she snarled at him in pain, twisting in her dance to turn the full force of its power on him.

He had no shields of his own, but the black lightning slammed into a shield around him anyway, his companions protecting him as he struck out. Shadow and electricity played around them as he met Ambrose once more, his sword lashing out at her as she struck at him with magic and shadowy claws alike.

Every blow he launched, she parried. Every strike she returned with, he blocked. He was faster and stronger and could see the future —but she had three *centuries* of combat experience on him.

The world shrank down to a single dark-red blade and half a dozen shadowy claws as David fought for his life. He sheared the claws off one hand, but she simply dueled him with the other as she regrew them.

She pushed him back a step. Then two. Then he forced her to fall back. Despite her magic and inhuman vitality, he could keep this up for hours…and he was starting to realize she *couldn't*.

"David!" Mason suddenly screamed as the defensive shield around him collapsed and he realized he'd missed a critical shift in the battle around him. A second vampire, the glow of power around him easily equal to the one around Ambrose, had joined the battle.

The second ancient vampire had disrupted the shield David's allies had maintained around him, and Ambrose's power slammed home. Pain tore through him as black lightning slammed into his skin, and her grin returned, exposing long, sharp teeth.

"*Mine!*" she snarled, and dove at him with her fangs.

David could regenerate injuries that would kill even other supernaturals, but he was only slightly more resistant to injury. His body, however, had adapted to handle the power and speed of his Empowered movements, and lightning, while painful and potentially lethal, wasn't *crippling*.

Fire still burning in his muscles, he struck. *Memoria* flashed out in a straight-arm thrust that met Ambrose in mid-charge and ran clean into her heart. She collided with him, the force of the impact throwing him to the ground, but the sword was still buried in her chest and her fangs didn't connect as she gasped impotently at him for several eternal seconds.

And then finally died.

THE MAGE DUEL continued around David as he shoved Ambrose's body aside and sprang back to his feet with the sword in his hand. Riley was bearing the brunt of the fight, much as he had done against Romanov the night before, but this time, the vampire he was dueling wasn't trying to protect his minions as well as fight.

And a Mage's reserves didn't replenish overnight. Riley was still badly weakened by the energy he'd expended to take down Romanov. Even with Young and Mason in support, he was barely holding his own, and to David's Sight it was clear that the Elfin Lord was weakening fast.

The Patriarch they were fighting saw the same thing. A new flurry of blows, fire and lighting and shadow alike, hammered down on Riley, pushing him back step by step as the unknown vampire's laughter echoed off the hills.

"So, this is all the Lord General has?" he mocked Riley. "It seems I should not have been so afraid of Petrov after all!"

Bright light flashed as Riley threw a burst of power back at the vampire, stabilizing on his feet and holding up his sword.

"I am a servant of the Secret Fire, wielder of the flame of Anor. You cannot pass," he gasped out. "I will not yield."

"I am Nazario Santos Cortez," the vampire told him, "and I do not require you to yield. Simply to *die*."

A single lance of pure black shadow blaze from Cortez's palm, cutting through the shields of the three Mage's to hammer into Riley's chest and fling the Elfin Lord back thirty feet or more. The magical aura around Riley vanished like a popped soap bubble.

"McCreery, Wilbur—*now*!" David snapped, charging toward where Riley had fallen. "Mason, Young, cover him."

The two Mages threw up a doubled shield over the Elfin Lord, focusing their efforts on defense as Cortez laughed, his voice clearly magically amplified as it echoed off the trees and mountains.

Then the artillery arrived. Wilbur had clearly been paying attention to the battle, as the first six shells bracketed the vampire lord *perfectly*, the explosions silencing his laughter and his magic with equal force.

David knew there was a small but significant chance the vampire had *survived* being blown to pieces by six 155mm howitzer shells, but Cortez was definitely out of this fight.

And then, as the second salvo slammed home into the lead elements of the vampire formation, the remaining Pendragons came sweeping silently over the mountain. Hellfire missiles ripple-fired, silver-laced explosions walking their way along the armored vehicles and advancing vampire infantry.

The silver-laced explosions were ONSET's usual blast-fragmentation warheads, but the containers they'd received after the previous night's engagement had included some of the original Hellfire missiles: with anti-tank warheads.

Most of the stolen M1 Abrams were already gone, the primary target of every heavy weapon and Mage David commanded. The remainder didn't survive the Pendragons' pass as missile after missile reduced tanks and APCs and chunks of mountain to burning debris.

And then more artillery shells arrived as David hoisted the limp—but still alive, according to his Sight—form of Elfin Lord Jamie Riley over his shoulders.

"Fall back to the final surface position," he ordered as the helicopters swept back around, cannon blazing in the night.

"And McCreery?"

"Sir?"

"One pass with the cannons. Then get the *hell* out of here."

"What about you?" she asked.

"We hold," David said flatly. "One way or another, we hold or we die."

FOR TWO MINUTES, the guns pounded the vampire assault, six massive shells slamming home every fifteen seconds as Major Wilbur's battery wore their barrels out. With two Familias leaders dead—or at least cripplingly wounded—in the same span, the vampires paused under fire, taking cover in the remaining APCs.

It was long enough for David's people to complete their withdrawal to the final dug-in position around the main bunker entrance. What was left of them, anyway.

ONSET Six was gone, wiped out by Ambrose before she'd killed their commander.

ONSET Fifteen was better off, with both Mason and two of her three agents up. Pierre Dupond wasn't dead, but the big Empowered had been rushed back into the Mountain along with the other wounded. David didn't know enough to say if he would pull through or not.

His own team was intact, though with McCreery currently leading the helicopters to safety, he only had Stone and Hellet. They were down to six ONSET agents on the ground from twelve, a brutal winnowing he was sure was going to cause problems later.

The Elfin were even worse off. Klein was dead. Silas, the leader of the scouts, was missing, and his five companions were dead. They'd started with forty Elfin Warriors, plus Riley and his Second. They now had nine and Young, though many were wounded instead of dead.

There were a lot of dead Elfin and ONSET people on the slopes of Mount Scott tonight, and David doubted it was any reassurance to anyone that there were *far* more dead vampires and Thralls. Every stolen M1 Abrams was wrecked. Most of the Strykers and Bradleys were gone as well, as were a massive number of the M113 APCs.

"We're done," Wilbur told him. "Gun six just blew her barrel to pieces. Two of my people are injured, but no fatalities and she's still mobile. We are out of here."

"Drive fast, drive safe," David replied. "And, Major?"

"Yes, Commander?"

"Thank you. And you should probably lock down your CBRN systems."

Wilbur was silent.

"Seriously?"

"I have no idea how this is going to go down, Major. Make certain your people are safe."

"Understood. Locking down our radiation seals. Good luck."

Mason, Young and Santiago approached him. His "leaders" were a quarter of his remaining people. It wasn't a good place to be.

"What do we do now?" Santiago asked.

"Well, unless whoever's left in charge over there is *completely* useless, they're discovering about now that we collapsed the silo entrances earlier today," David replied. "The only way into the Mountain is through us."

"Lovely," Young snapped. "Riley's in there. He'll live, but..." She shook her head. "He's vulnerable."

"I know. So are we all. Leitz." He poked the analyst. "Any idea on what we're looking at for numbers?"

"Looks like they're abandoning the APCs and bringing up the remaining Strykers and Bradleys," she reported. "Most likely because those have grenade and missile launchers. Half the damn hill is on fire, David; it's hard to get any kind of count, especially with vampires."

"Eyeball it," he ordered grimly.

"Three, four hundred," Leitz answered. "Can't get better than that."

David whistled softly. He'd lost most of his people getting this far, but they'd taken out over *six hundred* vampires and Thralls.

"They're moving," she warned them. "APCs are sweeping on the silo doors, but you've got the Bradleys and Strykers heading for you."

"Understood."

THE VAMPIRES HAD STARTED with forty of the more heavily armed light armored vehicles, but only sixteen of them were left to make the rush, still evenly split between the Bradleys and Strykers.

The Strykers moved first, their remote-controlled grenade launchers and machine guns spitting fire to try and keep everyone's heads down. Vampire commandos moved with them, using the armored vehicles for cover while peppering the barricade with bullets whenever someone tried to return fire.

One of the Elfin Warriors popped up with an anti-tank missile and managed to launch it, the weapon blasting the first Stryker to pieces, before taking at least three separate silver bullets and collapsing in a crumpled heap.

"Keep your heads down," Santiago snapped at his people. "Wait until they're closer; we're only going to get one decent shot to push them back."

It turned out they should have been wondering just what the *Bradleys* were doing. The eight M2s had been using the more lightly armed Strykers as screen and had spent the entire night shooting with their 25mm chain guns and machine guns.

They had to be running low on chain gun ammunition, but none of them had used their *other* primary weapon. Now, the last eight of the armored fighting vehicles crested the hill in an even line, trained their turrets on David's final fallback position, and launched their anti-tank missiles.

He was flung back as the warheads exploded, shattering the sandbagged position, his ears ringing from the explosions as he tried to establish what was going on. The Strykers were adding to the confusion by dropping smoke grenades into the defensive position.

"Fall back!" he shouted, almost unable to hear his own voice. "Fall back into the bunker!"

Vampire commandos landed in the wreckage of his position even as he spoke, impossible leaps carrying them from beside the advancing armor to on top of his people. *Memoria* flashed out, the smoke only a minor impediment to his Empowered vision, and two of the vampires died before they even knew they'd reached him

"Everyone fall back!" he bellowed again, charging into the growing concentration of the enemy. A machine gun chattered and he sidestepped, allowing Stone's fire to tear apart a vampire about to shoot him, and he charged forward.

There were two Elfin Warriors desperately lost in the smoke. He grabbed their shoulders and pointed, sending them to safety.

Here was Hellet, smashed to the ground by a trio of vampires, one of who was tearing at her armor with fingers and fangs. David shot two of them with his off hand, his wounded shoulder barely absorbing the recoil, and decapitated the third, grabbing the Mage and half-carrying, half-dragging her toward the bunker.

By the time they reached the massive, only partially open entrance, he wasn't sure how much of the crowd around him was vampires versus his own people—then there was a flash of power as Young and Mason charged into action.

First, they blasted the smoke away, and then they rained fire and lightning on the vampires intermixed with the retreating defenders. It bought David and his people distance, but that was all. More of the vampires were pouring into the tunnel behind him, and his hands were full carrying Hellet's half-conscious form.

"Someone help me!" he snapped—and then Stone was there.

"Get us through the inner door. We've got to get under cover."

"They are *right* behind us," Mason told him. "Whatever you're going to do—"

"We've got to *move*."

"They're using shaped charges to breach Silo C," Leitz reported in his head. "I've got nothing. What do we do?!"

David pulled through the inner door after Stone, the last of the survivors to make it, and saw it begin to close. It was thoroughly oiled and moved smoothly and quickly, but it still seemed to take an eternity.

And when it finally closed, he pulled the remote detonator from inside his armored vest and clicked the button. There was no complexity to this. All of the codes had been input before he buried the bomb.

The surface of Mount Scott disappeared in nuclear fire—along with the remaining vampire vehicles and any portion of the assault that wasn't under the surface.

[35]

THE ENTIRE BUNKER TREMBLED AROUND THEM, THE MOUNTAIN ABOVE THEM shifting as a massive chunk of its surface was removed and scattered. The tremors continued but slowed, and David looked over at Mason.

"Kate?" he asked quietly.

"The door is sealed." She gestured at the big metal barrier to the outside world. "Some of them...a lot of them made it into the tunnel, but they're not getting any further."

"That wasn't what I wanted to know."

She sighed and nodded.

"I can't tell if the cleaner worked from in here," she admitted. "I can tell you it triggered, but I don't have a lot of experience with trying to contain the radiation from a *nuclear explosion*."

When they'd buried the bomb, Mason and Riley had put together a spell that *should* have limited it to the heat and blast effects, cleaning the radiation before it could cause long-term catastrophe. Even if the spell hadn't entirely worked, it should, thankfully, have reduced the impact of what was already a "clean" weapon by nuclear standards.

"We'll need to get back in touch with the outside world, but right now, I need to know what's going on."

"I can tell you that much," Jenna said softly, the white-robed vampire seeming to appear from nowhere. She carried a computer tablet in her hands that she turned to show him. It was displaying the feeds from multiple security cameras throughout the hardened complex.

"Just over a hundred of them made it into the tunnel and survived," she told them, gesturing at the big door behind them. "The entrance has collapsed, someone will need to bring in major earth-moving equipment to get us out, but they also can't get in. They are trapped until you decide what to do with them."

"Then that's it, isn't it?" David asked. "We did it.

"Sadly, no," the other of the two Sisters told him, Gabriel helping the Arbiter into the room. "Because despite our collapsing the entrances, they managed to open Silo C, and there are now about a hundred commandos and Mages, all from Familias Reginald, I believe, making their way in from there. They are *not* contained."

"Let me speak to these, Commander," the Arbiter told David. He looked...injured. Drained. There was something wrong with him, something that hadn't been there before. "There has been...so much death. I don't know if I can take any more.

"Let me talk to them, convince them to agree to my Truce, and I will bind them as I have bound the others before," he promised. "Deal with Joseph Reginald—you must—but leave these to me. I will make them harmless; I swear it to you."

"His oaths are bound in magic and blood," Gabriel snapped, despite the Arbiter's angry glance. "He is sworn to preserve the race; this many deaths so near him is destroying him, Commander."

"Please, Gabriel," the old vampire said weakly. "My weakness is not a weapon to be used."

"No," David agreed, "but it's part of the calculation, as Gabriel well knows." He glanced over at his handful of remaining people. All of the remaining Agents had made it in, but Hellet was badly injured, clearly bitten.

"Do we have any antivenom?" he asked, his gaze on his Agent.

"If you don't, we do," Jenna told him. She flashed a smile at him as he looked at her in surprise. "Where did you think your people got the formula, Commander? You haven't had that much opportunity to study vampires, after all."

The Arbiter crossed over to Hellet and knelt by her. Magic flickered from his hands as he studied her, and then he looked up and met David's gaze with his strange black eyes.

"She is too injured, Commander," the vampire whispered. "Her body wars with itself, but she is beyond even magical healing now. If you let the virus take her, she may live. If you give her the antivenom I gave your people, she will die."

The Arbiter touched the Mage's head gently.

"There are things we can do to encourage the transformation, but she will either turn or die, Commander. Even my power cannot save her."

That was...one hell of a choice.

"Help her," David snapped. "Then talk to your people."

He turned to the Elfin.

"Santiago, keep what's left of your team here, just in case. Mason, Fifteen and Thirteen are with me."

David shook his head grimly.

"Joseph Reginald was one of ours once. One way or another, Omicron will deal with him."

Leaving the Arbiter to speak to the trapped vampires, David led the ONSET Agents deep into the underground complex. The Keepers had provided them a map that Leitz had loaded into their AR systems—systems that were shielded well enough to survive the EMP of the surface nuke—to guide their way to Silo C.

The last thing David was expecting to hear during that journey was his phone ringing.

"What the hell?" he exclaimed aloud, carefully adjusting the balance of his sword to pull out his Omicron-issued smartphone. A number was flashing on the screen—a number with no name attached.

The phone was linked into a government directory, and only a handful of people had the number who *weren't* in Omicron. All of them were programmed into the contacts. His phone had only run like this once before...

"David White," he answered crisply, still following the path on his HUD.

"Commander, you can guess who this is," the softly accented voice of Caleb Dresden, Patriarch of the Familias Dresden, said in his ear. "So, you survived. I wondered if you'd nuked your own position."

"I had alternatives," David replied. "What do you want, Dresden?"

"I need to know something, Commander. Something very, very important."

"I don't have time for this," David snapped. "Get to the point."

"Is the Mountain Crèche intact?" Dresden asked. "Are the children of my race alive, despite the fact you just blew up their safe haven?"

"Yes," David told him. "Despite your people's attempt to kill everyone here."

"*I* have not participated in the attack," the vampire said dryly. "Some of my people appear to have, which I will...deal with, if any have survived. Certainly, my allies have.

"But Familias Dresden will not wage war on Omicron," the Patriarch of that Family concluded. "You have defeated the massed forces of the Familias. I'm sure there's some cleanup you're still doing, you aren't almost running for nothing, but I recognize when the war is over, Commander White."

Was the vampire suggesting...

"You know my price," Caleb Dresden said quietly. "If the Committee will lift Standing Order Twenty-one and provide a blanket amnesty for actions prior to the Truce, I will bind my Familias to the Arbiter's Truce. I would see my family be citizens once more.

"And I will not sacrifice their immortality for nothing," he finished. "And the fact that I suspect I am the only remaining Patriarch except Sakura, who has conceded to me, leaves me many options in a more peaceful future."

"I can't promise anything," David told him. "That's up to the Committee."

"I know," the vampire leader confirmed. "For the moment, I guarantee a complete cease-fire on the part of every vampire outside the Mountain. If the Committee agrees to the Truce, we will provide a full detailing of our arms and facilities and engage in a cooperative process of disarmament.

"If you can pound sense into your leaders, *I* now have the power to force the Vampire Familias of North America to honor the Arbiter's Truce. Thank you for that, Commander White. It's always nice to have someone *else* destroy one's enemies."

Dresden chuckled.

"I'll hang on to this phone for a while," he promised. "Though, believe me, I'll know the results of the Committee meeting before any attack could be launched on me.

"I hope we speak again in better times, Commander White."

The phone clicked to silence.

DAVID DIDN'T HAVE a lot of time to process the conversation with Dresden before they reached the chokepoint they'd been heading toward—and discovered that the vampires had made it there first. He yanked Mason bodily back out of the line of fire as his prescience twinged, then a fusillade of bullets smashed down the hallway.

"They look pretty dug-in," Stone noted. "That's a lot of bullets."

The two ONSET Commanders traded glances. They were down to five: David; the two Mages from ONSET Fifteen, Mason and Bella Samuels; Mason's flame elementalist, Tsimote; and Stone.

It wasn't much to contain a hundred vampires from trying to break forward.

"We need to throw them back," David said softly. "Grenades?"

"You won't be able to throw them without getting shot," Stone replied.

"But we can *move* them," Samuels, Mason's junior Mage, pointed out. "Commander Mason and I can drift them down the hallway, and then Tsimote can blow them."

"I can detonate them from a distance," the elementalist confirmed, fire flickering around his hands as the man tried and failed to contain his hatred of vampires. "It will be good to send more of these scum to their graves."

"Control yourself, Tsimote," David warned. "This...might well be the last time we fight vampires."

"Then I shall have to kill as many of them as I can tonight, won't I?" Tsimote replied, his tone sending a shiver down the Commander's spine. "I can detonate many grenades. How many do we have?"

Combing out everyone's gear produced a total of twenty fragmentation grenades. Only a quarter of them had silver in them, the rest would only injure or shock vampires unless they were very close, but they'd make a hell of a bang.

"Here we go," Mason said with a heavy breath, wrapping magic around the cluster of explosives and sending it floating down the hallway, moving faster and faster as it shot around the corner and launched toward the vampire position.

Tsimote had his eyes closed, his mind and magic somewhere else as he followed the collection of grenades, and an unpleasant smile on his face. Gunfire echoed down the hallway, but the small Japanese man ignored the sound as he focused on his task.

"And...now," he murmured.

Twenty grenades went off simultaneously, an ear-shattering cacophony, and David charged in the aftermath.

The others followed him, gunfire and magical strikes flickering past him as he closed with the vampires. Most of those in the chokepoint security area were down, some dead, some only shocked. Others saw him coming and opening fire.

He twisted around bullets, grunted as his armor absorbed a lightning strike, conducting it away from him into the ground, and then cut the attacking vampire Mage in half with *Memoria*. The demon-forged blade flashed in the dim light, reflecting magic away from him as he carved through the defensive position.

Stone's machine gun echoed around him, heavy silver rounds smashing the vampires who tried to attack him to the ground as David fought. More magical fire flickered, and then suddenly no one in the room was moving.

The passage toward the collapsed exit from the Silo was empty, and there were moans around him—but the surviving vampires were staying still on the ground, raising their hands above their heads in surrender.

"Bind them, move them out of the way," David snapped. There had been a *lot* of death tonight. He wasn't going to refuse surrenders, not at this point.

Mason and Samuels quickly set to work, leaving Tsimote and Stone to watch the passageway with David. Keeping Tsimote away from surrendered vampires clearly struck everyone as a good idea.

"Parlay!" a voice shouted out of the tunnel. "Parlay. I would speak with you, Commander White."

[36]

"Cover me," David ordered his people, then stepped forward.

"All right, if you want to talk, come where I can see you," he shouted back.

A tall, fair-haired man dressed in an eighteenth-century frock coat over a very modern bulletproof vest walked along the tunnel until he could be seen. He wore a large pistol of some kind on one hip and a dueling sword on the other, but his hands were well clear of the weapons and he was smiling.

Whatever the joke was, David wasn't getting it.

"Who are you and what do you want?"

"I am Joseph Reginald," the vampire said, his voice perfectly calm as he identified himself as one of the first men to take on the task of defending the United States from the supernatural. "I did your job once, Commander, a long time ago when the job—and the world—was simpler!"

"I know who you were," David replied. "And how many of our problems did you create, Master Reginald?"

The vampire chuckled.

"A few," he admitted. "I *tried* to fix some, too, but I won't pretend the USA started our little war, Commander. If you were expecting me to reveal some dark secret, some purge of the vampires alongside the Natives, there isn't one.

"There was no compromise that could be reached between us. Blood will tell, we had to feed—and men like you and I had to protect the people. Violence was the only end."

"And so here we are."

"Here we are," Reginald agreed. "Buried under a mountain by the nuclear weapon you chose to detonate on your own head. How far-reaching will the consequences of that be, Commander?"

"One way or another, the Familias ends tonight," David told him. "Dresden has surrendered. The Arbiter has surrendered. You are all that remains. It's over."

"Do you even know what 'it' *is*?" Reginald asked. "You know so little of what drives the vampires who live in your country. So little of how we are organized. Did you even know the Arbiter existed before he came to you?"

"Before he betrayed us?"

"We didn't," David admitted. "I don't know if I'd call his actions betrayal, though. His oaths, according to him, are to preserve the species. He did not believe this was a war you could win."

"Given that we are now standing underneath a nuclear blast crater in one of our country's greatest natural treasures, it appears he may have been right," the old vampire replied. "But I, too, have oaths."

"There's no way out," David told him. "Every entrance is collapsed. We're only getting out of here when Omicron comes to dig us out. Even if you could kill us all, you could not escape."

Reginald was silent for several seconds.

"I wish I could believe you were lying," he said conversationally. "But I still do not have it in me to kneel again, Commander White. I have not walked the shadows for two hundred years to bow once more to lesser men."

"You could tell us so much, you know," David replied quietly. "You *knew* the Founding Fathers. You're a historian's walking wet dream!"

The ex-Judge laughed.

"I don't think most of America wants to hear *my* opinions of your

'Founding Fathers,'" he noted. "I knew them as men, after all, not legends. And they were far from perfect men."

"And perhaps that's what we need to know," the younger supernatural told him. "The truth. It's worth more than dead men, isn't it?"

"Perhaps. But my oaths do not permit to yield the Familias Reginald without a fight, Commander. I did not forge a new Familias from *nothing* to surrender.

"I have a proposal, Commander. A simple one, even a logical one for a man of my time," Reginald told him, the grin at a joke no one else heard returning to his face.

"You and I duel. If I win, your people let mine go. What's a hundred vampires on the loose when the rest have surrendered? We'll disappear; there aren't enough of us left for the Familias to continue as it has.

"If you win, my people will surrender. This war ends forever. My children live, bound by the Arbiter's Truce."

"We've already won," David pointed out. "Why would I fight you?"

"Because if we fight, you will lose more people, Commander White," Reginald replied bluntly. "How many Elfin Warriors and Omicron Agents burned with the vampires on those slopes? How much bloodshed has this night seen, Commander? Would you add to it when it can just be you and I to end this whole affair?"

David considered it in silence, studying the young-looking ancient facing him.

"Don't do it," Mason told him over the radio. "They can't take us; it's already over."

"But they *can* kill more of us," David replied, subvocalizing into his microphone. "We could lose any of us."

He could lose Kate Mason, which he wasn't prepared to consider after making it this far.

"We can end this," he continued to his fellow Commander and lover. "*I* can end this."

He glanced back at her and saw her sigh—and nod.

Commander David White turned back to Joseph Reginald and smiled grimly.

"All right, 'Your Honor,'" he told the vampire. "Let's do it your way."

REGINALD'S SMILE broadened and he gracefully shed the old frock coat, gesturing a minion forward to take the garment and leaving him clad in a white dress shirt and an armored vest.

"You heard the deal with Commander White, Cody," the vampire Patriarch told the man taking his coat. "If I fall, you all surrender. You understand?"

"Yes, milord," Cody replied.

"And take my gun as well," Reginald told the younger vampire, unstrapping the big automatic and passing it over. "This isn't going to be walk ten paces and turn, is it, Commander?"

"No," David replied. He gestured Mason to him and passed over his own gun. "You heard my own promise," he told her softly.

"I'm not sure you have the authority to let them go," she pointed out.

"I probably don't. But you'll do it anyway."

She sighed.

"Yes. Don't make it necessary," she warned him. "I might let him go today, but if he kills you…"

Mason's tone suggested all kinds of retribution for any vampire foolish enough to cause David permanent harm, and he chuckled at her, meeting her eyes with a smile that was momentarily warmer.

There were words they couldn't say. Not while they were being recorded, and everything they said on duty was recorded. From Kate's eyes, though, he knew they both knew what they were.

"I don't plan on dying today," he said firmly, then he bowed slightly to his lover and drew *Memoria*, stepping out to face the vampire Patriarch.

"Shall we, Lord Reginald?"

"Call me Joseph, Commander," the old Justice told him as he drew his own sword and approached into full view of both groups of supernaturals. "You and I, we understand each other better than most."

"Do we?" David asked softly, extending his sword towards Reginald. "We aren't friends. We aren't even on the same side."

"No. But we both understand duty. Honor. Oaths. I spent a long time after I was Turned trying to honor both who I had been and what I had become."

"You seem to have reconciled yourself to this," David replied, waiting for the vampire to make the first move.

"Now, perhaps. I tried differently once—but then Oscar Nelson tried to kill me," Reginald said softly. "You would have liked him, Commander. He was a man without give, without flexibility. And unlike you, he never learned any better.

"Not once he tried to kill me and left me no choice but to forswear who I had once been."

The vampire moved, his limbs and blade a blur of speed as he crossed the space between them in a fraction of a moment, his sword driving for David's neck even as it lit up with the turquoise glow of the vampire's power.

David was moving in the same instant, *Memoria* flashing through the air to intercept the blue-green blade. The glow of the two blades' power flickered in the dim light of the underground tunnel as they clashed, Reginald's sword thrown aside into the wall.

The vampire leapt backward as David tried to turn the moment of imbalance to his advantage, the dueling sword flickering out to trap the ONSET Commander's leaf-bladed sword and deflect it. Glowing with magic, the tip flickered across the space between them a dozen times in as many seconds, each strike driving toward another vulnerable point on David's body.

And each strike met *Memoria*, David blurring from parry to parry as he smoothly met every blow the vampire launched. A parry turned into a riposte and the vampire bent backward, folding nearly in half to allow the blade to whistle harmlessly above him.

Reginald sprang back upright, the momentum propelling his blade forward in a thrust that no human strength could have deflected. David saw it coming and…wasn't there, sidestepping in a blur and then grabbing the blade with his free hand.

Magic *crackled* up his fingers, lightning shocking him with pain as he closed his grip around the narrow blade and yanked. Reginald came stumbling toward him and David brought *Memoria* flashing around in a one-handed blow that should have taken off the vampire's head.

The vampire released his sword, sliding backward and throwing up his arm to block David's strike with his forearm. The crash of the impact echoed in the corridor as the demon-forged blade hammered into the armored bracer Reginald wore under his shirt.

Turquoise magic flared in the tunnel, flinging both men away from each other. Even David's Empowered strength barely managed to retain his grip on *Memoria*, and the glowing dueling sword slammed point-first into the concrete wall, embedding itself six inches deep.

The vampire Patriarch smiled at David again and ripped off the torn sleeve of his dress shirt. A green-enameled bracer covered his entire right forearm, glittering in the underground complex's dim light. A gesture from Reginald lit up the hilt of his dueling sword with power and flicked the weapon back into his hand.

"I'm no Mage, Commander, but I've mastered a few tricks over the years," the vampire told him. "Come. You can do better."

"If you can't, this isn't going to last much longer," David replied levelly, but he moved to the attack regardless. The vampire had carried the offensive at a speed no regular human could match...but David was actually *faster*.

The dueling sword was primarily a thrusting weapon. *Memoria* was a slashing blade, requiring more movement and arc for a proper strike, but David still unleashed a flurry of blows that pushed Reginald back, the vampire blocking with blade and bracer alike to buy himself time as he retreated,

David slipped past the vampire's guard, the blade sliding over the bracer on Reginald's right arm, but the Patriarch managed to flash his left arm across to smash *Memoria* downward, revealing a second enchanted green bracer as he tore the blade from David's grip.

Reginald's sword flashed out toward the Commander, but David stepped *into* the strike this time, twisting his torso away from the blade as he grabbed the weapon with both hands and pulled in opposite directions.

Old and enchanted or not, the weapon wasn't strong enough for that. The blade snapped in two, and David tossed the pieces aside as he kicked *Memoria* back into the air. Catching the sword, he slashed at Reginald again as the vampire stared at his shattered weapon in shock for a critical fraction of a second.

The vampire dodged backward *just* fast enough to avoid losing the top half of his head, but not fast enough to prevent the demon-forged blade from opening up his face from cheek to cheek in a massive bloody gash.

A gash that would not easily heal, since *Memoria* impeded regeneration.

One hand pressed to his face, Joseph Reginald stumbled back and shoved his other hand out, palm open.

"Wait!" he snapped. "Wait, please."

David paused, the demon-forged sword at the ready. With his hand over his eyes and blood pouring down his face, he wasn't sure the vampire was a threat, though the duel had been implied to be to the death.

Reginald used his free hand to tear off a piece of his shirt, slowly and crudely binding the gash across his face and wiping the blood from his eyes. Once he was able to see, his hands covered in his own blood and the rough bandage already turning red, the leader of Familias Reginald faced David once more and, slowly and carefully, bowed.

"I yield," he said simply. "I will not sacrifice immortality on a point of pride, David White. I yield and will bind the Familias Romanov to the Arbiter's Truce." He exhaled heavily, the pressure sending more blood pumping into the bandage.

"It is over."

It was, of course, not quite so simple.

Disarming Familias Reginald's collection of commandos and Mages took over an hour, even with them being *mostly* cooperative. Then Gabriel found them halfway back to the main entrance, the

Guardian looking askance at the slowly moving collection of unarmed vampires.

"I see your morning has progressed," she told David dryly. "So has my master's. He and my sister are busy disarming the vampires trapped in the entrance tunnel."

"We're going to need somewhere to keep them all," David replied. "No offense, but I'm not letting several hundred vampires run around freely until we actually have rules in place for just what you people can and can't do."

Gabriel shook her head.

"You know the rules we've agreed to," she pointed out. "We feed on animal blood and live by the same laws as the rest of the supernatural community." The vampire's mouth twisted in what might charitably have been called a smile.

"We may break the latter to enforce the former on occasion, but no one will know anything, I promise."

"I know what you've offered and the oaths they've promised to swear," he told her. "But until Standing Order Twenty-one is lifted, I don't have the authority to let them go."

She shivered.

"What happens, Commander White, if the Committee refuses to change?" she asked softly. "If you are ordered to kill us all?"

"I won't," he assured her. "But I know that wouldn't change much. Which is why your master and I need to talk. He and I need be ready to go to Washington."

The Arbiter's bodyguard sighed.

"He is...not well, Commander," she told him. "His oaths have power, David White, and he swore to preserve the race. If this all turns out as planned, he has *succeeded*, but those spells only sense so many of our kind dead around him."

"The fate of your people, Miss Gabriel, is going to rest on him," David replied. "I can only argue so far, speak so strongly for his integrity. *He* must convince the Committee of Thirteen that the vampires of North America will keep their oaths and become citizens once more."

"He will go with you," Gabriel promised. "Jenna and I must come as well. He will need...coddling. And he will not appreciate it, but we must make certain he is strong enough to speak for us all."

"That is for you and him to decide. The promises that I have made will see him delivered safely to the Committee of Thirteen.

"What happens there..." David shook his head. "That is where we learn if all of this was for nothing."

[37]

Twenty-four hours of carefully coordinated digging, magical lifting, and demolitions later, the outer entrance of the main tunnel was finally opened up, allowing the pale light of a Rocky Mountain dawn to filter into the underground complex.

Mostly ignoring the earth-moving equipment and uniformed Anti-Paranormal troops, David walked out onto the side of Mount Scott and looked down on his handiwork.

It was horrifying.

A trail of devastation started near the main road, a half-mile-wide trail of shattered and burnt-out trees that led up the mountain until it met and merged with the utterly destroyed blast zone of the nuke. The old parking lot was gone: the concrete, the sandbagged defenses, the bodies, even the attacking vehicles vaporized when the bomb had gone off.

As he looked toward the road, he could see the burnt-out hulks of the armored vehicles the Familias had brought to try and retake the facility from Omicron. There were few visible bodies now, and most of the ones he could see had been burnt to a crisp.

The best part of a *thousand* vampires, beings that could easily have been immortal, had died there. Some of those beings had witnessed the birth of the nation whose officers had destroyed them. There was no question in battle, no regret then, but the thought of the knowledge and memories that had died there struck David like a blow as he looked out over the slope.

"Congratulations, Commander White," Major Warner told him, the redheaded Mage seeming to appear from nowhere. "You now join Commander O'Brien in a very select, very short list."

"Which is that?" David asked softly.

"Two, actually," she replied. "You have waged all-out supernatural war on American soil…and you have detonated a nuclear weapon in the line of duty."

David winced. Michael O'Brien had led the counterattack to the Montana Incursion, when the Masters Beyond had managed to launch a major supernatural invasion into a thankfully desolate and remote area. He'd also, during nuclear tests in the seventies, lured the first High Court demon to enter the world into a blast site and triggered a megaton nuclear warhead in its face.

"How bad is the fallout?" he asked.

"Literally?" Warner chuckled. "Not bad. The containment spells you dropped on the bomb worked. The radiation was contained; the spread of radioactive material is close enough to zero that we can publicly pretend it wasn't a nuke."

He winced again.

"Metaphorically, I don't think we really know yet," she continued. "This was *not* what you were supposed to use the bomb for, David. Detonating it inside the complex wouldn't have been as noticeable!"

"It wouldn't have carried the day, either," he pointed out.

"No. There will be consequences for this, David," she warned. "I hate playing the terrorist card, but the bastards gassed an entire fucking National Guard base. Officially, they gassed the base and tried to steal a MOAB—and were shot down over Crater Lake National Park, triggering the bomb."

Even a MOAB—the bunker-buster known as the "Mother of All Bombs"—wasn't as powerful as the nuke they'd set off, but it would cover for what had actually happened.

"The terrorist card plays into a lot of hands I'd rather not have given that kind of ammunition," Warner noted, "but the Familias didn't exactly give us a choice."

"So, what happens now?" David asked. "Between the fledglings, the Keepers, and the surrenders, we have over seven hundred vampires in the Mountain. They've promised a Truce, to observe the new code the Arbiter wants to impose, but so long as—"

"So long as Standing Order Twenty-one exists, that won't change anything," his boss agreed. "David, you *know* some of those vampires were involved in gassing the base. All of them, except some of the Keepers and fledglings, have killed. What do you expect us to do?"

"We need to choose, Major, between whether we want revenge for the past or peace for the future," he told her. "We have a chance to end this war, to make peace with a group that *should* be our own people. Would you be able to look the family of the next Agent to die fighting vampires in the eye and tell them we *could* have had peace but we chose war?"

Warner sighed and nodded.

"You realize you're going to have to push this?"

"All the way to Washington," David agreed. "We need to put the Committee and the Arbiter in the same damned room. Let them look *him* in the eye and condemn his species to death, if they have it in them."

"I'll talk to Ardent," Warner promised. "I'll get you the damn meeting. What do you need from me?"

"A Pendragon with a blacked-out passenger compartment," David said. "We need to get three vampires and me to Washington DC by this afternoon—and you and Ardent need to get the Committee to agree to meet us when we get there."

She laughed.

"Who is supposed to be giving orders here again, Commander?" she asked, but she held up a hand when he started to apologize. "You have the plan, you have the momentum. We'll have that Pendragon here ASAP and we'll get you and your vampires to Congress.

"Everything after that is up to you."

McCreery took the controls of the helicopter once it arrived and hopped it *into* the tunnel, solving the problem of how to get the vampires into the blacked-out passenger compartment.

"Our ride is here," David told the two Sisters standing outside the Arbiter's quarters. "Is he ready?"

"I am ready," the Arbiter answered for himself, opening the door and stepping out. He wore his dark red priestly robes and leaned on a plain wooden walking stick. The two younger vampires stepped up to support him, but he waved them away.

"I am old and sore, my dears; I am not helpless or dying," he told them. "Are you ready, Commander?"

"How much do I need to be ready for?" David asked. "I'm just the man getting the door open for you, Arbiter. You're the one who gets to make the pitch."

"If you think your words will have no impact on what happens today, Commander White, I have a bridge in San Francisco for sale," the old vampire replied. "Come, let's go, then."

Stone fell in with them as they headed toward the exit, where Kate and Samuels were waiting. The two Mages were going to remain behind, along with a company of Anti-Paranormal troopers—roughly half of the AP troops *left* after the last six months.

"Keep them safe, Commander Mason," David told her.

"You certainly set a sterling example of what to do, Commander White," she replied. "One way or another, they'll be waiting for you when you get back."

"I know," David replied. "We'll be in touch, Commander."

"I know," she echoed. "Good luck."

He found himself once more meeting her gaze and leaving words unsaid. This, he knew, was *exactly* why anything between them was a bad idea. That just hadn't stopped it happening anyway.

"McCreery?" he said loudly.

"We're fueled and ready to go. All windows in the passenger compartment are blacked out. ETA at Washington DC is eight PM tonight."

"All right. Let's go."

[38]

There was absolutely nothing on the outside to make the four-story white stone building look at all different from a dozen other small office buildings scattered through Washington DC likely housing some small government department no one had ever heard of.

It was just down the street from the Capitol and had a helicopter landing pad on the roof, but that wasn't really a clue to the building's true nature. The fact that it didn't have *any* kind of sign on the outside was a hint that it wasn't exactly normal, but it was hardly the only office building in DC without identifiers.

Landing on the roof just after dark, however, David and his companions found themselves swiftly met by six Capitol Police officers in black suits, all of them openly carrying the distinctive M4 Omicron carbine. All of the six—so far as David could tell—were human, but *something* had been done to their suits.

He was pretty certain he could take them all, but he doubted it would be as easy as a supernatural who hadn't been paying attention might presume.

"Commander, we need to see your identification," one of the officers told David as soon as he exited the helicopter.

David calmly handed over his ID folio. No one standing on the roof of *this* building wouldn't be cleared to see Omicron-issued IDs. The officer skimmed the documents and then handed the folio back.

"Thank you, Commander White. We understand you are escorting three…individuals who will be giving a presentation to the Committee?"

"That's right."

"We'll need them to surrender any weapons they are carrying," the officer said flatly.

David glanced at the three vampires in the helicopter.

"Did any of you even bring weapons?" he asked.

The Arbiter chuckled.

"We did not," he assured them. "But, of course, we will permit the officers to search us. Indeed, I insist. The security of the Committee is of paramount importance to any supernatural citizen of this country."

From the USCP officer's expression, that wasn't the response he'd expected from demanding the vampires surrender their weaponry. He nodded anyway and gestured for his people to search the Arbiter and his escorts.

The officers patted them down quickly and professionally before pronouncing them clean.

"Follow me, please, Commander, sir, ladies," the leader told them. "Colonel Ardent and the Committee are waiting."

"Thank you," David replied.

"You have no idea how wrong it feels to be letting *vampires* in here," the man half-whispered to David. "Are you *sure* about this, Commander?"

"We've been at war with them for two hundred years, Lieutenant," David told him. "It's time to try something different while we're all still here."

"True that," the office allowed. "I don't know if I agree with what you're doing, Commander White, but it's *you*. Good luck."

"Thank you," David repeated.

THE INNOCUOUS OFFICE building contained the in-the-know staff and bureaucracy that enabled thirteen Senators and Congressmen to act on behalf of the elected government of the United States of America in the affairs of the supernatural.

It also contained, on the ground floor and buried behind multiple layers of electronic, physical, and magical security, the luxuriously adorned meeting room in which the Special Committee for Supernatural Affairs met.

The Capitol Police escorted David and the three vampires down to that room and stopped outside.

"Do all of you really need to go in?" the officer asked, glancing hesitantly at the three vampires.

"No," the Arbiter replied instantly. "The Commander must come, obviously, but I can leave my escorts behind."

"We'd appreciate it," the USCP Lieutenant admitted.

"You are nervous about permitting vampires into the presence of the Committee, I understand," the Arbiter told him. "Anything in my power to make you more confident in our goodwill, I will do."

"There isn't anything else I can think of," the Lieutenant admitted. "Go on in. They're waiting."

David led the way, the Arbiter falling into step behind him as he stepped into the meeting room before he could think about just what he was doing.

The room was large enough for each of the Committee members to bring multiple staff members and even had seats and folding desks for them. Nonetheless, there were only fourteen men in the room today: the thirteen members of the Committee and Colonel Ardent himself.

Their seats had been arranged into a semicircle, with a single table and two chairs in the center, where everyone could see them.

"Take a seat, Commander White, Arbiter," Ardent instructed. "You sought this meeting, so I leave it to you to explain to the Committee just what it is you have promised in their name."

"I promised only that I would bring the Arbiter's Truce before you," David told them after taking his seat and watching the Arbiter slowly and carefully do the same. "We are faced with an opportunity, gentlemen, to end the long-standing conflict between us and the vampires, to recognize them as citizens again—with all the responsibilities and rights that entails."

"There was a reason, Commander White, that our predecessors passed Standing Order Twenty-one," Senator Albert Day told David. The Senator was a stereotypical politician David had met before, a paunchy man of middling height with shockingly white hair around a large bald patch.

"We have evidence that vampires cannot be trusted, that they must kill to survive," he continued. "We do not enjoy having ordered the death of a race, but the preponderance of evidence suggests that they truly are the rabid dogs we have treated them as.

"Does this...'Arbiter' argue against that?"

David glanced at the old vampire, who nodded to him and leaned forward.

"I am very old," he said softly. "I was at the French Court when we decided to support the Revolution that birthed your United States. I saw the Crusades firsthand. I have seen empires rise and fall, from Alexander's to Kaiser Wilhelm's.

"And for most of that time, all that you have said has been true of my species," he admitted flatly. "A small number of us were forced to avoid human blood to raise the next generation, but most found humans simply easier to find and feed on than other sources."

"We are supposed to believe this has changed?" Day demanded.

"I have *made it change*," the Arbiter stated harshly. "I have spent a hundred years researching the ability to store and transport animal blood that would work for vampires. Thirty years acquiring the slaughterhouses and building the logistics infrastructure.

"The network is in place for every vampire in North America, not just the United States, to never need to touch human blood again. That allows what the Familias has termed the Arbiter's Truce: if you will lift Standing Order Twenty-one and pardon their actions before today, they will forswear human blood and honor the laws of this nation."

"And what proof do we have this oath would be kept?" Ardent snapped.

"I will bind their oaths in magic and blood," the Arbiter told them. "Some of the adults may elude that oath, but I swear to you: no *teknon* will leave the Crèche without swearing that oath. Let my people be citizens again, gentlemen, and I have made it possible for them to live without death."

The breath fled the vampire in a rush and he half-collapsed onto the table.

"My apologies," he forced out. "I am weak tonight. I can only beg of you, Congressmen, Senators: so much has been sacrificed to convince the Familias to agree to this. Do not throw it away. Give my people a chance."

The room was silent.

"Commander White," Day said slowly. "You were bitten by a vampire once, correct?"

"I was," David confirmed. "I survived because of an antivenom we have on hand—an antivenom I recently learned the Arbiter here provided us the formula for."

From the old vampire's twitch, that hadn't been a piece of leverage he'd planned on using.

"At least one ONSET agent has been infected as we speak," David continued. "If we cure her, she will die. If we permit her to turn, Standing Order Twenty-one would require us to euthanize her. We would lose one of our competent and loyal Mages."

"In exchange for *safety* from these bloodsucking monsters!" Senator James Clay, a massive black man with a shaven head, snapped. "They are rabid and infectious. I cannot believe we are even considering this!"

"Senator, the Arbiter and his Keepers have forsworn human blood for decades, centuries in many cases," the Commander pointed out. "They are proof that vampires do not need to kill to survive. You have all been briefed on my Sight: I swear to you that what the Arbiter has said is true."

David looked around the room and shook his head.

"A thousand vampires died on the slopes of Mount Scott in the last three days," he reminded them. "Many of them were younger, survivors of Vietnam or other eras still in conscious memory...but others were not.

"Men and women died on the slopes of Mount Scott who fought in both World Wars. Men and women died who lived through Prohibition. Who listened to Abraham Lincoln give speeches. Who fought in the Civil War—or in some case, the Revolution!

"There is a woman standing outside the doors of this room who saw the Declaration of Independence signed as a child. The Arbiter here *invaded Persia* with Alexander the Great.

"They are living history, and living history that we have fought and destroyed for years," David told them. "With reason, at that. We did not start this war: they did. Now they are offering to surrender, to give up that which makes them feel powerful in exchange for allowing them to once more be *people*.

"Until today, that living archive of history was unavailable to us behind a shield of blood and war. Now *they* are offering to yield, to compromise.

"We can seek vengeance for what has happened—or we can consider the fact that sixty percent of the vampires in North America are now dead as justice enough and look to the future.

"I did not promise them safety." David admitted. "I promised merely that I would present their cause to you and demand a hearing."

The room was quiet for a long time.

"Commander White, could you please escort the Arbiter outside?" Day finally asked. "Do you have a full copy of the text of this... 'Arbiter's Truce'?"

"I do. Colonel Ardent should have a copy," David said, gesturing toward his boss.

The Colonel inclined his head toward David.

"I will have a staff member bring in copies to enable your discussion," he said calmly. "And then I believe that I too should leave you to your deliberations."

THE GUARDS SHOWED David and the vampires to a seating area, where the Arbiter gratefully took one of the old wooden chairs with a sigh of relief.

"Are you going to be okay?" David asked the old vampire, who seemed to be feeling every century of his age right now.

"I will live," he confirmed. "Recovering from this kind of blow will take time, time I have not had."

"Your oaths?" David questioned.

The Arbiter nodded.

"You will learn," he noted. "Be wary, Commander, of swearing by your immortality. Magic takes such things very seriously."

"I am not immortal," David objected.

"You are as immortal as any vampire," the Arbiter pointed out. "You will see. And remember, Commander White, that I will be there when you need me. I owe you that much.

"When I need you?" David asked. "I can't see that—"

"We lose almost half of all vampires to suicide when the last of their mortal relatives die," the vampire stated harshly. "Institutions help, but you and many others among ONSET's senior Agents will live a long time." He smiled.

"You will likely outlive ONSET itself."

"That is something we are planning for," Ardent's calm voice interrupted the discussion. "The potential immortality of many of our Commanders represents an asset we would be foolish to waste."

The Arbiter leveled his dark gaze on ONSET's commanding officer and smiled.

"Indeed," he agreed softly, studying the Colonel. "Though I will warn you, Colonel, the swiftest way to lose an immortal is to stop regarding them as a person."

Ardent bowed his head in wordless concession.

"The potential for recruiting vampires to our ranks is a benefit of this potential truce," he murmured. "As Commander White pointed out, your knowledge and experience could add a great deal of value to our country."

"If we all stop shooting each other on sight, that is," the Arbiter replied. "I have done all I can. The rest, Colonel Ardent, is up to your Committee."

The Colonel shrugged.

"That depends as much, I think, on whether Caleb Dresden meant his surrender," he admitted. "While the strings are still being followed, your younger friend owns at least three men in that chamber. Most of the rest can be convinced, and we only need seven. It's not even a new law, really. Just…changing a standing order."

"Caleb meant it," the Arbiter admitted, then smiled. "Caleb wrote half the damn Truce. I don't know what hooks he has in the Committee members, but if he has them, they'll vote for peace."

"I hope they'll vote for peace regardless," Ardent replied. "While your people have been distracting us, even more damn minor portals are opening. People are dying, Arbiter—people we could save if we didn't have to split our attention."

It was disturbing just how calmly the Colonel said that.

"So, we wait," David told them both. "And see what the Committee thinks."

IT WAS WELL past midnight by the time the Capitol Police guards returned.

"Just the Arbiter and White again," the Lieutenant told them. "Come on. I think even the Committeemen want to just go home and sleep at this point."

David smiled humorlessly.

"We all do. You have no idea what my week has been like," he replied. "Let's see what they have to say."

He and the Arbiter followed the police officer back into the meeting room. Ardent had clearly taken a different route, the Colonel already having rejoined the Committee as David and the vampire were led back to the table in the center of the room.

"We have reviewed this proposed 'Arbiter's Truce'," Senator Day told them. The Senator looked and sounded tired. "Your people, Arbiter, have done a solid job of assembling a document that addresses many of our potential concerns and issues.

"*If* it can be trusted."

Day's words hung in the room.

"Some of us feel that the Vampire Familias should be given a chance," he continued. "Others feel that the vampires have demonstrated beyond question or challenge that they cannot be trusted. Why should we regard this as more trustworthy than you have demonstrated yourselves to be?"

"The strength of the Familias is broken," the Arbiter admitted into the silence. "Commander White shattered the vast majority of their forces and numbers on the slopes of Mount Scott. Dresden has agreed to disarm his people, turning over their illegally acquired weapons to you.

"We are no longer capable of fighting this war. There are oaths that can bind our people in blood and magic. They will be sworn.

"We will turn over our weapons, and Omicron will maintain control of the Mountain. Much of the organization of the Familias will simply disintegrate without the need to rely on each other to survive.

"I cannot guarantee anything," the Arbiter warned them. "All I can promise is that we will try. That the failures will be lone actors, not soldiers with an army behind them.

"An entirely different scale of problem, wouldn't you say?"

Day nodded and looked around the room.

"Having heard his words, does anyone wish to change their vote?" he asked.

From the table, David could only see a few of the members of the Committee. One of those tapped something on a screen in front of them, but he couldn't see if any of the others responded.

The Senator studied something on his desk, then nodded.

"By a vote of eleven to two, Standing Order Twenty-one is lifted," he told them. "Omicron will remain authorized to use lethal force against vampires in the defense of themselves or others, but the shoot-on-sight order will no longer apply."

David heard the Arbiter's concealed sigh of relief, but he could also feel the vampire's continuing tension.

"By a vote of ten to two, with one abstention, the Special Committee on Supernatural Affairs agrees to accept the Arbiter's Truce as an interim solution," Day announced. "We will designate a team of legal experts to work with representatives from the vampire community to draft legislation to lay out the exact position of our vampire citizens in the United States, but the Truce will act as our guide until that legislation is passed into law.

"By a vote of thirteen to zero, the facility known as the Mountain must remain under Omicron control, with no armed vampires permitted at the site," he concluded. "We will permit the Keepers to continue their training and will make an effort to deliver future discovered fledgling vampires to them, but they will do so under the protection and security of the United States government."

The room was silent, and the Arbiter bowed his head across the table.

"Thank you," he told them. "I swore an oath to preserve my species, gentlemen. I understood—I have understood for a long time now—that we could no longer live hidden in the shadows, a parasite upon our nation.

"That is why I am here. To find a better way—a better path that we must find together."

"I won't pretend this is going to be easy on you," Day told him. "Your people have made themselves no friends in Omicron. It will take time to rebuild trust; you will have to prove yourselves again and again for us to begin to see you as safe."

"It will be done," the Arbiter said flatly. "That is my oath to both you and my people. We will have peace."

JOIN THE MAILING LIST

Love Glynn Stewart's books? Join the mailing list at

GLYNNSTEWART.COM/MAILING-LIST/

to know as soon as new books are released, special announcements, and a chance to win free paperbacks.

ABOUT THE AUTHOR

Glynn Stewart is the author of *Starship's Mage*, a bestselling science fiction and fantasy series where faster-than-light travel is possible–but only because of magic. His other works include science fiction series *Duchy of Terra*, *Castle Federation* and *Vigilante,* as well as the urban fantasy series *ONSET* and *Changeling Blood*.

Writing managed to liberate Glynn from a bleak future as an accountant. With his personality and hope for a high-tech future intact, he lives in Kitchener, Ontario with his partner, their cats, and an unstoppable writing habit.

VISIT GLYNNSTEWART.COM FOR NEW RELEASE UPDATES

facebook.com/glynnstewartauthor

OTHER BOOKS BY GLYNN STEWART

For release announcements join the mailing list or visit **GlynnStewart.com**

STARSHIP'S MAGE
Starship's Mage
Hand of Mars
Voice of Mars
Alien Arcana
Judgment of Mars
UnArcana Stars
Sword of Mars
Mountain of Mars
The Service of Mars
A Darker Magic
Mage-Commander (upcoming)

Starship's Mage: Red Falcon
Interstellar Mage
Mage-Provocateur
Agents of Mars

Pulsar Race: A Starship's Mage Universe Novella

DUCHY OF TERRA
The Terran Privateer
Duchess of Terra
Terra and Imperium
Darkness Beyond
Shield of Terra
Imperium Defiant
Relics of Eternity
Shadows of the Fall
Eyes of Tomorrow

SCATTERED STARS
Scattered Stars: Conviction
Conviction
Deception
Equilibrium
Fortitude (upcoming)

PEACEKEEPERS OF SOL
Raven's Peace
The Peacekeeper Initiative
Raven's Course
Drifter's Folly (upcoming)

EXILE
Exile
Refuge
Crusade
Ashen Stars: An Exile Novella

CASTLE FEDERATION
Space Carrier Avalon
Stellar Fox
Battle Group Avalon
Q-Ship Chameleon
Rimward Stars
Operation Medusa
A Question of Faith: A Castle Federation Novella

SCIENCE FICTION STAND ALONE NOVELLA
Excalibur Lost

VIGILANTE
(WITH TERRY MIXON)

Heart of Vengeance
Oath of Vengeance

Bound By Stars: A Vigilante Series (With Terry Mixon)

Bound By Law
Bound by Honor
Bound by Blood

TEER AND KARD

Wardtown
Blood Ward

CHANGELING BLOOD

Changeling's Fealty
Hunter's Oath
Noble's Honor
Fae, Flames & Fedoras: A Changeling Blood Novella

ONSET

ONSET: To Serve and Protect
ONSET: My Enemy's Enemy
ONSET: Blood of the Innocent
ONSET: Stay of Execution
Murder by Magic: An ONSET Novella

FANTASY STAND ALONE NOVELS

Children of Prophecy
City in the Sky

CPSIA information can be obtained
at www.ICGtesting.com
Printed in the USA
LVHW100221121022
730384LV00037B/204